crossing danger

A SHELBY NICHOLS ADVENTURE

Colleen Helme

Book Cover Art by Damonza.com Copyright © 2015 by Colleen Helme
Book Layout ©2013 BookDesignTemplates.com

Crossing Danger/ Colleen Helme -- 1st ed.
ISBN-13: 978-1511632454
ISBN-10: 1511632453

Dedication

To Wendy Tremont King
For giving Shelby a voice

ACKNOWLEDGMENTS

I would like send a big thanks to my family for your never-ending support and encouragement. It means the world to me!

To Melissa, thanks for being such a great idea-bouncer and first-draft-reader, I couldn't do it without you!

To Kristin Monson, I'm so lucky to have such an amazing editor who catches my mistakes and makes these books the best they can be.

To my husband, who is my biggest fan! Thanks for your encouragement and patience through this process.

To all of my friends, who put up with listening to me talk about Shelby *all the time.*

To my amazing fans! You keep me writing and inspire me to do my best with each book. I hope you enjoy this adventure!

Shelby Nichols Adventures

Carrots
Fast Money
Lie or Die
Secrets that Kill
Trapped by Revenge
Deep in Death
Crossing Danger
Devious Minds
Hidden Deception
Laced in Lies
Deadly Escape
Marked for Murder
Ghostly Serenade

Devil in a Black Suit ~ A Ramos Story
A Midsummer Night's Murder ~ A Shelby Nichols
Novella

Contents

Chapter 1

I stood inside the small women's locker room dressed in white drawstring pants that ended several inches above my ankles, and a robe-like top that crisscrossed to close in front. Luckily, I wore a black tank top underneath, since there wasn't anything besides a white belt to hold it together.

I tied the belt in a knot and let out a breath, hoping I'd done it right. The white training uniform was a bit stiff, and worse, felt like a poufy marshmallow around me. I let out a disgusted huff, knowing that I looked like the womanly version of the Pillsbury dough-boy.

Billie Jo waited just outside the door, but it was hard to step out there dressed like this. Did I really need to do this? Especially since I'd know what everyone was thinking about me? Reading minds often came in handy, but not in situations like this.

Of course, the fact that a serial killer had recently taken me hostage and nearly killed me certainly helped. It was time to learn some self-defense, so nothing like that could ever happen to me again.

So what if I looked silly, and that with my 'superpower' of reading minds I'd know what everyone thought of me. I could take it. Besides, I had to start somewhere, right?

I took a calming breath and opened the door.

Billie smiled encouragingly before glancing down at the way I'd tied my belt. Her brows drew sharply together, and she was thinking it looked like a disaster. No way did she want me out on the mat looking like that. "Here...let me help you with that. Tie it this way..." She demonstrated how to do it, then pulled it tight. "Okay. Now you're good to go."

"Um...thanks," I said.

She didn't miss the embarrassed flush creeping up my neck and was thinking I should just suck it up and be grateful she was there to keep me from looking like a dork. With an indulgent smile that contradicted her thoughts, she turned and led the way to the mat.

Swallowing my pride, I followed behind, noting that her black skirt-like pants with the waist-high belt looked ten times better than my outfit. Compared to her, I looked like I was still in my underwear and had forgotten to put my pants on.

A vision of getting out there and everyone laughing at me crossed my mind but, given how Billie made sure my belt was right, I didn't think she'd let me embarrass her like that. Still, once we got to the mat, I let out a relieved breath to find I wasn't the only one wearing white training pants.

Billie did a quick bow before stepping onto the mat, so I bowed as well. I followed her to stand in a line before the teacher, or Sensei, as everyone called him. He wore the same black pants as Billie but, on him, they seemed more dignified and masterful. He was also a big, tall and brawny kind of guy. With his long, gray-black hair pulled back into a ponytail, he intimidated the crap out of me.

He caught my gaze and nodded a cool greeting while I tried to hide my jittering nerves. After he introduced me to the rest of the class, we began with a few stretches and warm-ups. Then he taught us that the most important part of Aikido was learning how to fall safely and then roll around to get back up.

Besides Billie, there was only one other woman in the class. Her name was Melissa, and she was a second-degree black belt like Billie. With the two of them paying special attention to me, I began to relax and actually started to enjoy myself. Even the rolling-around part didn't seem so bad. They showed me some basic techniques, and my confidence grew.

Near the end of class, Sensei asked if I had any questions, so I blurted out the one thing I'd been thinking about all night. "Yeah. I was just wondering...if someone was to get me in a choke hold with his elbow around my neck and start dragging me backwards, would I be able to get away?"

His gaze caught mine, and his eyes narrowed. He was thinking that, from the fear in my eyes and the tone of my voice, it probably wasn't a rhetorical question. No. I had the look of someone who'd been there, and a spike of anger rushed over him. He'd seen it more times than he liked, and it always made him furious.

"Yes you can. I'll show you how." He turned his gaze to Melissa and asked her to help him demonstrate the technique. Since she was about my size, and he was huge, I was interested to see how she could possibly take him on and come out on top.

He stood behind her and clamped his elbow around her neck beneath her chin. "The first thing you do is tuck your chin down so they can't choke you." She did this, and Sensei proceeded to explain how she needed to pull down on his elbow and step back, then grab his wrist and forcefully push outward with his elbow still bent. "At this point, you will break his arm."

Whoa! That sounded pretty awesome, and I couldn't help smiling with wicked delight. He demonstrated the technique a few more times, adding different variations to the attack, and then asked me to practice with him. Him! The biggest guy in the class!

I nervously licked my lips and, as he put his arm around my neck, that feeling of helplessness washed over me. But he patiently talked me through the moves and, after breaking his hold a few times, confidence replaced my fear. I even forced him to the mat once. Who would have thought? By the end of class, I was pumped. This was the right place for me, and I could hardly wait to come back and learn more.

As I changed my clothes, I envisioned how fun it would be to take Ramos down. Since I had an appointment with Uncle Joey the next day, I could even try it then. With that happy thought, the fact that I had to see Uncle Joey didn't seem so bad.

He was the crime boss who knew my secret that I could read minds, and Ramos was his hit man and bodyguard. We'd shared a few life-and-death situations together over the last several months, and now we had a complicated relationship... complicated because, as much as I didn't like the whole mob-boss thing, I still liked Uncle Joey.

Ramos also held a special place in my heart, especially after what happened a few weeks ago. My breath hitched just thinking about how he'd saved me from being burned alive. In fact, he'd risked his own life to save mine, nearly dying in the process. How could I ever turn my back on either of them?

In my head, I knew it was wrong to work for a mob-boss and his hit man but, so far, that didn't stop me from going to his office every time he called. At this point, helping him out was like second nature to me, and I didn't even question it. Only... now it looked like I was part of his organization, and if he went down, I'd probably go down with him.

It kind of made my chest hurt, but thoughts of jail time for being in his employment still didn't stop me. Nope. Not even a little. Somehow, Uncle Joey had gained my loyalty and trust. It was somewhat disconcerting to realize that, no matter how wrong it was, I still couldn't bring myself to stop helping him. Whoa, was I ever in too deep, or what?

The door opened a crack, and Billie peeked in. "Hey Shelby, are you dressed?"

"Um...yeah," I said, grateful for the interruption. "Just putting on my shoes. Why?"

"I just got done with the weirdest phone call from Addie Matern. Remember her? She's the Attorney General's secretary?"

"Of course," I said.

"I've been trying to reach her for the last several days, and she just texted me that she was leaving town. For good. I called and convinced her to meet with me before she left. I don't know what in the blazes has gotten into her, but with your premonitions, you might be able to figure it out. Is there any way you can come?"

"Um...well..."

"Please? If she takes off now, we might never have what we need to take down Grayson Sharp."

"Okay...sure."

Billie was a reporter for the newspaper, and I'd helped her with a few of her stories. She in turn had helped me out a few times. She didn't know the truth that I could read minds, instead believing that I had 'premonitions' and that's how I figured things out. It was the same thing I'd told Detective Harris, or 'Dimples' as I liked to call him.

It hit me how complicated my life had become. Not only did I help Uncle Joey whenever he needed me, but I had started my own consulting agency, and it sometimes involved helping the police and now Billie. My plate was pretty full. Still, I couldn't turn her down. "Where's the meeting?"

"Same place as before...Gracie's Tavern. I'll drive us out, and then bring you back here for your car when we're done."

"That should work." I finished tying my shoes and then sent a quick text to my husband, Chris, telling him I'd be a little late.

During the drive, Billie told me what was going on with the investigation into Grayson Sharp, the Attorney General, and his not-so-law-abiding ways. "That weasel won't resign," she complained. "And it looks like the legislature and the county attorney's office are dragging their feet about investigating him...even though they said they would."

Billie also worried that she might have to shoulder some of the blame since she hadn't turned her evidence, in the form of a thumb-drive, over to the proper authorities. "That thumb-drive Addie gave me won't be enough without her testimony to back it up, so she can't leave town. You have to talk some sense into her."

"So...you didn't turn the thumb-drive over as evidence?"

"Uh...no. I probably should have, but I was worried that someone might lose it...you know...on purpose?"

"How much of it did you print in your article?"

Her lips turned down with disapproval, and she glanced at me. "Well...maybe if you'd read it, you'd know."

"Hey...I had a lot going on right then. At least I helped you."

"Okay, okay...sorry." She knew I was right and that she needed to calm down. "I mentioned a few of the cases that made it to the attorney general's office, which he had dismissed for no good reason, and stated that all of the accused businesses had made sizeable donations to his campaign. It was enough to get the ball rolling without disclosing the details on the thumb-drive. I figured I'd save those for insurance, in case they dropped the investigation. But without Addie, I don't know if any of that will matter."

"Yeah...I can see how that could be a problem."

We pulled into the parking lot and hurried inside the tavern. Addie was already there, and relief poured over her to see us. With her wide eyes and pale face, she looked ready to bolt and, from her thoughts, I gathered that if we hadn't come in just then, she would have.

Billie smiled to put her at ease, but the tension radiating from her was hard to miss. "Hey Addie, thanks for stopping. What's going on? Why are you leaving?"

She glanced between the two of us and nervously licked her lips. "I can't be a part of this. I thought I could help, but it's too involved." She was thinking about the threatening notes and the phone call from a man who told her to leave town or she'd be dead before the day was out.

"Besides, my mom needs me back home right now. My dad's got some health issues, and she really needs my help around the house."

That wasn't true, but the caller had also threatened to hurt her family if she didn't do the 'right thing,' so it only made sense to use that as the reason for her abrupt departure. "I'm sorry I have to go home, but you've got the thumb-drive. You really don't need me."

"But we do," Billie protested. "The thumb-drive won't go far without your testimony. Besides, you don't need to worry. No one knows you gave me that thumb-drive, so you're perfectly safe."

"Safe?" she blurted. Then realizing her outburst might give her away, she continued. "I mean...yeah...so if it goes to trial, I'll come back and testify. I promise." She checked the time and stood. "Well...I've got to go. At this rate, I'm going to be up half the night driving, and my mom's expecting me as soon as I can get there. See you."

She grabbed her jacket and hurried out of there like someone had lit a short fuse in the seat of her pants. As the door shut behind her, Billie turned to me. "Looks like someone got to her, and she's running scared."

"Yeah...I think you're right. And whoever it is, they know about the thumb-drive. What did you do with it anyway?"

"It's..." Billie glanced at me. "It's in a safe place." But she was thinking that locking it in her desk drawer at work might not have been such a good idea. In fact, she hadn't checked on it in a while, and a shiver of alarm passed over her. "Do you mind if we stop by my office on the way back to the dojo? I just want to make sure it's still there."

"Sure." I nodded, hoping that my gut feeling was wrong this time, and that the thumb-drive hadn't been stolen. Billie was hoping the same thing, so when we finally arrived at her desk, she quickly unlocked the drawer and yanked it open.

Even though we'd both expected to find it empty...not seeing the thumb-drive there was still a blow, and Billie frantically searched through each of her drawers. "Damn!" she said. "It's gone!"

"Are you sure that's where you put it? You didn't give it to your boss for safe-keeping, did you?"

She shook her head and silently berated herself, thinking it was a good thing she'd made a copy. "No, and I guess if someone stole it, they'll know what's on it."

"Yeah," I agreed. "Which must be how they got to Addie. Do you think they might suspect you made a copy? That could be real dangerous for you. I mean, look at how bad they scared her."

Her eyes narrowed, and she placed her hands on her hips. "How did you know I made a copy?"

"What? Are you kidding me? Of course you'd make a copy. You're a famous reporter...that's just something you'd do." I smiled, hoping she'd buy my explanation, and that throwing in a little complement wouldn't hurt either.

She was thinking that if I'd figured out she'd made a copy someone else could figure it out too. That could be bad.

"Don't worry, I won't tell anyone. And since most people don't know you as well as I do, I'm sure your secret's safe with me."

"That's good to know," she said, thinking I was sure good at picking up on things, since that was exactly what she'd been thinking.

"Well...we'd better get going," I said. "It's getting late."

"Wait. Did you get any other premonitions about Addie? Like...who's behind this or anything helpful?"

"Sorry...no. I only picked up that someone had threatened her if she didn't leave town."

Billie pursed her lips and nodded, then turned to leave. I followed her back to her car, and we drove to the dojo in silence. Mostly because Billie was thinking hard about the case and wondering who had taken the thumb-drive from her locked office desk and also threatened Addie. By the time she let me out at the dojo, I knew where she'd hidden the copy of the thumb-drive. I also knew who she thought was behind it.

"Thanks for your help, Shelby," she said.

"Sure. Let me know if you need anything else." She nodded, and I hurried to my car. As I drove home, I worried about Billie. It looked like things were escalating, and I didn't want to see her get hurt. Had I done enough to help her?

Maybe I should have warned her about Addie's threatening notes and phone calls...but then she would have wanted to know how I knew all of those details. There was just no easy answer. I could check up on the person she thought was behind it, though, and find out more about them.

I got home and greeted Chris with a kiss, glad to be home where I didn't have to worry about keeping my mind-reading a secret, at least from him. My kids were a different story, but no way would I ever let them know their mom could read their minds. I shuddered at the thought.

"How was class?" he asked.

"Great! I learned how to break someone's arm. Do you want me to show you how?"

"Um...no." He was thinking *do I look stupid?*

I chuckled. "You don't think I'd really break your arm, do you?"

"You might," he said, but hurried on to add, "Not on purpose though." He was thinking my enthusiasm might get the best of me, and then who knew what could happen?

"I wouldn't break your arm...geeze."

His smile widened, and mischief brightened his eyes. "Okay then...you can show me."

What a tease. I had him do the choke-hold on me and then pushed my way right out of it. I got a good hold on his arm and pulled it back and down. "This is where I could break your arm if I wanted to."

"Yeah," Chris said, his voice a little strained. "I can feel that...you can let me go now."

I let up on him and tried to keep the satisfied smirk off my face. What was it about pushing a man around that gave me so much pleasure? "Let me show you something else. Grab my wrist like you're trying to drag me away."

His lips turned down in a frown, but he did as I asked. This time I put my other hand over his and twisted his wrist until he staggered back. "With this hold...I can break your wrist."

"Yeah...I get it...lots of breaking things."

"Isn't this great?" I asked, letting him go. "And this was just my first class. Imagine how good I'll get after a few months?"

Chris rubbed his wrist. "Yeah, that's true." He was thinking that maybe he should take lessons too, just so I couldn't beat up on him.

I snickered. "That could be fun. Maybe the kids would like to learn too. Some basic self-defense is always a good thing, especially for a girl. Where are the kids anyway?"

"I think Savannah's in her room, and Josh is playing video games downstairs."

"Did he get his homework done first?" I asked. This was a rule I tried to enforce, and I hoped Chris had checked up on him.

"I think so," Chris said. But he really had no idea.

"You don't know?"

"Um...no, but I think he was working on something earlier, so he probably did."

His mind was blank, so I knew he was blocking me out. "Okay...good." I hated the role of "the mean parent," so I let it go and yelled down the stairs for Josh to come up. Being fourteen, he wasn't enthusiastic about losing his place in his game, so it took him several minutes before he came upstairs.

At twelve, Savannah was more than happy to see what I'd learned. It was also surprising that she had some of the same thoughts about beating up the guys that I did. As I showed her the wrist-grabbing move, she was thinking about the boy at school who'd grabbed her by the arm and shoved her into the boy's bathroom.

I caught my breath to 'hear' that, and hot indignation surged over me. "Let's practice that again so you've got it down before school tomorrow. In fact, I think you should start coming to Aikido with me." I knew seventh grade was rough, but seriously? Who were these boys?

"Cool," she said, excited about the prospect of breaking someone's arm, or at least causing some pain so no one would want to mess with her.

"You got that right," I said, giving her a high five.

Josh thought it was cool too, but he wasn't as enthusiastic as me and Savannah. His voice had dropped an octave, and he was growing like a weed. He'd even passed me up by a couple of inches. He'd also never had the same experience of getting shoved into the bathroom like Savannah had.

That's when it hit me that men didn't experience life the same way as women. Walking to a car at night, or being alone on a dark street, wasn't a big deal to them. But I always felt fearful at times like that, and I thought most women did.

Good thing I was taking Aikido. Knowing how to defend myself would help me feel more in control and, after what I'd been through recently, it was definitely what I needed to cope with the times those dark memories fell over me like a shadow.

"Hey beautiful," Chris said, lifting my chin to gaze into my eyes. He always seemed to know when I got lost in the dark and knew just what to say to bring me back. I smiled up at him, amazed that he put up with me most of the time.

The fact that I could read his mind had been a real trial for us, but somehow we'd managed to make it work, and my relationship with him was better than ever. Especially now, when he was thinking that I was beautiful, sweet, and...did I buy his favorite ice cream when I went to the store?

I narrowed my eyes. "I bought some ice cream, but I got my favorite this time."

"That's okay," he drawled. "I especially like your flavor." This time, he wasn't talking about ice cream.

"Did someone say ice cream?" Josh piped up.

"Yeah," I said, pulling away from Chris with a knowing smile. "Dad's going to dish it up for everyone."

"Sweet," Josh said. His voice cracked, and we all laughed.

The next morning I got out of bed, surprised to find my muscles stiff from my workout at the dojo. At least I felt confident that if anyone grabbed Savannah's arm today, she could handle herself. That put me in a good mood.

After Chris and the kids left, I got ready for my appointment with Uncle Joey. I only felt a little guilty that I hadn't told Chris about it. But I'd learned that, where Uncle Joey was concerned, telling Chris as little as possible beforehand worked best, mostly because I didn't want him to worry about me. I could fill him in after I knew what was going on...if I needed to. So really...it was for his own good that I didn't tell him to begin with.

I had no idea what Uncle Joey wanted this time but, for the first time in a long while, I felt I stood on equal footing with him. Like I could speak my mind about whether or not I'd do something he wanted. Gone were the days when I might have groveled or tried to run. We were both in a different place now...and I was grateful for the change.

I pulled into the parking garage and walked with confidence to the elevators. On a whim, I peeked around the corner just to see if Ramos' motorcycle was there. The sight of it brought a bit of longing to my heart.

The autumn leaves were cascading to the ground, leaving trails of color in the breeze. Even though the weather was a bit cooler now, it was still warm enough to go riding through the leaves, and I could imagine how nice it would be to sit behind Ramos and enjoy a brisk ride.

Full of nostalgia, I headed to the elevators and soon exited on the twenty-sixth floor. The words "Thrasher Development" spanned above the double doors and, with a smile, I pushed the door open and stepped inside.

"Shelby!" Jackie greeted me warmly. "How are you doing?"

"Great. How are you?"

"Things are going okay. I'm still here, even though Joe wanted me to quit." She was thinking that now that everyone knew she'd married Joe, he thought it was inappropriate for his wife to be his secretary, and it drove her crazy. "Can you imagine someone else running this place? There's no way I'm going to let that happen."

"I totally agree," I said. "If he knows what's good for him, he'll keep you right where you are."

"Exactly," she said. "Anyway, he's with a client right now, but he should be done soon. You want a Diet Coke?"

"Sure." I followed her to the end of the hall and through a door that opened up into a swanky apartment. It was done in black and white, with splashes of color on the walls and couches, and I knew Ramos often stayed there.

As if thinking about him conjured him up, Ramos entered the kitchen from a back room. He stopped in surprise, and a small grin spread over his lips. "Babe."

"Hey," I replied. My stomach did a little flip-flop, and my heart raced. He had that effect on me. "We're just here to get a Diet Coke." I didn't want him to think I was stalking him or anything.

"Oh...yeah, I see that."

Jackie grabbed a couple of cans out of the fridge and set them on the counter while shaking her head. She was thinking that if we didn't stop drooling over each other, she was going to be sick.

"How have you been?" he asked.

"Good." I reached for the soda, but he got it first. "Hey...that's mine."

He smiled, but didn't let it go, so I took the other can, and Jackie rolled her eyes before opening the fridge for another one.

"I'll have you know I'm learning self-defense, so you'd better watch out." He raised his brows, so I continued. "Yeah, I could probably break your arm if I wanted."

"Really? You think you could take me?" He was thinking he'd like to see me try, and if I managed to take him down, he'd certainly be impressed.

"Sure," I said.

"Okay then, show me what you've got."

The living room floor was covered with thick, white carpet, and Ramos moved the coffee table to the side so there was lots of open space. I slipped off my shoes and set my purse on the counter, visualizing how fun it would be to throw Ramos over my shoulder. But since I didn't know exactly how to do that yet, I decided to do the wrist-grab thing to take him down.

"Okay," I said. "First you have to try and grab my arm."

Ramos suppressed a grin before lunging for me. I squeaked and tried to jump out of the way but, before I knew what was happening, he'd grabbed me around the waist and, in one smooth move, pinned me to the ground. Even though the carpet was soft, it kind of knocked the breath out of me, and I stared up at him with surprised shock. As he easily held me down, a satisfied smirk twisted his lips.

"How did you do that?" I asked, a little breathless.

Before he could say a word, the flash of a camera caught me full in the face. I blinked up to find Uncle Joey standing there with a big grin on his face and his phone in his hand.

"Crap!"

Ramos grunted and quickly got up, then offered me his hand. After helping me to my feet, I glared at Uncle Joey. "You did not just take a picture of me."

"I did," he grinned. "But it might be a little blurry. Do you want to see it?"

"Yeah...sure..." I reached for the phone, but he held it out of my grasp while he pushed a few buttons.

"There it is...what do you think?"

He handed me the phone, and I nearly fainted to see myself in such a compromising position. The look of shock on my face wasn't very flattering either. Before he could object, I found the delete icon and got rid of the photo.

"Shelby? Did you just delete that?"

"Of course I did! What were you thinking?"

He couldn't hold it in any longer and burst out laughing. "You should have seen your face. As long as I live, I'll never forget that look."

I glared at him, but he only laughed harder. I scowled before handing Uncle Joey his phone and turned toward the kitchen. "Where's my Diet Coke?"

"Um...on the counter," Jackie said. She was trying not to laugh, even though it was killing her. She also thought maybe that would teach me a lesson about keeping my distance from Ramos. After all, I was a married woman.

Clenching my teeth, I slipped on my shoes, grabbed my purse and soda, and took off out the door. They all followed behind, each entertaining amused thoughts about my little incident with Ramos. Jackie stopped at her desk, and Ramos continued down the hall to the security room, a happy grin on his face.

By the time I got to Uncle Joey's office, I had loosened up a bit, realizing that the whole episode was probably all my doing...and even a little funny if I thought of it that way. Why did I ever think I could take Ramos? Of course, I hadn't expected Uncle Joey to be there with his camera. Whew! That was close. Thank goodness I'd deleted it.

I took a seat in front of Uncle Joey's desk and eyed him with new understanding. He hadn't gotten where he was by coincidence. He knew how to be at the right place, at the right time, to take advantage of situations just like mine. I hadn't missed Ramos' thought of how Uncle Joey had 'let' me delete the photo either and, right now, I was glad I was on his good side.

"I hope you're not too upset with me," he began, taking in my observant stare. "But I couldn't resist having a little fun."

"Oh no...it's okay...I mean, what can I say? It was pretty silly of me to think I could take Ramos. Of course, in my defense, all I really wanted to do was show him some moves I'd learned at Aikido last night. I decided to take a martial arts class after what happened with that guy who tried to kill me. It kind of spooked me, you know? So I thought this might help, so that maybe next time...of course, hopefully there won't be a next time, but since I'm still working...uh...well, you never know what could happen."

I swallowed, grateful I hadn't said, *since I'm still working for you,* like I was thinking, and I clamped my lips tight. I usually didn't open up so much to Uncle Joey but, for some reason, I couldn't seem to stop the words from pouring out of my mouth. What had gotten into me?

"That's good, Shelby. It shows a lot of initiative on your part and should help you cope with everything you've been through lately."

"Yeah." I sighed, relieved he understood. "I think it's helping a lot."

"Good. I'm glad. Well...shall we get down to business?"

"Yes, of course."

"Do you remember the man who left this little note at my wake?" He pulled a note from his desk drawer and handed it to me.

Just a few weeks ago, Uncle Joey had survived an explosion but faked his death to find out who had tried to kill him. At his wake, a man approached the casket, dropped a note, and quickly left. I'd seen the whole thing, and grabbed the note to show Uncle Joey. He'd been on edge ever since then.

"Yeah, sure I do."

"Did he look anything like this guy?" He pushed a grainy, black-and-white photo in front of me.

It showed a man in dark glasses leaving the building. From the side angle, it was hard to see his features but, after a moment of study, I nodded. "Yeah...it looks like him. The dark glasses hide his eyes, but it's the same jaw and hair. That crease down the side of his face is one of the things I remember most about him. So yeah...it's probably him."

Uncle Joey rubbed his chin, thinking that having Blake Beauchaine show up after all these years wasn't a good thing.

"Weren't you thinking about sending Ramos back to Seattle to check up on him?" I asked.

His lips twisted in annoyance that I'd read his mind, but he let it go and answered my question. "As a matter of fact, I was. I don't know why he's here in town unless it's to check up on me. Now that I'm not dead, we might have some unfinished business he wants to take care of."

"Where did you get this photo?" I asked.

"Yesterday, a large envelope addressed to me was left in the lobby downstairs. Someone who works in the building noticed it and brought it up. After I opened it, Ramos went through the surveillance cameras to see who'd left it."

"What was in the envelope?"

"It was the newspaper article about the explosion on the yacht," Uncle Joey answered. "I don't know if it's a veiled threat that he wants me dead, or just a reminder that he's watching me. Either way, I'd sure like to know what he's doing here."

"Yeah," I agreed. "But at least you know who it is, right?"

He nodded and glanced my way, not at all comforted that it was his old college roommate. Not after what had happened back then. He thought they had leveled the playing field all those years ago, and he didn't want Blake poking around in his business.

"Thank you Shelby. Once I find him, I might need your help to know what he's doing here. I'm sure he wouldn't tell me the truth." Uncle Joey was also thinking he might have to figure out a way to draw Blake out but, with the right incentive, he could do that.

"Okay...sure. Just let me know. Is there anything else?"

"Not at the moment, but I'll keep you informed."

"Well, I'd better get going then."

I said goodbye to Jackie and got on the elevator, uncomfortable that Uncle Joey was unsettled about this Blake Beauchaine person. Mostly because if this guy worried him, it was bound to be bad, and that meant I could end up right in the middle of it.

Chapter 2

I exited the elevator in the parking garage and, without even thinking about it, walked around the corner to look at Ramos' motorcycle one more time. From the way it was parked, it looked like he'd been using that instead of his car lately, which made perfect sense to me. I'd certainly be riding it on a day like today if I could.

Sighing, I turned to leave and came face to face with Ramos. "Babe," he drawled. "It looks like you're drooling just a little. Want to go for a ride?"

My breath caught and, even though I knew I shouldn't, I nodded my head and grinned like a fool. I didn't have any control when it came to Ramos and going for a ride on his motorcycle. What was worse, he knew it.

"It shouldn't take long," he said.

"Okay...that should work for me." I hated that I sounded so eager, especially since I didn't know where he was going or why. Who knew what I was getting myself into? There might be guns involved. It could be dangerous. But did that matter? Nope. I'd risk it all for a ride with Ramos.

Before I could decide if that made me a bad person or was just something any warm-blooded woman would do, he popped the trunk of his car and got out the gear I'd need. As I held his soft leather jacket in my hands, all doubt flew out the window.

I quickly slipped my arms through the sleeves and pushed them above my hands so I could zip the jacket up. It was huge on me, but I didn't mind. It was soft and supple and smelled of leather and that musky scent that was all Ramos. Next, I slipped on the helmet and, to my delight, I even managed to snap the straps together under my chin like a pro.

Ramos straddled the bike and moved it forward for me to get on. In one smooth motion, I swung my leg over the seat and got comfortable. He started her up, and I held on tight as we shot forward. A thrill went down my spine, and my stomach clenched. We pulled onto the street and I couldn't help the bubble of laughter that escaped my lips. What a rush!

We drove through town, then into a residential area close to the university campus. The homes here were old and stately with huge trees and sidewalks. Ramos found the house he wanted and pulled down the driveway and around to the back. Dismounting from the bike, I took off my helmet and left it on the seat.

"This is where my computer expert lives," Ramos explained. "He's checking out the surveillance footage from yesterday."

"Oh." I nodded and followed him to the back door. He rang the buzzer, and we heard sounds of someone running up the basement steps before the door opened. A young man barely out of his teens, with curly brown hair and glasses, invited us inside. He glanced at me with suspicion but, thought since I was with Ramos, I had to be okay.

"Come on down." He left the door open and led the way into the basement.

At the foot of the stairs, a large room opened up to reveal a serious computer setup. A huge desk had about six computer monitors stacked in a semi-circle at various levels on top of it. The computer guy slid into his chair and rolled over to the keyboard. He quickly typed in a few commands. "Okay...I hacked into the system and found the guy you're looking for."

A clip showing Blake Beauchaine leaving the building came up on a monitor. "It looks like he went along the street a few blocks before heading down to the metro. I couldn't pick him up after that." We watched his progress on the monitors and saw how he seemingly disappeared at the station. "I've looked at all the camera angles, but I couldn't pick him up anywhere. It's like he vanished."

We watched the replay several times, trying to catch sight of Blake, but had no luck. "Sorry," the young man said. "I'll keep looking. Maybe he doubled back or something. If I find him again, I'll let you know."

"I'd appreciate it. The boss wants a complete background check on the guy. His name's Blake Beauchaine. He's here in the city somewhere, and we need to know where."

"Sure...I'll find him."

Ramos handed him an envelope full of money. "Thanks kid. I'll be expecting your call. We'll show ourselves out."

I followed Ramos outside, trying to pick up his thoughts about what was going on, but they were closed up tight. "What do you think is going on?" I finally asked.

"I don't know...but once the kid finds him, Manetto will know what to do."

"All right, but this whole thing worries me."

He put his hands on my shoulders and shook his head. "This is nothing for you to worry about. I mean it...forget about it. Now...are you going to make me sorry I brought you? Because it's a beautiful day for a ride, and I'd hate to see that ruined."

I let out my breath and smiled. "You're right. I'll try not to worry."

"Good." He was thinking that trying wasn't the answer he wanted, but he let it go. My problem was that I was just too tender-hearted for my own good. Hell, even he had taken advantage of that in Orlando. Maybe it was time I quit being so helpful and thought about myself for a change.

"I heard that," I said.

"I was counting on it." He slid his helmet on and started the bike. "We'll take the scenic route back."

The streets were covered in leaves and, as we zipped through them, they scattered across the pavement to mark our passage. Golden sunshine warmed my back. It was a timeless moment, and I let go of my worries to enjoy it.

By the time we got back to the parking garage, my soul was light and happy. "Thanks for the ride. So far, it was the best part of my day."

"Good," Ramos said, taking my helmet and his jacket. He caught my gaze, thinking that, for him, it was more of a tie between pinning me to the floor in the apartment and having my arms locked tightly around him on the bike.

I smiled, but my mouth went dry remembering the feel of his weight on top of me. I cleared my throat and tried to swallow. "Well...I'd better get going." His smoldering gaze sent a flash of heat from my head to my toes, and I started to back away before I lost my cool. "Uh...bye."

"Shelby, wait..."

I smiled, but no way was I going to keep standing so close to him when he looked at me like that. I mean...a girl can only take so much. I kept going backwards, only to lose my balance when I stepped off a small step I didn't know was there. Ramos tensed, ready to catch me, but I managed to right myself without falling on my butt, and the moment passed. Still, I couldn't stop my cheeks from turning red with embarrassment. "Oops."

"Are you okay?" Ramos asked, his eyes glowing with mirth and satisfaction that he'd rattled me.

"Yeah...I'm fine." My phone began to ring. "Uh...gotta go...see ya." A little breathless, I hurried to my car while digging through my purse, grateful for the timely interruption. I smiled to see it was Holly, my best friend. Maybe she wanted to go to lunch? This was perfect. I could tell her all about my motorcycle ride and, when she told me she would have done the same thing, I wouldn't feel so guilty.

"Hi Holly," I said.

"Shelby!" Holly shouted. "Something terrible has happened. I need your help. My brother just called and told me his daughter's missing. No one's seen her since yesterday!"

"Oh no. That's terrible. How old is she?"

"She's fourteen."

"How come he didn't know sooner?" I asked.

"Apparently there was a mix-up with his ex-wife. She thought Chloe was spending the night with him, but he had no idea. Listen, I'm headed to his ex's house to meet with him and the police. Is there any way you can come? Scott and I both want you there."

"Of course. I'm downtown, but I'll come right over."

Holly told me the ex's address, which just happened to be close to my own neighborhood, and we disconnected. As I drove to the house, the name, Chloe Peterson, seemed familiar, but I wasn't sure how I knew her. I didn't think I'd ever met her before, but maybe she went to the same school as my kids.

I turned down the street and found the place packed with several parked cars lining both sides. Next to a police car, I recognized an unmarked detective's car and hoped Dimples was the lead detective assigned to the case. He wouldn't have a problem with my involvement, where someone else might.

I found a place to park and let out a relieved breath to find Holly's car already parked up the street. At the house, the front door stood open, and a police officer blocked my way. "Ma'am, are you with the family?"

"No, but the family requested me. I'm Shelby Nichols."

"Shelby!" Holly interrupted, pushing past the officer. "Please...come in." She'd been watching for me and pulled me into the house. "I'm so glad you're here. Let me get Scott." She caught her brother's attention, and he hurried over to meet me. "This is my best friend, Shelby. She can help. She's really good at finding people. She has her own agency and everything."

His eyes held the torment of a tortured father's soul, and he caught my hand in his. "Thank you for coming. I don't know what's going on. I didn't know she was missing until the school called a few hours ago." He was thinking that if someone had abducted her, he wouldn't be able to live with himself.

"Don't worry. I'm sure between all of us we'll find her," I said.

His eyes filled with tears, and he swallowed, glancing into the living room at his ex-wife, Kira. She was holding it together lots better than him, but fear was beginning to take its toll.

A detective I knew too well talked to her and my heart sank. He was the only detective on the entire police force who didn't like me much. His gaze caught mine, and his brows rose with incredulity. What the hell was I doing here? Excusing himself, he hurried over to find out.

Holly caught his intent and quickly introduced us. "Detective, this is my friend, Shelby Nichols. She's a P.I., and we asked her to help."

"I know who she is," Bates ground out, clearly unable to keep his disgust from showing.

"Detective Bates," I said.

All at once, Holly understood the tension between us, and her eyes widened. I'd told her all about Detective Bates and his dislike of me at one of our lunches. She straightened to her full five-foot-ten height and glared at him. "I don't care how you feel about Shelby. She is staying to help us."

Caught off guard, Bates sputtered. "That's fine. I hope she can help."

"I can," I answered. "Now fill me in on what's going on. A girl's life is at stake here." That was enough to get past the awkward moment, and we all sat down in the living room to go over the details.

"I last saw Chloe yesterday morning before she went to school," Kira began, handing me a photograph of her daughter. "Everything was fine. It was just a normal day. I reminded her that I had to work late, and she told me she'd already arranged to stay at her dad's for the night, so I could stay as long as I wanted."

She was thinking that Chloe had been a little flippant when she'd said that and, deep-down, she knew Chloe resented all the times she had to work late. As guilt spiked through her, I caught that the main reason she told Chloe she worked late was because she was seeing someone, and my eyes widened with surprise. Did Chloe know this? That might be a good reason for her to run away.

"I didn't check with Scott, because I just assumed she was telling me the truth," she continued.

I picked up that Kira didn't like Scott much, and talking to him was something she avoided at all costs. It was easier for her to have Chloe do all the arranging and leave her out of it. "I didn't know anything was wrong until Scott told me the school had called, and he wanted to know if she was sick or something."

Scott shook his head in frustration. "Maybe if you'd called to let me know what was going on, this wouldn't have happened. What if someone's taken her? Who knows where she could be? You should have checked her story out with me in the first place. Why do you always do that?"

"Let's calm down and focus," Bates interrupted. "We need to try and figure out what happened." He was thinking that Chloe probably ran away just to see if her parents cared about her. He'd seen that a few times. "It looks like she may have run away. Has she ever done anything like this before?"

"No," Kira said. But she was thinking about the argument they'd had, and how Chloe had threatened to run away and go live with her father. She'd told Chloe she could stay with him more often if she wanted, but there was no way in hell she would ever allow her to live with him. That's why she didn't think Chloe had lied about going to Scott's house in the first place.

"What school does Chloe go to?" I asked.

"She's in the ninth grade at Hillside High," Scott answered.

"Okay." Now I knew why her name was familiar. She went to the same school as Josh. "Has anyone talked to her friends? Maybe she's at one of their houses."

"She's not," Scott said. "I called their parents right away. None of them has seen her. I even searched everywhere I thought she might go. Here, my place, the park, everywhere I could think of. I've called her cell phone a hundred times, but it goes straight to voicemail. I don't know what else to do. If she ran away, where could she be?"

"Did she have any money or take your credit cards?" Bates asked. "Have either of you noticed any of your cash missing?"

Kira hurried to her purse on the kitchen counter and pulled out her wallet. After rifling through it, she shook her head. "My cards and cash are all there. I'll check my office."

After she left, Scott lowered his voice. "I've given her some cash every now and then when she visits, but I haven't told Kira. I don't think it's enough to pay for a plane ticket, or even a bus ticket, unless she's been saving it up."

"If she bought a bus ticket, is there a grandparent or aunt and uncle she would go visit?" Bates asked.

Scott shook his head. "I've already called all the relatives, even on Kira's side. No one's seen her."

"What?" Kira asked, only catching the tail end of the conversation.

Scott explained that he'd called her parents and sisters, and a cold spike of resentment went through her. Then she realized it was something she should have done, and guilt flooded over her again. She glanced at each of us in the room, thinking that we probably all thought she was a terrible mother. Maybe she was.

Lately, Chloe had been whining about everything, and it drove her crazy. She'd even thought about how much easier her life would be without her...and now she was gone. Was it all her fault? What if something bad had happened to Chloe? What if she never came home?

"What about your boyfriend," I asked. "Would Chloe have gone to visit him, or would he have taken her somewhere?"

Kira's eyes widened with alarm, and her heart-rate spiked. How the hell did I know about him? She'd kept him a secret from everyone. Not even Chloe knew she had a man in her life.

Everyone turned their gazes to Kira and she immediately went on the defense. "How did you...this is insane...what makes you think I have a boyfriend?"

I raised my brows. "That's why you work so late, isn't it? To be with him? In case he had anything to do with Chloe's disappearance, you have to tell us who he is."

She flushed before gaining her composure, knowing she couldn't lie about him now without looking like a total failure. "I don't know how you found out about him, but I can assure you he had nothing to do with Chloe's disappearance."

Bates glanced at me, a fissure of unease rolling through him. I'd just done that "ju-ju" thing, and he didn't like it, but if Kira had a boyfriend, that put a whole new spin on things. "I'd like to talk to him," he said. "Just to make sure we've covered all our bases."

Kira swallowed, thinking this was terrible. No one was supposed to know about him. This whole affair was their little secret, and she'd promised not to tell anyone. If she did, he'd be furious. "Couldn't we just wait and see if she turns up? Give her a little more time to come home?"

"Kira!" Scott said. "How can you say that? This is our daughter, and she's missing!"

She dropped onto the couch, her head in her hands. "I know...I know. It's just...I can't believe this is happening. How could she do this to me...to us? She's normally such a good girl." She glanced up at us, tears rolling down her cheeks. "But maybe she did run away. We had an argument the other day. She threatened to go live with Scott. Since she's not with him, then where could she be?"

I caught a general feeling of disgust towards Kira from pretty much everyone in the room. In the back of her mind, she was even wondering if Scott had done this on purpose just to get back at her. Her reaction gave me a sick, queasy feeling, and I felt sorry for both Chloe and Scott. She was even trying to decide if she should give Bates her boyfriend's real name or tell him it was someone else...

"Shelby?" Holly asked, her voice a harsh whisper.

"Huh?"

"Is that okay with you?"

I realized I'd missed something, but quickly picked up that Holly wanted me to go to the school with her and talk with some of Chloe's teachers and classmates. "Oh, yeah...sure. That's a good idea."

Bates prodded Kira for her boyfriend's contact information. She hesitated before making her choice. "His name is Matt Swenson. I'll give you his number, but I'd appreciate it if you didn't talk to him at home." She gave Bates the cell phone number and slumped into the couch in defeat.

Scott stopped cold, shock sending a shiver all the way to his toes. This was insane. Matt had been a friend to him when he'd first started his career. He was also ten years older than Kira and, even though he was married and had a respectable career, he was known for his philandering ways. How could Kira do this with Matt? What the hell? How long had this been going on? Was this the real reason she'd wanted the divorce?

My eyes widened, and I slammed my shields tight, unable to handle the anguish pouring from both of their minds. This was a mess. I thought stuff like this only happened on TV shows, not in real life. I turned to Holly and motioned with my head to leave. She nodded, and we cleared out of there before Bates could stop us.

"Let's take my car," I said, relaxing my shields now that we were out of the house.

"Okay," Holly agreed. A twinge of guilt passed through her for leaving Scott to fend for himself.

"You can text Scott and tell him where we went in a minute. He'll be grateful that we're doing something since he's stuck there with the police and Kira. It'll be fine."

"Yeah." Holly nodded, feeling better. "That's true." She sent me a grateful smile. "I don't think I could've stayed with Kira one more minute or I might have strangled her. Can you believe the gall? Telling Bates to leave her boyfriend out of it?" She shook her head, then glanced at me with curiosity. "Hey...how did you know...was that...did you get a 'premonition' that she had a boyfriend?"

"Yup," I nodded. I'd told Holly right after I got shot in the head that I had premonitions. I didn't want her to know the truth that I could actually read minds. She was my best friend, but if she knew I could hear her thoughts? I wasn't sure I wanted to put that burden on her. Since then, I'd shared lots of stories about my psychic ability, but this was the first time she'd seen me in action.

"Wow...that is so cool. I mean...I know you told me you could do that, but I didn't know how it worked." She'd always given me the benefit of the doubt, especially after all the things I'd told her, but it was still something else to see it in person. A surge of hope swelled inside her, and I braced myself. "Have you seen anything about Chloe? Is she all right?"

"No...sorry. It doesn't always work like that. Most of the time, my premonitions are more like intuition, or a hunch, rather than a vision of the future. That's why it's really good that we're going to the school. If I'm around her friends, or in her class, I might be able to pick up something."

"Oh...okay. That makes sense. I'm just so worried. What if she's been abducted? And the longer she's gone...well, they say the chance of finding someone alive after twenty-four hours isn't very good."

"I know," I agreed. "But it might be true that she ran away. That's a different story. Maybe one of her friends knows where she is but hasn't told anyone. If we start asking questions, that might get someone to open up and tell us what they know."

Holly nodded and sent a text to Scott about where we were going. A few seconds later, she got a response and groaned. "Scott and Detective Bates are coming too. Scott says since we're not her parents, the school won't give us any information about Chloe without him there. I guess I forgot about that."

"Oh...yeah. That's right. At least we can still log in as visitors while we wait."

We were just getting our visitor badges when Scott and Detective Bates came inside. Although he didn't say anything, Bates was fuming that we'd left and taken matters into our own hands, thinking he was the investigator here, not me. I moved behind Scott after hearing that, wanting to stay out of his way until he cooled down.

After he explained the situation to the principal, Mrs. Pascoe, I realized he had a point. As a police detective, he had the authority to get the school's cooperation, and I was grateful he was there. I could let him take the lead and sit back and 'listen' easily enough. If I heard anything that merited further questioning, I could speak up at that point.

Scott handed the list to Mrs. Pascoe, but there were only two names written down. He wasn't even sure how close his daughter was with these girls, but they were the only names he could remember. At least when he'd called the girl's parents, they knew who Chloe was, so that was a good sign.

I mentally winced at his ignorance, realizing that most fathers wouldn't know that much about their daughter's friends. I didn't think Chris could say beyond a couple of names who Savannah's friends were either.

Mrs. Pascoe sent for the students, and we waited in her office for them to arrive. Bates glanced at me. "I'll ask the questions, and you can keep your mouth shut."

I raised my brow and glared at him. "What's wrong with you? Are you so afraid of my 'ju-ju' that you don't want to find out where Chloe is? If I need to ask a question, I will."

Bates' jaw dropped, but he snapped it shut as the door opened. Mrs. Pascoe ushered the girls inside the room, and they both hesitated to see all of us sitting there. She told them to take a seat and explained that Chloe was missing. "This is Chloe's dad and the police. They want to know if you've seen her, or if she said anything to either of you about why she's not here today."

"She's not in trouble," I added, to soothe their fears. "We're just worried about her. We think she might have run away." I smiled at the girls and continued. "Did she ever talk to either of you about that, or where she might go if she did?"

The girls looked at each other before one of them responded. "Oh...well...she talked about going to live with her dad..." Here she glanced at Scott, and he sent her a reassuring smile. "But she never said anything about running away."

"When was the last time you saw her?" Bates asked.

"Um...I guess after school yesterday." she answered.

"What was she doing?"

She pursed her lips and glanced at her friend, trying to decide if she should tell us the truth or keep Chloe's secret.

"Chloe might be in real danger," I said. "If you want to help her, you need to tell us the truth."

Her eyes widened, and she glanced at her friend again. After a quick nod, she turned back to me, deciding she'd better tell the truth, even if Chloe didn't want her to. "Well...we weren't supposed to say anything, but she sort of has a boyfriend."

"What the hell?" Scott shouted. "She's barely fourteen!" I glanced at him with shock before realizing he'd only said that in his mind. His gaze caught mine, but I pulled my attention back to the girls before he wondered what was going on.

"Who is he?" Bates asked. "Was she with him yesterday?"

"Yeah...well, we don't know his name or anything, and he doesn't go to this school. He just picked her up in his car after school yesterday."

"Does he pick her up all the time?" Bates asked.

"No...this was the first time." She was thinking that Chloe had talked about this guy she'd met, but she'd never gone out with him. "She was excited that an older boy was paying attention to her, but I don't think she'd ever gone out with him before. She would have told me."

"What kind of car did he drive?" Bates asked.

They glanced at each other and shrugged. "I don't know. It was an old car."

"Probably a Honda," the other girl answered, "Or something small like that. It was black."

"Okay...thanks," Bates said. "Anything else you want to tell us?"

They both shook their heads, then one of them asked. "Do you think she's all right?"

"Yeah," Bates answered. "We'll find her." He wasn't so sure about that but didn't want to scare the girls. "You can go now."

After they left, Scott's shoulders slumped. He could hardly believe a word they'd said. How could his little girl go off with some stranger? She knew better than that. If this kid had taken advantage of her in any way, he would kill him.

As we left Mrs. Pascoe's office, Scott questioned Bates about what he was going to do next. Bates wasn't as concerned now that he knew she'd left with a boy. "It doesn't look like she was taken against her will, so that's good. It means she'll probably come home when she's ready." He didn't want to admit that she still might be in trouble.

As we walked behind them, Holly turned to me. "Did you get anything?"

"Not really," I answered. "It looks like she's with this kid, but I don't know if that's good or bad."

Holly sighed. "Yeah. Poor Scott. I can't imagine."

Bates' cell phone rang, and he quickly answered it. As he listened, I picked up that something bad had gone down. "I'm on my way." He glanced at Scott, dreading what he had to tell him. "They found Chloe's backpack. It's at the scene of a murder." He was thinking *three murders*, and my stomach tightened with dread.

"What??" Scott sputtered. "Is she..."

"She wasn't there."

Chapter 3

Scott reached for Holly, clinging to her for support. Bates continued, "I'm going to the scene right now. I'll let you know what I find out. In the meantime, you should go back to the house and wait for my call."

In shock, Scott could barely nod his head in agreement. His thoughts were a jumble of emotions that went from shock and worry to disbelief and an overwhelming feeling of fear.

"Wait," Holly said. "I want Shelby to go with you. She might pick up something."

Bates pursed his lips, then huffed out a breath. "Fine." He sighed heavily. "She can come." He glanced at me. "As long as she stays out of my way."

It was hard not to roll my eyes, but I managed. "Give me the address. I'll take Scott and Holly home and meet you there."

Bates pulled out his notepad and scribbled the address down on a piece of paper. He shoved it into my hand and hurried back to his car, grateful to let me take them home.

I did what I could to soothe Scott and Holly's fear on the drive back to the house, promising to let them know what I found. After they got out of the car, I let out a relieved breath to have my thoughts to myself. Picking up on all that stress oozing from both of them had started to rattle me.

The scrawled address Bates gave me would have been indecipherable if I hadn't heard it in his thoughts, and part of me wanted to smack him upside the head. I plugged the address into my GPS and drove to that part of town. Turning down the street, I found the house easily because of all the police cars.

This run-down neighborhood was close to the light-rail tracks. Graffiti covered the houses, and garbage littered the streets. In fact, without police cars present, I never would have had the courage to park my car and get out.

I opened the glove box, pulled out my honorary police ID badge, and slipped it over my neck. Sitting quietly to gain some composure, I took a deep breath before getting out of my car, knowing I had to prepare myself for the sight of three dead bodies. Since the sight of blood made me queasy, I sure hoped I could handle it. Luckily, I hadn't eaten much today, so that should help.

A police officer stood in front of the door and ushered me inside, telling me not to touch anything without putting on some gloves. The shoddy living room held a battered couch and was littered with take-out food containers and empty beer cans, but the main attractions were the two dead bodies sprawled across the floor.

Without looking too hard at the bodies, I followed the sound of voices to a back room and caught the welcome sight of my favorite police detective, Harris, a.k.a. Dimples. Yes! Finally my luck was changing.

Dimples glanced up, and his eyes widened with surprise before he smiled. His dimples made big dents in his face, and for some reason, the tension left my shoulders. "Shelby! What are you doing here?"

Bates glanced up from his position by the third dead body and frowned. "I told her she could come. She's friends with the missing girl's family."

"Bates doesn't like that I'm involved," I responded, deciding to tell the truth, even if it hurt his feelings. "But I'm here because the backpack belongs to my best friend's niece, Chloe, and I was hoping I could help you guys find her."

"That's great," Dimples said. "We can use your help." He was thinking that Bates was an ass, and sometimes he just wished he could punch him in the face.

I smiled and nodded, but refrained from saying *me too* like I wanted. "So do you know who these guys are?"

"No ID on any of them," he responded. "But this kid is young. Probably sixteen or seventeen."

"I think this could be the kid Chloe left school with yesterday," Bates added. "It looks like there was a disagreement and they all started shooting each other."

I glanced at the boy with his wide-open eyes framed by a lock of dark hair dangling over his forehead. A sharp pang went through me. He was so young, only a few years older than Josh. What had happened to him? What had Chloe gotten herself into? "Where was her backpack?"

"In here," he said. "It was shoved under the bed. We found her school ID and phone inside, along with some of her school work."

"So...if they killed each other, what happened to Chloe?"

Dimples shook his head. "Without the backpack, we wouldn't have known she was even here. I think she probably took off."

"But if that's the case, why hasn't she shown up anywhere?" I asked.

Bates shrugged. "Maybe she has something to hide." He was thinking that they'd found evidence of drugs, but it looked like someone had taken them and run.

My breath caught with outrage. Chloe wouldn't have run off with drugs or money. How could he even think that? "I'm sure Chloe wasn't involved with drugs. Maybe someone else was here. Maybe this person forced her to go with them."

Dimples nodded, thinking that was what he'd concluded too, especially since she hadn't shown up at home. Now besides a triple homicide, this could also be a kidnapping, and if that was true, he didn't have much hope for the girl getting out alive. Not if she'd seen something she shouldn't have. But if that were the case, why wasn't she lying here dead too? Unless she ran, and her pursuer took a shot at her. That meant her dead body might be out in the yard somewhere.

"We need to search the area, just in case she's nearby," Dimples said. For my sake, he didn't add that they needed to search for a dead body too.

Bates understood what Dimples meant and left to organize the search.

I sighed with despair, and my gaze was involuntarily drawn to the body. The sight of his lifeless eyes, combined with the heavy, coppery smell of blood, started to turn my stomach into a woozy lump. "Is there anything else you can tell me?"

"That's all we have for now, but we've put out an AMBER Alert on Chloe. Hopefully we'll find her." He said that for my benefit, since he didn't have much hope of finding her alive.

"Oh...uh...good...that's good," I stammered. "Uh...I should probably go. There's not a lot I can do here."

Dimples frowned, thinking it was too bad that I hadn't picked anything up with my premonitions. Usually, I was better than this.

"If I pick up anything, I'll be sure to let you know."

His eyes widened, but his mouth quirked into a half grin. He was thinking he should be used to how I did that by now, even though it always took him off-guard. "Sounds good."

I left with a quick wave and got the heck out of there before I threw up. Standing next to my car, I inhaled deeply to calm my stomach. To take my mind off the grisly scene that seemed tattooed into my brain, I focused on the neighborhood. If Chloe got out of there alive, where would she run to get away from that house?

With the tracks so close, getting onto the light-rail train was probably her best bet. I didn't know where the next station was, but I could do some exploring and find out. I walked toward the tracks and, about a block away, the street dead-ended at some concrete barriers.

I leaned over the barriers and peered up and down the tracks, spotting what looked like a station on the other side not too far away. Hope flooded over me. Maybe Chloe came this way and hopped on a train.

In order to check it out, I'd have to climb the barrier and cross the tracks. I glanced both ways to make sure a train wasn't coming and clambered over the slab of concrete. After landing on the other side, I concentrated on picking my way over the tracks. Now was not a good time to get a foot trapped in the rails.

Halfway across, I caught sight of a shoe lodged in a tight space between the rails, and my heart stopped. It looked exactly like the kind of shoe a fourteen-year-old girl would wear. Was it Chloe's? Without being able to see in the dark, she might have gotten stuck and left it there. Before I could pull it out, the ground began to vibrate underneath me, and I glanced up to find a train roaring toward me.

My breath caught and I froze. Damn! With my heart pounding to beat the devil, I swallowed my instinct to run, and carefully picked my way back over the rails. At the edge of the track, I realized that the concrete barrier was higher on this side, and my stomach clenched. I could still reach the top, but it would take a little more effort to climb over. With the rumbling train getting closer, I found the motivation to heave myself up to the top and kick my legs over to the other side.

As I landed, my shaking legs barely supported me, but I backed away, counting the seconds before the train blew past. I'd made it to ten and let out a breath, relaxing my tight shoulders. That wasn't so close...I had plenty of time to get out of the way. Still, I decided to go back to the house and tell Dimples about the shoe. After being that close to the train, there was no way I was going to try that again.

Back at the house, I was relieved to see Dimples talking with a police officer on the front porch. I approached, and his brows rose in puzzlement, but he excused himself and hurried to my side.

"I thought you left," he said.

"Yeah...well, I took a detour." I explained about the shoe and my close call with death. "It could be hers, so I think someone ought to get it...as long as it's not me."

Dimples shook his head. "I'll get someone down there to retrieve it." He was thinking finding the shoe was good detective work as long as it was Chloe's, but it was most likely just someone throwing a shoe onto the tracks...and I'd almost gotten killed over that?

"I wasn't actually crossing the tracks to get the shoe," I explained, not liking how stupid he made it sound. "I didn't even see the shoe until I got onto the tracks."

"Then what were you doing on the tracks?"

"I just thought if she was trying to run away, she'd probably go that way and hop on a train. It's what I'd do. So maybe if you figure out the time all of this happened and then link it to the times the train stops there...you could figure out what train she might have gotten on."

"I like your train of thought." Dimples grinned, pleased at his pun. "We could check the video feed on the surveillance cameras at the station too. Way to go, Shelby." He playfully punched my arm.

I smiled, grateful my idea had merit. In fact, this could be our big break. We could find out where she went and, even better, we could find her. Who knew I'd be so good at this detective work? "Thanks. Let me know what you find, okay?"

"I will. Thanks Shelby." Dimples didn't want to tell to me that my idea was a long shot, and worse, he doubted that they'd find anything. He also hated to get his own hopes up, but it was worth taking a look. He was so tired of dealing with death, that he truly wanted a happy ending this time.

Hearing that kind of put a crimp in my style, and I headed to my car, wishing I really did have premonitions so I'd know if Chloe was still alive. Now I had to talk to Holly and Scott and let them know what was going on. I didn't want to give them false hope, but I didn't want them to think she was dead either.

I made it back to the ex's house and filled them in on what we'd found. Three dead people kind of shocked them, but since none of them was Chloe, they took it in stride. They were also grateful that I'd been there and could fill them in, since Bates hadn't gotten back to them.

By the time I left, I was tuckered out. Besides seeing those dead bodies and nearly being killed by a train, dealing with so many emotional thoughts had taken a toll on me, and I was ready to go home and take a bath.

Since it was just after three-thirty in the afternoon, I knew my kids would be there, and I couldn't wait to see them. Desire to grab hold of them and give them each a big squeeze rushed over me.

I pulled my car into the garage and got out, noticing a couple of scrapes on my palms from the concrete barrier. Now that I knew they were there, they started to sting. Dang! Why did I have to notice? I washed my hands in the sink, then went in search of my kids. Savannah was in her room and, after a big hug, I asked her about her day. "Did anyone try to throw you into the bathroom today?"

"Mom...how did...did I tell you about that?" She didn't remember telling me, but she must have if I knew.

Oh hell. I kept the smile on my face and shrugged. "I'm sure you did. How else would I know? But that's not the point. I was just wondering if you got to use your new Aikido skills."

"Oh yeah...no. Not today anyway. When's the next class?"

"Tomorrow. We'll go together, all right?"

"Sure." She was thinking it might be fun to take a class with me. It also might be weird...

"Good," I said, not wanting to hear anything bad about me right now. "Well...I need to find Josh. Have you seen him?"

"Um...I think he's in his room." She hadn't seen him, so she didn't know, but his room was a good guess.

"Okay...thanks." On my way to his room, I decided to take something for my headache first. Normally, things didn't bother me so much, but right now, my nerves were a little frazzled. I'd also missed lunch, but with the vision of three dead bodies so fresh in my mind, I wasn't sure I could eat anything anyway.

After swallowing my pills with a big glass of water, I kicked off my shoes and headed downstairs. Josh had a great set up in the basement with a large bedroom and connected bathroom. Besides the laundry room, the rest of the space had an entertainment center on one end, and a pool table on the other.

On a nice day like today, he was usually outside shooting hoops. Or at a friend's house playing soccer. Or shooting pool down here, or playing video games. But he wasn't doing any of those things, which puzzled me. Maybe he wasn't even home.

His bedroom door was shut, so I raised my hand to knock...and froze. I heard voices but couldn't make out what they were saying. Then I sucked in my breath. I recognized Josh's voice, but the other was unmistakably female.

With shock and dismay, I twisted the door knob and barged into his room. Josh jumped a little, but it was from surprise, not guilt. The girl flushed and lowered her eyes. They'd been sitting on the edge of his bed, but Josh sprang to his feet when I pushed the door open.

"Mom!" Josh said. "I...uh..."

"Chloe?" I asked. This was the same girl from the photo, only with shorter hair and no braces. Her clothes were rumpled and dirty, and she had dark circles under her eyes with smudges of dirt on her face. With a quick glance at her feet, I noticed one of her shoes was missing.

"Are you okay?"

Her eyes filled with tears, and she nodded, barely keeping it together.

"Everyone's looking for you. Your parents are frantic. What are you doing here?"

Her lips trembled, and she closed her eyes to gain control over her emotions. Finally calm enough to speak, she answered, "I'm in trouble and I didn't know who to turn to. I remembered Josh talking about you and that you helped people, so I was hoping you could help me."

"We should really get you to the police," I countered. "They're the ones who can help you."

"No! I can't." Her eyes widened with fear. "You have to help me. I'll even pay you. I haven't got much, but I'm sure my dad would pay your fee. Please...Josh said you'd help me."

Her pleading gaze turned to Josh, and he nodded. "That's right, mom. You have to help her. I promised her that you would."

I took a deep breath. "Yeah...okay. But just so you know, I'm already working for your dad to find you, so you don't have to pay me. How about we give him a call? He's worried about you."

"No!" she said. "Not yet. No one can know anything about where I am, okay? Promise me you won't tell him." She was frightened for her life and scared to death. What the heck had happened to her?

"All right, I promise, but you have to tell me what's going on."

She swallowed and nodded, but the trauma of her experience was so real she didn't know where to start, and her thoughts were muddled and erratic. With the way she was feeling, I was surprised she'd made it this far.

"How about we go upstairs and you can tell me what's going on while you eat something...you look like you're starving." I figured Chloe hadn't eaten since it had happened, and I knew Josh was always hungry.

"Okay," Chloe said. She let out a breath and, with it, the tension seemed to drain out of her.

Josh ushered her out the door, and I followed them up to the kitchen. "Would you both like a PB & J?" I asked. At her listless nod, I turned to Josh. "Why don't you get her something to drink? Oh...and get me a diet soda while you're at it."

"Sure," he said.

Doing something so normal calmed Chloe down, and once I got the sandwiches and drinks in front of her, she was ready to eat. I cleaned up the counter while they ate so Chloe could have some space before our talk. Just having her here and safe did me a world of good, but it also came with pangs of guilt that her parents had no idea she was okay.

As they finished up, I sat down at the table. "So, tell me what's going on and why you're so scared."

Chloe picked up her napkin and began to shred it. "I did something really stupid...and...now, I think my friend is dead." Big tears gathered in her eyes, and from the remorse flowing through her, I was afraid she would fall apart before she could tell me much of anything.

"You're doing fine," I prodded. "And you're safe now. What happened?"

"This boy I met picked me up after school yesterday and I guess he was showing off or something because he took me to this house where his friends live. He said it was a secret place and I could go there anytime I wanted to run away." She stopped, then let out a breath and continued. "My mom and I had lots of fights, so he knew I wasn't happy at home."

"Sure," I nodded. "That's understandable."

"Well...these two guys were already there when we got there, and they weren't happy to see us." She was thinking about the gobs of cash sitting on the table and nearly gagged. "Liam...my friend...tried to act like it was no big deal, but I knew he was nervous. He made a big show of taking me to the back rooms, then shut the bedroom door, saying stuff like we needed our privacy...you know...for the guys' benefit, but his hands were shaking.

"Once the door shut, he started to swear and run his hands through his hair. He said stuff like 'we shouldn't have come here' and 'this is bad' so I was getting totally freaked out. He tried to open the windows to sneak out, but they were nailed shut."

She squeezed her eyes closed, and huge tears ran down her face. I grabbed the box of tissues from the counter and set them next to her. After blowing her nose, she continued. "We could hear them arguing, so Liam opened the door a crack. They were talking about us. They were saying we'd seen too much and they had to clear out. One of them said they needed to take us somewhere and kill us so we wouldn't talk. The other one argued that he didn't want to shoot us, but in the end he agreed that we had to die. I was so scared, I didn't know what to do."

"I'm sure you were," I said.

"I never should have gone with him," she sobbed. "I knew it was wrong...but I went anyway."

"It's okay Chloe, you had no idea this would happen. You're safe now. I won't let anything bad happen to you. You can trust me."

Chloe caught my gaze, thinking she hadn't even gotten to the worst part yet. What would I think then? Could she trust me? At least I wasn't the police, but what if I insisted she turn herself in? She couldn't do that. They'd find her and kill her for sure.

"What happened after that?" I asked. "You need to tell me everything so I can help you."

She lowered her gaze and licked her lips, thinking that if she didn't trust me, who could she trust? Not her mom...and her dad would just freak out. The police were out of the question. That was the reason she'd come to me in the first place, so she might as well tell me the whole story.

"Liam closed the door and hurried to the closet. He moved some stuff out of the way and pulled out a gun. He said something like he'd shoot them first and they'd be sorry. He loaded the gun and told me to stay there, then opened the door and started shooting.

"I panicked and hid under the bed. I was so scared. I heard gunshots and shouting, then someone stumbled into the room and fell on the floor. It was Liam, and he was staring right at me. He tried to say something, but he was making this awful gurgling noise. Then he just stopped." She sniffed and wiped her eyes and nose.

"I couldn't hear anything in the other room, so I didn't know if he'd killed them or not, but I couldn't seem to move. I waited as long as I dared, hoping those guys were both dead. Then I heard footsteps in the other room, and I was afraid they were coming to get me. I knew I couldn't stay there, so I scooted out the other side of the bed and peeked around the door.

"I could see down the hallway to the living room and caught a glimpse of someone else. He was muttering something like...you guys never learn do you? Then he started talking about how he'd just take their stash since they didn't need it anymore." Chloe swallowed and closed her eyes. This was the part that could get her killed, and she didn't know how to continue.

"It's okay...you can tell me," I said.

"He...he started coming down the hall, so I hurried back inside and hid under the bed again. I saw his shoes when he came in, and then his fingers when he reached down to check Liam's pulse. He seemed pretty upset because he started swearing." Chloe paused, taking another tissue to wipe her face.

"He pulled out his phone and started talking to someone. He said that the three idiots killed each other, but he'd take the cash and drugs. Then he said he'd do a thorough check of the house to make sure nothing could get traced back to them."

Her wide-eyed gaze caught mine. "I knew I had to get out of there before he found me, but I was so scared. After he left the room, I got out from under the bed and watched for a chance to leave. I saw him in the living room, putting all the cash into a bag and...that's when I saw it." Her face crumpled.

"What? What did you see?"

"A badge...a police badge attached to his belt along with a gun. He was a cop!"

"Good grief! No wonder you didn't go to the police. How did you get out?"

"When his back was turned, I slipped into the other bedroom. There was a window in there that wasn't nailed shut, so I pushed it open and popped out the screen. I thought I could hear him coming, so I got out of there as fast as I could.

"I remembered the train station nearby and ran that way. I made it to the concrete barrier and saw him running toward me. I heard the train coming, but I knew if I didn't get to the other side he'd catch me, so I hopped over the barrier and ran across the tracks. My shoe even got stuck, but I pulled my foot out of the shoe and made it across. With the train between us, he couldn't follow, so I ran hard to the station and jumped onto the train as it pulled up."

"You lost him," Josh said, impressed that, for being in such a bad spot, she'd managed to escape.

"Yeah," she agreed, turning her grateful gaze to Josh. He'd been so understanding and sweet. She'd always thought he was cute, but now she realized how tall he'd grown...and his eyelashes were so long...

"Where did you go?" I asked.

She pulled her attention back to me and blushed. "I...uh...rode the trains for a while, until I figured out which one would bring me closer to home. By then it was late, and I didn't know where to go. Since I'd left my backpack, I was afraid he'd find out where I lived and watch for me, so I ended up at the library.

"There's a place in the top of that old building, like an attic, that's kind of a lounge with a couch and chairs, so I hid there until everyone left. That's where I spent the night. I had all night to figure out what to do. That's when I remembered that you were a P.I. so I came here after I snuck out of the library and waited on your deck. That's where Josh found me after school."

Josh was thinking she was sound asleep and nearly had a heart attack when he woke her up. Now he knew why. He glanced at me. "What are we going to do?"

"Um...well," I answered. "I think I need to call my friend, Detective Harris. I know we can trust him, and he'll figure out a safe place for Chloe until we get this figured out."

Chloe's eyes widened, and her gaze jerked to mine. "What? Are you sure?"

"Yes. It's the only way to find this cop you're worried about. Besides, your parents need to know you're okay. I'll talk to him first. Then we'll go from there."

Her shoulders slumped, and she nodded. "Okay."

"How about I get you some clothes, and you can take a shower while I'm gone. Savannah's close to your size, and I'm sure she's got some sweats you could borrow. What do you say?"

"As long as she won't tell anyone," Chloe answered. She was thinking a shower sounded wonderful and, now that I'd figured out what to do, she was more than ready to let someone take care of her.

"Come on...Savannah's room is upstairs."

I introduced Chloe to Savannah, only telling her that Chloe was in trouble and needed our help. Savannah willingly lent Chloe some of her clothes. Once Chloe was in the shower, I told Savannah the whole story, and how witnessing her friend's death and barely escaping with her life had brought her to us.

"Since she left her backpack there, she's afraid this cop is looking for her. That's why she didn't go home or tell anyone," I concluded.

"That's terrible," Savannah said. "What are we going to do?"

"I'm going to talk to Dimples," I said. "But we have to keep her a secret until I do."

"Yeah...I get that." She felt bad for Chloe but was glad I could help her. Maybe the fact that I was a P.I. wasn't so bad after all...as long as no one tried to kill me again. She still had nightmares about that substitute teacher.

"Oh...honey...uh...thanks, I'm sure you do." I hoped my response made sense since I had basically answered her thoughts instead of what she'd said. A pang of guilt washed over me, and I gave her a big squeeze. "I'll head down to the police station. Maybe you guys could watch a movie or something until I get back."

"Yeah, sure. We'll take care of her."

I smiled and hurried downstairs, glad Savannah wanted to be so helpful. Josh had gone down to his room but hurried up when I called to him. From his thoughts, I knew he'd been straightening his room and the basement for Chloe, since he didn't want her to think he was a slob. Well...that was interesting.

"I'm headed to the police station."

"Okay...I'll make sure Chloe's safe."

"Thanks, Josh."

Chapter 4

I drove to the police station, knowing my kids would do everything they could to help Chloe feel at home. It was a comforting thought, and I was grateful I could trust them. From Chloe's thoughts, I'd gathered a sketchy impression of the cop...or at least the guy she thought was a cop. But he wasn't anyone I'd ever seen before. Could he be from another precinct?

One thing I knew for sure: Chloe's parents needed to know as soon as possible that she was all right, and this was the best way to do that. I entered the police station and made my way to Dimples' desk. I couldn't see him right away, and my heart sank. Why hadn't I called first?

Bates had no trouble spotting me, and I cringed under the barrage of mean thoughts directed my way. It made me mad enough that I walked right over to confront him. "Why do you hate me so much?"

"Huh?" His eyes shifted back and forth, taking in the curious glances sent our way. "Would you knock it off? I don't hate you. Okay?" His thoughts of *geeze you crazy woman...get a grip* contradicted his words. "What are you doing here? Did you find out something about Chloe Peterson?"

"I'm...I'm looking for Dimp...uh...Detective Harris. Is he around?"

His eyes narrowed. He knew I had something. "If you know anything about Chloe, you need to tell me."

"Yeah...right." I turned my back on him and sauntered to Dimples' desk, knowing I never should have talked to him in the first place. He was a hopeless case, and I needed to resign myself to the fact that he would never change.

I sat down and called Dimples' cell number, satisfied to see the pained look on Bates' face. He knew he could be nicer to me but, for the life of him, he didn't think he'd ever said anything mean to my face. So why did I act like he had?

"Hello?"

"Hey, it's Shelby. I'm sitting here at your desk. Where are you?"

"Oh...I'm just downstairs. I'll be right up."

"No...wait," I said, needing to talk where Bates couldn't hear. "I'll come to you. Just tell me where you are."

He chuckled. "Okay...but you won't like it. I'm in the dead files room. You still want to come?"

Goosebumps popped up all over my arms. Damn! I hated that room. Too bad that was probably the safest place to tell him about Chloe. "Yeah...sure. I'm on my way."

As nonchalantly as possible, I walked into the hallway. Bates wondered where I was going and decided to follow me. I caught his gaze and shook my head slowly back and forth, then hurried down the stairs. It freaked him out a little, but I wasn't sorry. If he thought I was crazy, then so be it.

The dead files room was at the end of the hall, and trepidation caught in my throat. Drawing a deep breath, I pushed through my fears and opened the door. The light was on, and Dimples stood in front of a filing cabinet.

"Hey," he said, turning to greet me. "I'm just about done."

I nodded as a cold chill settled around me like a shower of ice water. Hunching my shoulders, I rubbed my arms. "Why is it always so cold in here?"

"Uh...it's in the basement?" Dimples answered. He sent me an apologetic smile. "We don't have to talk here. Once I'm through putting these away, I can meet you someplace else."

"No, no, it's fine."

"Okay." He turned back to his files and rubbed his chin. "You know...you were instrumental in solving four of these cases. Have you ever considered helping with some of these others? I've got one that's just..." He sighed. "It's this one right here. Filing it away down here just makes me feel like a failure...you know?"

His tone softened my heart. "What is it?"

"About a year ago, this guy was found dead in an underpass of the freeway. It's close to the soup kitchen and the park where a lot of homeless people hang out. His wallet, jacket and shoes were gone. From the forensics report, he was shot in the chest at close range." Dimples brought the folder to me and opened it to reveal a picture of a handsome, smiling man.

As I stared at the photo, the dawning realization that I knew him nearly knocked me over. His hair was shorter, and his face more lean, but his eyes were the same. "Oh my gosh! That's Tom Souvall. I went to school with him. We graduated the same year!"

"No kidding?"

"Yeah. I didn't know he'd died. This is awful." I could hardly believe it. I'd had a huge crush on him, and we'd dated for a while, but after high school we lost touch. He even took me to prom, and I'd always had a soft spot in my heart for him. "So you never caught the person who did this?"

"No. All our leads dried up. We finally came to the conclusion that it was a random act of violence, probably by a homeless drug-user who got close enough to kill him for some quick cash."

"But what was he doing in that part of town?"

"He went down there occasionally to help at the homeless shelter. He liked to bring food and help serve people. His wife said his older brother was homeless and died from a drug overdose, so that was the reason Tom wanted to help where he could."

"That's just so sad," I said.

"Yeah. He has two kids. I was the one who had to tell his family. I'll never forget how devastated they were. I promised them that I'd find the person responsible..." He let out a huge sigh. "But I didn't. I feel like I let them down."

"I'm sorry. If you want...I'll take a look, but don't hold your breath."

His eyes lost that touch of sadness, and his face brightened. "Thanks Shelby. I really appreciate it."

"Sure," I said, tucking the folder into my purse.

"Now...what was it you needed to talk to me about?"

"Oh...yeah. Um...just a sec." I tiptoed to the door and yanked it open just to make sure Bates wasn't standing there. He wasn't...and it kind of disappointed me, but I just shrugged and headed back to Dimples. He was wondering what the heck I was doing. "It's about Chloe. I know where she is."

"You do? Is she okay?"

"Yes, but there's a slight problem." I told him everything, ending with the fact that she was now at my house, and a cop was probably after her.

"Oh man, seriously? Did she give you a description of the cop?"

"Yes. But he didn't look familiar to me...I mean...he didn't sound like anyone I've met here, but I was thinking that if you had pictures of all your cops somewhere, like on a roster, I could take a look. Maybe one of them would match?"

Dimples' brows drew together in confusion. I was talking like I'd seen the guy. That didn't make any sense, unless I was lying and I had seen him. But that didn't make any sense either.

"Um...or...I guess we could show Chloe the pictures. Anyway...what should we do? Her parents need to know she's okay. But we don't want the cop to know where to find her, right? Since he might want to kill her?"

"Yes...of course. We need to keep her safe." He was thinking that the first thing he needed to do was tell Chief Winder.

"Before we tell everyone she's been found, we should figure out who the cop is, right?" I asked. "Why don't you let me take a quick look at the roster while you talk to the chief...just in case I pick up something with my premonitions?"

"Uh...okay...sure," Dimples agreed, slightly dazed that I knew he was going to talk to the chief.

I followed him upstairs to his desk, passing Bates, who outwardly ignored me but was mentally keeping track of my every move.

Dimples sat in front of his computer and pulled up the resource file with the names and photos of every cop in the precinct. "Okay...here you go."

"Wait. He wasn't in uniform...shouldn't that narrow it down?"

"No...everyone in the photos has on a uniform whether they wear them to work or not."

"Oh...okay."

He vacated the seat, and I quickly sat down to begin the process. Scrolling through the photos and remembering Chloe's mental images made it hard to decipher who it could be. There were a few that could be a match, but that didn't make it a sure thing.

By the time I got done, I had two names that were best guesses, and I didn't think Chloe would fare any better. It could be neither of them, and I hated wrongly accusing an innocent cop. On the other hand, I could just talk to each of them. After a few questions, I'd know who the real bad guy was. That could work...as long as Dimples would go along with it.

He'd been in Chief Winder's office for a while now, but I didn't dare interrupt, so I went back through the roster again. Finally, the door opened, and Dimples stuck his head out and motioned me inside. I logged off the computer and grabbed my notes.

"Shelby, have a seat," Chief Winder said. "We need to notify Chloe's parents that she's safe. If they will cooperate, I'd like to keep a tight lid on this so that no one else finds out. Harris and I would like you to help us with that. Right now she's at your house and no one else knows. Is that correct?"

"Well...my two kids know. They're home with her. But they're the only ones."

"Okay. This is what we're going to do," he said. "Harris will head over to the parents' house and fill them in. If they're okay with it, I'd like to know if you're willing to keep Chloe at your place until a decision is made.

"Given the delicate situation, I don't want to put her under police protection, so it's up to her family to keep her safe until we find the cop who may be after her. In the meantime, I want her to look at the roster and see if she can identify the cop."

"Okay," I agreed. "I can take the roster home with me to show her."

"Good." Chief Winder held out a large binder. "Everyone in the department is in there."

Taking the heavy binder I said, "Just so you know...he might be watching her house in case she shows up."

"Yeah," Dimples agreed. "I'm sure he'd recognize her from the AMBER alert. If we hadn't found her backpack, we wouldn't have known she'd even been there. He must have missed it under the bed. That was our lucky break."

A shiver ran down my spine. That was lucky, but I had a feeling Chloe would have found me anyway. She was one gutsy kid. "I'll be going then. Let me know what happens."

I held the heavy binder under my arm and made a quick exit, noting that this time Bates blatantly stared at me. He was thinking that the chief better let him in on what was going on, or he was going to be really mad.

As long as he left me alone, I was okay with that. It took longer than I liked to get home since I got stuck in rush hour traffic. I pulled into the garage and hefted the binder inside the house where I plopped it on the kitchen counter. "I'm home!" I called.

Savannah rushed into the kitchen making little shushing noises. "Mom...she's asleep."

"Oh? Where?" I asked.

"On my bed. After her shower, she looked so tired. I told her she could lie down if she wanted, and she fell asleep. Just like that."

"I'm sure she was exhausted," I said.

"So what's going on? What are we going to do?"

"Hey," Josh said, coming up the stairs. "Yeah...what's going on?"

"I need to talk to Chloe..."

"I'm here," Chloe said. At the sound of her voice, we turned toward the stairs and watched her descend. Her face was still pale, but the nap and shower had done her some good and, even better, the fear in her eyes was gone. "What happened?"

I snatched up the binder and set it on the table. "I brought this home for you to look through. Hopefully, you'll be able to identify the cop you saw at the house. Detective Harris is talking to your parents to decide where you'll stay until we find him. But you're more than welcome to stay here if you want." I explained the details of the plan, while she sat down at the table and opened the binder.

I picked up that Chloe wasn't sure how comfortable she'd be staying with us, but when Josh smiled at her, she changed her mind. Maybe it wouldn't be so bad with him here. He was really cute, and she wondered how she'd missed that.

I glanced at Josh, and he flushed that I'd caught him staring. "I'm going to go shoot some hoops."

"Okay," Chloe said, responding before I could, and sending him a shy smile. Hmm...

She finally turned her attention back to the pictures, and a gnawing fear crept over her that she wouldn't be able to identify the guy at all. Her glimpses of him at the house were quick and fleeting, and she realized that, besides the general hair color, she wasn't exactly sure of his features.

"Here's a pen and paper," I said, setting them down beside her. "Don't worry about being absolutely sure about him. Just write down the name and page numbers of anyone that looks close, and I'll take it from there. Once I interview them, I'll know who it is."

She glanced at me, her eyes wide with skepticism. How could I be so sure?

"I have a knack for that sort of thing," I explained. "That's why I'm so good at my job."

"Oh," she said. "Okay."

With Chloe occupied, Savannah and I started making dinner. It needed to be something easy, so I threw some potatoes in to bake and got out a couple cans of chili. As the smell of potatoes began to permeate the air, I finally got the call I'd been waiting for.

"Hey. What did they decide?" I asked Dimples.

"I'm here with them now. The plan is that they want Chloe to stay with Holly for now. Since Holly's family, a visit to her place wouldn't seem suspicious, and they can see Chloe anytime they want. In the meantime, we'll keep up the pretense that we're still looking for her and so will her parents."

"Okay. That makes sense."

"So this is what we're thinking," Dimples continued. "Holly's here, but she's headed home. In a couple of hours, when it's dark, you can take Chloe over there. Just make sure she stays out of sight. Has she picked out anyone from the pictures yet?"

"Um...no," I said. "I think it's going to take a while, but I'll call you with a name when I have one. I was wondering if I could be there when you talk to them...you know...so I can tell if it's them or not? Just in case she's not sure. You'll let me do that, right?"

"Yes," Dimples said. "And Shelby...if you get any feelings...or premonitions about anything, don't hesitate to call me. I don't want anything bad to happen to Chloe."

"Thanks. I won't, and I'll call you as soon as I have a name."

We disconnected, and my heart warmed that Dimples believed in me and my premonitions. Lots better than anything I'd heard from Bates. I told Chloe the plan, and she was disappointed that she wouldn't be staying here. I think it was mostly because of Josh.

"I've been through this binder twice," she said. "And I've narrowed it down to two guys. It's just so hard to know from a picture. I think if I saw him in person, it would be easier to tell." She pursed her lips in frustration.

"Let me see," I said. She showed me their pictures, and both men were the same ones I'd picked out. "This is good. I can let Dimples know, and he can check into what they've been up to. Maybe tomorrow I can talk to them, and we'll know which one it is by then. This is great."

"Really?" she asked.

"Yes. Soon you'll be back home, and your parents will probably ground you forever...but at least you survived. I have to say, I'm impressed that you could take care of yourself and think so fast on your feet. You did an amazing job to get out of that situation...and coming to see me...that was genius."

Her lips turned up in a small smile, but even my kind words did little to dispel the gloom of what she had gone through. She closed her eyes, thinking it was stupid she'd put herself in that position in the first place. Her parents were going to kill her. And Liam had died...right in front of her. It was horrible.

"So what was it like staying in the library all night?" I asked, hoping to take her mind off Liam. "I think it would be kind of scary."

"Yeah...it was a little. But the lounge area is really small, and I put a chair up under the doorknob so no one could get in. Before I did that, I found one of my favorite books and a flashlight and read most of the night." She was thinking she mostly kept reading so she wouldn't have to think about what had happened or replay the scene of Liam's death over and over in her mind.

"I'm so sorry that happened to you," I said. "But you'll get through this. I know...I've seen someone die before too, right in front of me, and it definitely leaves a mark, so if you ever need to talk...I'm here."

"Really?" she asked, surprised.

"Yeah," I admitted. "It was awful." Actually, I'd seen quite a few people get shot and killed, but I wasn't about to tell her that. Not when I was trying to forget them myself. "It's better if you don't dwell on it. But please feel free to talk to me if you need to...I really do understand how it feels."

"Thanks Shelby," she said, gazing at me, her eyes wide with awe. "So you're doing okay?"

"Yeah," I said, smiling. "And you will too, just give it some time." My phone rang, and I checked the caller ID. "It's Holly. I'd better answer." I pushed the button and barely said hello before she started talking.

"Shelby! Oh my gosh!" she exclaimed. "I can't believe Chloe is really there. Is she all right?"

"Yes...she's good."

"I can't tell you how grateful we are that you've got her. All of us. And my poor brother. It's been a nightmare."

"Yes," I agreed. "I'm sure it has...but she's here and she's safe. What time do you want me to bring her over?"

"Um...Detective Dimples said to wait until it got dark."

"Holly! You didn't call him Detective Dimples did you?"

She chuckled. "No...but you've told me enough about him that the minute I saw those dimples, I knew exactly who he was. I'm glad you know him. Oh, and he's lots nicer than Bates."

That brought a smile to my lips. "Thanks for saying that, but I think Bates is okay as long as I'm not around. Anyway,

I'll text you before we leave, but we should be there after dinner, probably around seven, seven-thirty?"

"Sounds great. Give Chloe my love...and just a sec...here's Scott."

"Shelby!" Scott said, sounding out of breath. "Thank you...I don't know what to say...but I'm so relieved..."

"Thanks is fine...hey...I'm sure you want to talk to Chloe...here she is."

I handed her the phone, and she swallowed before taking it. "Dad...I'm so sorry...I never meant..."

He cut off her apology, telling her how grateful he was that she was all right and how much he loved her. I busied myself with dinner to give her some privacy. She spoke to her mother as well and, a few minutes later, handed me the phone, wiping tears from her eyes. "I'm going to use the bathroom."

"Sure," I said.

I glanced through the roster at the pictures of the men one more time. With both of us picking out the same people, I had to believe it was a good sign that it could be one of them. I pushed Dimples' cell number and waited for him to answer. He picked up after the first ring.

"Okay...I've got the names. Are you ready?" I rattled them off, and he didn't sound surprised or upset, but what did I know since I couldn't hear his thoughts? "Do you know either of them?" I asked.

"Yeah. I know them both."

"Do you think one could be involved?"

"Shelby...I just don't know. I'm still in shock that she saw a cop in the first place. I don't want to believe one of our own could be involved in this, but if they are...well...I guess we'll find out. Can you come down to the precinct tomorrow?"

"Sure...but how are you going to get them to meet with us without scaring them off?"

"Leave that to me. Just be ready. I'll call you in the morning and set up a time to talk to them. Be careful tonight. Bates is the only one besides me and the captain that knows we have her, so she should be safe, but we can't be too careful."

"I will," I said. "See you tomorrow." We disconnected, and the enormity of what we were trying to pull off filled me with doubt. It was too bad the police couldn't do any more to protect her, but this plan should keep her safe.

"Did you give him the names?" Chloe asked. She had perked up quite a bit, now that she knew her parents weren't furious with her.

"Yes."

"Did he know them?" She was worried that he'd believe the cop over her, especially if they were friends.

"We'll get to the bottom of it, Chloe. If it's one of these guys, we'll find out."

As she nodded, Josh came inside. "Hey," he said, wondering how long Chloe was going to stay. It was kind of nice having her here...and a little weird too.

"Chloe's going over to Holly's house after dinner," I said.

"Oh," he answered, relieved and disappointed at the same time.

"Hey...do you have Mr. Johnson for math?" Chloe asked.

"Yeah. I do."

"Me too. Do you know what the assignment was for today?"

"Uh...let me look," Josh said. He picked up his backpack from the floor by the table, and she followed him into the living room where they sat side by side on the couch. Soon they were talking about their teachers and classes.

I let out a relieved sigh that they were getting along so well. It was good for Chloe to have some normalcy right now. I also picked up that undertone of attraction and interest from both of them, and my heart did a little flutter. It was tempting to intrude on their thoughts...but that just seemed wrong on so many levels, so I resolutely put up my shields.

It was a relief when Chris came home and I could tell him what was going on. He'd heard about the AMBER alert and was shocked to find Chloe at our house. "I don't know if they can keep this a secret for long, especially with the reporters and TV crews watching the family's every move."

"Yeah...well, hopefully we'll know which cop it is by tomorrow."

We had a pleasant dinner, and soon it was time to take Chloe to Holly's house. She and Josh had spent all their time together before dinner, and I had a feeling we'd be seeing more of her once this was all done.

Chloe said her goodbyes...mostly to Josh, and we got into the car. As I pulled out of the garage, I made sure she kept her head down. I couldn't see any strange cars on the street, but it was dark and I didn't want to take any chances. With Holly's house just around the block, it was a quick drive, and I didn't catch sight of anyone following. Still, I pulled in the driveway and all the way to the back of the house.

Chloe jumped out and ran to the back door, but I took my time, closing the door and listening for anyone thinking about us being there. Of course, if they were in a car, I wouldn't be able to hear them, but I had to try. Hearing nothing, I let out my breath and went inside.

Holly smothered me with a hug as soon as I entered. She couldn't stop thanking me for my part in finding Chloe, and I kind of felt bad since it was Chloe who'd found me. I tried to tell her that, but she wouldn't hear of it.

Holly's husband, Dave, said hello and her three kids took Chloe downstairs. I knew the kids were dying to hear all the gruesome details, and I hoped Chloe could handle it. I sat down at the kitchen table and Holly got me a diet soda with crushed ice. She knew me so well.

"Scott's coming over a little later, but no one should suspect anything since I'm his sister," Holly explained, setting the soda in front of me.

"What about Kira?" I asked.

She pursed her lips. "Yeah...she's coming over too, but not until about eleven and only for a few minutes. She's taking this pretty hard and doesn't want to mess up. So...do you have any leads?"

"Chloe picked out a couple of cops who looked similar to the man she saw," I said. "So it's not a sure thing, but I'll be going in tomorrow to question them. So it should be resolved by then."

Dave was thinking that didn't sound like a sure thing at all. How was I going to know who it was just by talking to them? What kind of a plan was that? He didn't like any of this and thought Chloe should be under police protection with someone who had a gun and wasn't afraid to use it. Of course, if it was a cop...that just made it all worse. Could he protect her if a cop showed up? Beneath those sentiments was his real worry that his family could be in danger as well. He had a shotgun; maybe he'd better get it out.

"The police don't know the extent of who's involved, so the best way to keep Chloe safe is to keep her out of their system. Having her come here is really the best option," I said, meeting his gaze. "I think she'll be fine staying here with you. I know I wouldn't want my child with anyone else. I really think this is the best plan, and I'm sure nothing will happen to you or your family."

Dave sat back, surprised that I'd responded to his worries. "Oh...I didn't know that. I am glad we can help her, I just hope we can keep her safe here." Holly's brows creased, and she shot him a glance that sent guilt flowing over him. She was thinking it was the least they could do for their niece after what she'd been through, and if he didn't like it, he could...

"Well, I'd better be going," I said. "Thanks for the soda. I'll call tomorrow."

Holly thanked me again and I hurried out to my car, hoping they wouldn't get into an argument since they both had valid points. I pulled out of the driveway, watching closely for anything suspicious, but that didn't stop the shiver of unease that ran down my spine. Dave was right to be concerned. Somewhere a dirty cop was out there looking for a missing girl, and I couldn't shake the feeling that he was already watching me.

Relieved to enter my garage without incident, I hurried inside, grateful to be home. I let Chris and the kids know everything went well and Chloe was safe. Chris and Josh were watching a football game, and Savannah had homework, so now was the perfect time to take a bath. I was exhausted, both mentally and physically, so a bath sounded wonderful.

I hurried to my bedroom to change, and there, sitting on the bed, was the folder of my old flame and his unsolved murder. I had forgotten all about it. Picking it up, I flipped it open for another look at his picture. His eyes held warmth and a touch of mischief, like he was ready to laugh about something.

Memories of him from our time in high school flooded my mind. I smiled, remembering the car he drove back then. It was a convertible, and he would take me on long drives. Most of the time, we ended up at the lake, where we'd skip rocks and hike around until we found a good spot to watch the sunset. He always carried a camera and took a ton of pictures. Most were of me. He called me 'sunshine,' because of my blond hair, and said I was the most photogenic person he'd ever known. I still had a few of those photos, and I always wondered what he'd done with the rest.

I also remembered the way he smelled. Like a cross between Irish Spring and fresh-cut grass. I used to ask him what cologne he was wearing since I loved that smell so much, and he would never tell me. No matter how many times I pestered him about it. It drove me crazy. Now he was gone, and my heart ached to know he was dead...and worse, someone had murdered him.

With a sigh, I read through the report. It was basically the same thing that Dimples had already told me. His wallet was taken, but they'd never had any hits on the credit cards, so whoever it was didn't use them. They figured some homeless people took his jacket and shoes, so that made sense in a sick sort of way. But it still broke my heart. The detectives had done a good job following leads, and my hopes sank. How was I ever supposed to solve this case?

I came to the crime-scene photos and chewed on my bottom lip. Did I really need to look at these? Taking a deep breath, I quickly glanced through them, then closed my eyes and put them away. Seeing his lifeless body propped up against a freeway pillar like that brought tears to my eyes. Maybe I shouldn't have told Dimples I'd help him. It was just so sad. Of course, I might feel better about it if I found the killer. But what if I couldn't?

My cell phone rang, startling me. The caller ID said it was Dimples and I froze. Had something happened to Chloe? "Hello?"

"Shelby," Dimples said, his voice strained. "It's Billie. She's been shot."

"What?"

"I don't know if she's going to make it. They just took her into surgery. Can you come to the hospital?"

"Of course. I'll be right there."

I hurried through the hospital doors and rushed to the waiting room where Dimples sat with his head in his hands. "Drew?" I'd never called him by his real name, but at that moment, it felt right.

"Shelby." He stood and gathered me into a tight hug. I felt his regret and anguish that he might lose the woman he loved. He hadn't realized it until this moment, and now he might lose her. What if she didn't make it and he never got the chance to tell her? Shards of pain hit him in the chest and made it hard to breathe. She'd wormed her way into his heart, and now he couldn't think about living without her. Why had this happened? He was the one that was supposed to get shot, not her.

I held him tight, hating that this was happening to him. A moment later, he took a deep breath and let it out, then loosened his hold on me. Still holding my arm, he pulled me down into the chair beside him, and then shook his head. Tears pooled in his eyes, but he blinked them away and pursed his lips, working hard to gain control.

"Don't forget that Billie's a fighter," I said, struggling not to cry myself. "We have to believe that she'll come through this. Don't give up on her. Okay?" He nodded and inhaled deeply to pull himself together. "Good. Now tell me what happened. Who shot her?"

"I don't know. I just...I had just finished talking to you and Chloe's parents. Bates and I were watching the house after...just to see if anyone suspicious was around. Since I was going to be late to her place, I called, but she didn't pick up. It worried me a little, but I figured she was busy and would call me back when she got a minute." He shook his head, thinking he should have left right then, and maybe now she wouldn't be in surgery.

"I left about a half hour later. Bates said he'd keep an eye on things so I could make it up to Billie. When I got to her apartment, the door was ajar and the place was trashed. I found Billie..." He swallowed, thinking of all that blood and how at first he thought she was dead. "She was barely hanging on."

He leaned forward with his head in his hands, and I patted his back, then put up my shields. His grief and pain were more than I could handle, and I didn't want to break down in front of him. He needed me to be strong, so I concentrated on that. I could cry about Billie later.

"I think I may know something about it," I said.

Dimples' head jerked up. "What? What do you mean?"

"Billie's been working on the case against the attorney general, Grayson Sharp. She had a thumb-drive with incriminating information that was stolen from her desk in her office. She made a copy and hid it in her apartment. I think that's what they were after. Maybe she walked in on them and they shot her."

Dimples eyes hardened. "If Grayson Sharp is behind this...he will not get away with it. I will make sure of that."

"I'll help you," I said, worried that he might take things into his own hands. "But be careful who you talk to about this. You don't know who's in his pocket. He's got a lot of influence."

"Maybe. But he's not above the law."

"That's right. So we need to figure out how to stop him through the proper channels, and you're just the person to do it." I hoped he'd take that to heart and not do anything stupid.

Dimples nodded, but he was thinking how much he'd like to walk into his office and shoot off his kneecaps. After that, his questioning would begin. Then if he didn't like the answers, he'd keep shooting different body parts until he was satisfied.

"Don't do anything stupid, okay? Like...shoot him?"

He blinked, pulling away from his bloodthirsty thoughts, and focused on me. "Uh...no...of course not." But he wondered how I knew what he was thinking. Just like I'd read his mind.

"Good," I said. "Because you were looking like you had murder in your eyes, and it kind of scared me."

"You got that from my eyes?" he asked. I nodded, and he let out a breath. Of course I did. What was he thinking? It was the stress. If he knew Billie was going to make it, he wouldn't feel so helpless and imagine such stupid things.

Now I sighed. I didn't want to make him feel worse...and yet...I was...and at a time like this. Ugh! Maybe I wasn't as good at comforting people as I'd hoped. I certainly didn't want to make him feel bad.

Just then the doctor came into the room and approached us. "Detective Harris?"

"Yes." Dimples braced for bad news, and I caught my breath.

"Billie made it through surgery and that was huge. She's not out of the woods yet, but she's young and strong. Her chances of making it through this are pretty good. We just need to see how she does in the next few hours."

He went on to describe her injuries and what they'd done, but I barely followed. Dimple's relief mixed with my own nearly sent me to my knees. Before I knew it, the doctor had left, and Dimples caught me in a hug.

"She's going to make it," he said, his breath warm against my neck. He pulled away and smiled, his dimples doing that crazy dance that always cheered me up. "The doctor said I could see her, so I guess I'll call you in the morning. Tomorrow, we can figure out exactly what happened."

"Okay," I agreed.

"Thanks for coming." He gave my hand a squeeze, then rushed down the hall.

I walked out of the hospital a little lighter than when I walked in, relieved to know that Billie would be okay. Someone had nearly killed her for that stupid thumb-drive, and it made me furious.

If it was that important, I should probably go over there and see if they got it. If they didn't, I could take it for safe-keeping. It wouldn't be hard since I knew exactly where it was. The police might still be there processing the crime scene, so I'd be safe, and I knew Billie would want me to get it...if it was still there.

I drove to her apartment before I chickened out. There weren't any police cars left in the parking lot, and I cursed my luck that I'd missed them. But now that I was there, I might as well go upstairs and take a look. She lived in a third-floor apartment with outside stairs on both ends. It had a nice, open feel with apartments on both sides of the open staircase with plenty of room to walk through to the other side on each floor. I'd be able to see if anyone was around, so it should be all right.

By the time I got to the top of the third floor, I was a little out of breath. No wonder Billie was so skinny. I'd hate lugging groceries up here. Her apartment was at the other end of the floor and, as I got closer to the doorway, I caught sight of the yellow crime scene tape flapping in the breeze.

I trudged to her door anyway, since I'd come so far, and tried the knob. Of course it didn't turn, but it also didn't look like it was shut tight. With a little push inward, it popped open, and I caught my breath. It'd done it now.

My pulse raced and I glanced both ways before ducking under the tape and stepping inside. I pulled my coat sleeves over my hands so I wouldn't leave fingerprints and pushed the door shut behind me. Hardly daring to breathe, I stood in the dark and let my eyes adjust.

I'd never been in Billie's apartment before, but what I'd seen from her thoughts helped me get a picture of where things were supposed to be. This was nothing like that. The place was a wreck. Overturned furniture and broken knickknacks littered the floor. Stuffing spilled out of the couch where it had been ripped apart, and pictures on the wall hung askew.

Remembering my stun flashlight, I pulled it out of my purse and flipped on the light. The mess seemed even worse now that I could see it better. Stepping carefully, I rounded the corner to the hallway and into the second bedroom which she had made into an office.

The computer was gone, and everything on the desk had been swept off onto the floor. I shone the light into the mess and let out my breath. The little box lay on its side, open and empty. Relieved to find it, I picked it up and gently closed the lid. The key was missing, but that didn't matter. I had a copy of the key that would open the secret compartment inside.

This was the box that had once belonged to Sam Killpack, a P.I. who had been murdered, and a case I knew well since I had been the main suspect. Somehow, Billie had managed to keep it after the murder investigation, and I knew she'd hidden the thumb-drive inside the secret compartment.

I hesitated, then stuffed it into my purse, hoping I hadn't just made a huge mistake. Leaving it here might be the safest place for it, but I couldn't take the chance of it getting lost or taken by someone else.

A sense of urgency filled me with the need to get out of there. Since I knew the shooter hadn't found it, I was a sitting duck if he came back to look again. I hurried to the door and pulled it open a crack, checking the hallway and staircase. Finding the way clear, I ducked under the tape and pulled the door closed, making sure it locked behind me.

I took off down the hall in a rush, but as I started down the stairs, I picked up someone's thoughts. He was thinking about a woman with blond hair wearing jeans and a black jacket with a large bag over her shoulder. My breath caught. That was me. I glanced toward the parking lot, but it was too dark to see anyone.

He was trying to figure out my identity and what I was doing there. I wasn't someone he'd seen around. Maybe I had come to check out Billie's apartment. Had I gone inside? He turned his attention to taking a few snapshots of me with his phone, so I hustled back up the stairs like I'd forgotten something. He swore in his mind that he hadn't gotten a good shot of my face and decided to follow me.

There was another staircase at the end of the hall, so I hurried toward it and crept down the stairs as fast as I dared while he ran up the stairs on the other side. Once he reached the third floor, I doubled back on the ground floor and ran to my car. I jumped inside and peeled out of there, hoping I'd gotten away before he had a chance to snap a photo of me or my car.

Breathing heavily, I clenched the steering wheel so hard my knuckles turned white, and it was sometime later before I could relax my grip enough to peel my fingers off. Who was that guy? Maybe he was working with the police...or he was a P.I. hired to watch her place for some reason...or, worst case scenario, the guy who'd shot her. Either way, it was a good thing he didn't get my picture.

It was almost midnight when I got home. Instead of going to the hospital with me, Chris had stayed with the kids. Mostly because neither of us wanted them home alone in case a dirty cop showed up at our house looking for Chloe.

Now besides that, I had Billie's thumb-drive to worry about, and my stomach clenched with dread. The last time I had a thumb-drive that didn't belong to me hadn't turned out so well. Even worse, what was I going to tell Chris? He'd be furious that I'd gone to Billie's in the first place, let alone taken the box. But...it was late. Maybe he'd be asleep in bed. Even if he was half asleep, I could tell him about Billie and wait until tomorrow for the thumb-drive part.

I entered my house and automatically locked the door behind me. The kitchen light was still on, so I flipped it off. As I made my way up the stairs, I crossed my fingers that Chris was asleep and pushed the door open. The lamp beside the bed was on, and Chris sat up as I came in, dashing my hopes.

"Hey," he said, smiling anxiously. "How's Billie doing? Is she going to make it?"

"Yes," I said. "Dimples is with her, and they're pretty sure she'll pull through."

"That's a relief. So what happened?" he asked.

"Her place was ransacked. Someone was looking for something, and I think she might have surprised them."

"That's crazy. What were they looking for?"

"My best guess is that whoever shot her was probably looking for the thumb-drive with the information about the attorney general."

"The one she got from that secretary?"

"Yeah. I told you someone stole the one from her desk at work, right?" At his nod I continued. "Well she made a copy and hid it in her apartment."

"Wow. That's nuts. Do you know if they got it?" he asked.

I hadn't decided what to tell him about my visit to her apartment. I didn't want him mad at me, but I also didn't want to lie to him. He noticed my hesitation and his brows drew together, so I quickly answered.

"Um...not exactly. I'm going to help Dimples look through her apartment tomorrow." This was mostly true...since I didn't know for sure if the thumb-drive was in the box I'd taken, and I was sure Dimples would want my help tomorrow.

Chris' lips twisted and his eyes narrowed. "Why do I get the feeling you're not telling me everything?"

My eyes widened, and he knew at that moment he'd caught me. My shoulders sagged in defeat, and I crawled onto the bed beside him. "I went to her place after I left the hospital."

I told him everything, even the part about the guy who'd seen me from the parking lot, and felt his muscles tighten with tension under me. Before I lost my nerve, I pulled the box from my bag. "I have a key to this...so we can see if the thumb-drive is in it."

Chris closed his eyes. Besides nearly getting caught...probably by the bad guy, he was thinking about all the laws I'd broken and...*what the hell?* He rubbed his forehead like he always did when I upset him and tried to reign in his thoughts about how stupid that was, and how was I going to explain it to Harris? Did I even think before I did stuff like that? If the police found out, I was in so much trouble.

I cleared my throat and tried not to feel bad. He hadn't said a word...and that made it even worse. "I thought the police would be there...you know...working on the crime scene...and they'd let me in, or I wouldn't have gone in the first place.

"And contrary to what you think, I didn't break in...the door wasn't closed tight so it just popped open. I thought if someone could get in that easily, I'd better get the box while I could and make sure the door was closed and locked up tight before I left. It was the least I could do for Billie."

"Uh-huh," Chris said, resigned to what I'd done, but not entirely over it. "Well...I guess you might as well check the box, right?" He was thinking I could tell Dimples that Billie had given me the box for safe-keeping. As long as it didn't show up in the crime-scene photos, I wouldn't end up in jail.

"What? You think he'd put me in jail?"

"Probably not," he said. "I just thought that to scare some sense into you." He sighed, then tightened his hold around me. "I'm just grateful nothing bad happened."

He was thinking that Billie had nearly died, and there I was poking my nose into the crime scene. It was just one more thing that he hated about what I did. But he also knew he couldn't ask me to stop.

Guilt rushed over me, and I frowned. Was it really that bad for him?

"Um...let me get the key," I said. His arms loosened, and I pulled away. I found the key in my jewelry box and sat beside Chris. The key fit perfectly into the lock and, somewhere inside, a spring popped, pushing a false drawer open. "It's here. Billie will be so relieved."

"That's good," Chris said, trying to be supportive. "So...what are you doing to do with it now?"

"Leave it there." I pushed the drawer with the thumb-drive back inside, then put the box under the bed and the key back in my jewelry box.

"Aren't you going to look at it?" he asked.

"Not tonight. It's enough to know it's safe."

I changed out of my clothes and put on my pajamas, then headed into the bathroom to wash my face and brush my teeth. I listened for Chris' thoughts, but he had closed them up tight, probably because he didn't want to hurt my feelings. That just made me feel worse.

I came out and slipped under the covers, then turned out the light and snuggled up next to him.

"I don't like what you did," Chris said. "You took a big risk and almost got caught." He sighed and put his arms around me. "What if that guy had wanted to shoot you instead of take your picture? I don't want you to end up in the hospital like Billie did tonight." He was also thinking he didn't want to go through what Harris had either.

"I know...but I'm fine. Nothing happened, and I got the thumb-drive."

Chris sighed, then nodded. "Yeah...I get it...you did it for Billie."

"You're right," I said, laying my head against his chest. "I felt so helpless sitting in the hospital with Dimples. He was so sad and scared. When the doctor told him she'd pull through, he changed. He really loves her. I don't think he knew how much until this happened. Worse...he never told her. So...now at least he'll get to tell her how he feels. Who knows what will happen between them after that? Wouldn't it be cool if they got married?"

He chuckled and pulled me close. "You always like to look on the bright side of things. I guess that's one of the things I love about you, even if you sometimes drive me crazy." He playfully nipped at my lips with his, then deepened the kiss until we were both breathless.

I felt it the moment he let go of his anger. His love crashed over me with such force that it took my breath away. He was thinking that right now, he didn't want to worry about the future and what could, or couldn't, happen. What he needed most was to live in this moment and enjoy holding me in his arms.

Chapter 5

First thing the next morning I called Dimples to see how Billie was doing. "Better," he said. "She even woke up and talked to me for a few minutes."

"That's great."

"Yeah...actually, I'm still here at the hospital. I think I'll stay a little longer, but I'd like to meet you at her apartment later. Maybe you'll pick up on something that we missed. Does that sound good?"

"Uh...sure," I agreed. "But I could come to the hospital first if that's better."

"Well...Billie would probably like to talk to you, but she's pretty wiped out." He hesitated, and I could hear someone else talking before he came back on the line. "She wants you to come here. Will that work?"

"Sure, tell her I'll be by around nine-thirty or so."

"Okay," he said. "And...thanks again for coming last night."

"You bet."

After Chris and the kids left, it was close to eight o'clock, and I was tempted to go back to bed for half an hour. Yesterday had worn me out, and I hadn't slept well last night. But now that I was awake and thinking about all my worries, I didn't think I could go back to sleep anyway.

I gave Holly a quick call to check on Chloe and let her know I was meeting with Dimples this morning. She reported that everything was going well for now, but I could hear the tension in her voice.

"Did Scott and Kira make it over for a visit?" I asked.

"Yes, and they came late, so I don't think anyone noticed. I've had a few calls from the media this morning already, asking for information, but I've referred everything to the police like Dimples said to do."

I puffed out a breath. "You know it makes me nervous when you call him Dimples, right?"

"Yeah," she chuckled. "Why do you think I do it? Anyway...other than that, we're just waiting for news, so keep me in the loop, okay?"

"Sure," I agreed. "How's Chloe holding up?"

"Better since Scott brought over her phone last night."

"What? Wait...she's not texting her friends is she?"

"No of course not...just her parents and...Josh," she replied.

"Josh?" That surprised me, but I should have seen it coming. "Oh Josh...right."

"Scott brought the phone over. I guess he got it from Dimples. Chloe's supposed to text him a few times during the day, which I can certainly understand."

"Oh, for sure...me too. Well, I'll let you know what happens with...uh...Dimples today."

She laughed and we disconnected, but it made me think that maybe I shouldn't call him that anymore. I wasn't sure I could do that since it was such a habit, but I could probably try.

I ate breakfast and mulled over everything I needed to do. Finding the dirty cop for Chloe was imperative, but so was finding out who shot Billie. I also had the thumb-drive and needed to figure out what to do about that, but if I could talk to Billie about it, maybe she'd help me figure it out. Then there was the guy who'd seen me last night. It would certainly be nice to know who he was.

The file on my old flame, Tom Souvall, sat on my dresser where I'd left it last night, and I knew that his murder case would have to take a back seat for now. There was also Uncle Joey's old friend Blake Beauchaine to consider but, until Uncle Joey asked for something specific, there was nothing for me to do about it.

With all that to worry about, it didn't help my mood that the sky was covered in gray clouds and it was raining off and on. The drop in temperature meant it was time to turn the heat on in the house. I had put it off as long as possible, not wanting the good weather to end. I loved fall, but a dreary day like this meant winter was coming for real.

At least I had some really cute boots to wear, and I'd wanted to get a motorcycle jacket...black leather, of course. Maybe when this was all over I could see what they had at the mall. That cheered me up enough to get into the shower.

The hospital doors swooshed open for me, and I hurried inside, anxious to see how Billie was doing. As I got to her room, I stopped to glance through the glass in the door. Dimples slouched in the chair beside her bed, his eyes closed and his head slumped forward. But he sat close enough to hold Billie's hand, and my heart warmed to find them like this.

Billie's pale face gave her a vulnerability I'd never seen before, and I sighed with gratitude that she'd survived. With her dark hair framing her face, she reminded me of a princess waiting for her prince charming to kiss her awake. My mood lightened and I smiled, knowing how much she'd hate that image of herself.

Dimples jerked his head up as I came inside. He quickly let go of Billie's hand and checked his watch. "Wow...is it nine-thirty already?"

"Um...yeah," I said. "Did you stay here all night?" He glanced at the floor, embarrassed to admit it, and nodded. "How's Billie doing?"

"Good. She's doing really good."

Our voices woke Billie, and her eyes fluttered open. She glanced in my direction and smiled. "Shelby." Her voice was weak and scratchy. "I'm so glad you're here. Drew told me you came last night." She glanced at Dimples and smiled tenderly. "He's been here all night."

Her voice got stronger, and she reached for his hand. He automatically took it, and I picked up that Billie was grateful he'd stuck with her. Maybe he really did love her, even if he hadn't said the words. If that was the case, then getting shot might not be so bad.

He squeezed her hand and smiled, making those dimples swirl like magic. Wow...maybe he really was her prince charming.

"So...um...what happened last night?" I asked.

That brought her focus back to me and, since she didn't want Dimples to hear what she had to tell me, she thought this was the perfect time to send him home. "Drew's already heard this." She turned to him. "Honey, you look a little rumpled. Why don't you go home and get cleaned up. Shelby can keep me company for a while."

"Uh...is that all right?" he asked. He hated leaving her, but he wouldn't mind changing his clothes and taking a shower.

"Of course it's all right," I assured him. "Go. She'll be fine."

He nodded gratefully, then leaned over and gave Billie a tender kiss. "I have some things I need to do today, but I promise I'll be back as soon as I can."

"Sounds great," she assured him.

He nodded and turned to me. "Can you meet me at Billie's apartment in about...forty-five minutes?"

"Sure," I agreed.

"Good. See you then."

We watched him leave, and I caught Billie's feelings of love trail after him. Once the door clicked shut, I sat down in his chair and asked if there was anything I could get for her.

"No...but I do have a favor to ask you." Her raspy voice held an underlying desperation.

"Sure...anything."

"I need you to get the thumb-drive from my apartment. I don't want anyone else to find it."

"Not even Dimples?" I asked.

"No...if he knew about it, he'd have to turn it in as evidence, and I'm afraid something might happen to it. I just don't trust everyone in the police department right now...not when it concerns the attorney general's office. He's got all kinds of people in his pocket, and I don't want to put Drew in his cross-hairs."

"Don't worry. I...uh...already got it."

"What?"

I explained what I'd done last night, including the guy I caught watching me. "I don't know who he was but, to be honest, he didn't feel like a bad guy to me."

"Wow...that's crazy." She thought for a moment, but came up empty. "I hate to admit it, but I have no idea who it could be."

I shrugged. "Okay. Well...maybe he'll show up again. So now it's your turn. Tell me what happened to you."

Closing her eyes, she shook her head. "I walked in on a guy ransacking my apartment. His face was covered by a ski mask...so I didn't see what he looked like. I was pretty upset to find him there, so I pulled my gun on him. I didn't see the other guy until it was too late. He knocked the gun out of my hand and we struggled. The first guy picked up my gun and shot me. They took off after that."

"Oh Billie...how awful."

"Yeah...I got shot with my own gun...it's humiliating." She was thinking that Drew was so mad at her for that.

"Why would he be...uh...why would you be...humiliated?"

Her brow puckered and she thought, *duh*. "It was my gun. I probably wouldn't have been shot if they hadn't gotten a hold of it."

"Right," I said. "Yeah...okay. Well...so you want me to keep the thumb-drive?"

"Yes...at least for now." Her voice faltered with fatigue.

"Okay...but you know what that means. I'll probably have to lie to Dimples. Last night I told him about the thumb-drive and that it was probably what they were looking for."

"That's okay...just don't tell him you have it." Her eyelids began to droop. She'd worn herself out talking to me.

"Well, I'd better go meet him at your apartment. You don't think whoever broke in would come here to finish you off, do you?

"No...if anything...I'd think they'd go back to my apartment...but now...you have it...so I don't have to worry..." Her voice trailed off, but I heard her thinking *thanks Shelby*.

"You're welcome," I whispered.

The crime scene tape at Billie's apartment had been taken down, and Dimples opened the door to my knock. He'd showered and shaved, but his eyes held weariness from lack of sleep. With a quick greeting, he ushered me inside.

"Find anything?" I asked. A twinge of guilt flared, but I pushed it away.

"No. But they took her computer, so I think they were after the thumb-drive like you thought. So..." His gaze zeroed in on mine, and his eyes narrowed. "What did she tell you that she didn't want me to know?"

"Huh?" Guilt flooded over me with a vengeance, but I tried to act dumb. "What makes you say that?"

"Come on Shelby...I know how this works." At my wide-eyed gaze and continued silence, he ran his fingers through his hair and sighed. "Okay, I'll explain. First, she tells me she wants you to come to the hospital, but when I ask her why, she blows me off. Then once you get there, she tells me to go home and get cleaned up. Now it doesn't take a genius to know she's up to something, and you're in cahoots with her. So spit it out...what did she tell you?"

My mouth dropped open. I snapped it shut and tried to come up with a reasonable explanation. "That's because it's personal. She just needed to talk woman to woman...about what happened and other things...like...you and her."

His left brow raised, and he didn't say a word, letting the seconds tick loudly by. The way his eyes narrowed reminded me of the look I always gave my kids, or my husband, when I wanted them to know I wasn't buying their explanation.

"Okay," I caved. "But I'll have you know she trusted me to keep her secret. You might regret it."

"I'll take my chances."

"Fine," I shrugged. "She wanted me to get the thumb-drive without telling you."

He stilled, confused and a little hurt. "Why would she do that?

"Um...so you wouldn't get it." I shrugged. "Mostly because she worried that if the police had it, someone would conveniently lose it. Plus, I think she'd like to keep it out of the system so she can get her hands on it."

He nodded his head like he understood, but he was thinking we were both a little crazy to go to that extreme, and all the subterfuge was hardly called for. It also stung that Billie didn't trust him to keep it safe...he wasn't just 'the police' in this case...he was a lot more than that. And then there was me. Why hadn't I tried to talk her out of it? What was up with that? "So...did she tell you where it is?"

"No." It was the truth, but now he thought I was deliberately lying to him.

"Shelby..." he growled. How could I lie to him? After everything we'd been through together? What about our friendship? What about what was best for Billie? His brows drew down over his eyes, and loud thoughts of strangling me surfaced in his mind.

"She didn't have to because I sort of figured it out already," I quickly said. "So she didn't need to tell me." His jaw clenched, and his fingers tightened. Yikes! I decided I might as well tell him before he burst a blood vessel and had a stroke or something. "Okay, so...I got it."

His brows lifted in confusion. "You have the thumb-drive? How did you get it?" He was thinking that the only way I had it was if I'd come by last night, broken into her apartment, and taken it. Would I really do something stupid like that? What if those guys had come back? And going into her apartment was breaking the law. He'd have to arrest me.

Now I really didn't want to tell him the truth, so I figured it was better to fudge a little. "Oh, she gave it to me a while ago...for safe-keeping."

"But last night you said those guys broke in because of the thumb-drive."

"Well...yeah. I'm sure that's why they broke in."

"Then why didn't you tell me you had it? You're not making any sense!" Not only had his face gone red, but he was practically shouting at me.

"Um...well...the truth is, I didn't have it when I talked to you last night."

Dimples' eyes bulged, and his fists clenched again, so I decided to fess up.

"You're right...I came here last night after I left you at the hospital and got it. I thought maybe the crime scene people would still be here so I wouldn't be alone and it would be okay to look around. But I promise I didn't break in. When I got here the door wasn't closed tight. I just pushed on it and it opened...so you can't arrest me."

Dimples stared at me with his mouth wide open before he snapped it shut. His breath puffed out of his flaring nostrils, and his shoulders drooped a little. "You just lied to me. I can't believe it."

"Well...yes...but you were freaking out. How could I tell you the truth when you thought I was stupid to come get it in the first place?"

"I never said..."

"Oh, I know. You didn't have to say it...but I could tell you thought it was stupid and you'd need to do your duty and arrest me or something." I crossed my arms and took a deep breath. "But now that you know, don't tell Billie, okay?"

He shook his head, hardly believing I could ask him something like that. "I think you should give me the damn thumb-drive."

"No way...at least not yet. Just pretend you don't know I have it, and let's figure out who did this to Billie."

"Shelby...if it wasn't safe for Billie to have it, what makes you think it's safe with you?"

"No one knows I have it." I was a little worried about the man who sort of saw me last night, but since he didn't get a good look, it was probably okay.

Dimples closed his eyes and held the bridge of his nose with his fingers. Between not getting any sleep last night, and the trauma of Billie getting shot and nearly dying, a monster headache was coming on. Having this conversation with me just made it worse.

"Are you okay?" I asked.

"Do I look okay?" he snapped.

My breath caught, but then I realized he'd only said that in his mind, and I tried not to feel bad while he got his temper under control.

"Let's just say it's been a long night...and now this," he said out loud.

"Yeah...I'm really sorry. Let me talk to Billie about giving you the thumb-drive...or maybe I can make a copy and give that to you while I keep the original. Then she'd have access to it, and you'd both be happy."

"Just forget about it for now," he said, mostly because he was tired of the whole thing. Why did Billie have to do this stuff anyway? Not trusting him was hard, but he understood her logic. Still, didn't she know how hard this was on him? Now she was into something that almost got her killed. How could she do this to him?

"Did they get any fingerprints?" I asked, hoping to take his mind off Billie and me.

"Yeah...they'll run them today and let me know if they are a match for anyone we have in the system."

"Good. Maybe something will turn up."

He was pretty sure the guys who did this wouldn't be that stupid, but he nodded anyway and glanced around the trashed apartment. "I'm just sorry this place is such a wreck. I don't want Billie to come home to this mess."

"I'll help you clean it up before she comes home. When do you think they'll release her from the hospital?"

"I don't know...probably next week."

"Okay...that gives us plenty of time. Just call me when you're ready to start. We'll have it back to normal in no time, and she won't have to worry about it. Sound good?

"Sure, that should work."

"Good. Um...so, what's going on with Chloe? Did you find out anything about those two cops?"

"Oh yeah." He ducked his head. "I...uh...turned that over to Bates. With everything that happened to Billie last night, I just couldn't think about it."

Too shocked to respond, I stood there gawking at him.

He noticed my silence and pursed his lips. "He should be calling you. I told him to make sure he included you when he talked to them." We both knew that might not happen and, with a flush of remorse, Dimples whipped out his phone to call him.

"Wait," I said. "I'll call. You have enough to worry about. If he gives me a hard time, then you can talk to him."

"Are you sure?" he asked.

"Yes. In fact, I'll head over there right now, and you can go back to the hospital."

He shook his head. "I need to work on finding who shot Billie." A thought that maybe she might have some clues popped into his head. "Hmm...wait a minute...maybe talking to Billie is the best way to go. Do you think she has any idea who did this?"

I remembered her thoughts about who might have stolen the thumb-drive from her desk at work. "Yeah. I think she might. You should ask her."

He smiled, and it was a relief to see those dimples come out after so long. "Good. Then that's where I'll start."

We both headed to the door at the same time. He was thinking that he had the upper hand now that he knew our little secret, and he wasn't going to let Billie bulldoze him. She needed him, and he'd be damned if she tried to do this without him. "Call me if you need any help with Bates," he said.

I nodded and hurried to my car, grateful it wasn't me talking to Billie. Of course, talking to Bates wasn't going to be a picnic either. I just hoped he hadn't done anything stupid and accused any of those cops without me.

I strolled into the precinct with my I.D. badge around my neck, my head held high, and my best 'don't mess with me face.' I probably should have called Bates first, but with his attitude toward me, I was afraid he'd tell me not to come. Ugh! Today was not going how I'd wanted. My simple plan to talk to the cops, find the one who'd done it, and send Chloe home to her parents wasn't so cut and dry. Not with Bates in charge.

I rounded the corner and there he was, sitting at his desk looking over some paperwork. I listened to his thoughts for a moment, but he was only focused on the task before him and it didn't get me anywhere. Taking a deep breath, I marched over to his desk.

He caught sight of me, and his face scrunched up like he'd just taken a bite of something sour. His thoughts about me weren't much better and, if I had an inferiority complex, I would have burst into tears. Instead, I just got mad.

"Hello Bates." I tried to sound cordial, but it was hard when he was thinking such mean thoughts. Instead, I sent him a killer smile to make up for it. He picked up on my fake smile and frowned.

"You should have called," he said, sitting back in his chair. "I could have saved you a trip."

"What do you mean?"

He glanced around, then spoke in a low voice. "I checked out those cops...they were both on assignment in different parts of the city at the time Chloe would have seen them. So there's no way it was either of them."

"But...that can't be right. Dammit Bates! You should have waited for me."

He shook his head, thinking *don't get your panties all twisted in a knot,* and motioned me to an out of the way corner where no one could hear us. "It wouldn't matter. She must have gotten it wrong. Are you sure she saw a badge? Maybe what she thought was a badge was something else." He knew both cops and had even worked on a case with one. It couldn't be either of them. They were the good guys. They'd never do anything stupid like that.

I knew Chloe had seen the badge, since I'd seen it in her mind...unless her mind had played tricks on her and she'd imagined it? No, I couldn't go there. She'd been too traumatized to make something up like that. It could only mean we were looking in the wrong place. "Does the FBI or other kinds of agents wear badges on their belts?"

His eyes narrowed. "I suppose..."

"Maybe we should look there."

"Possibly," he said. "But you have to remember that she didn't get a good enough look at the guy for a positive ID. I mean...she picked two different people from the photos. What makes you think looking at other agents would be any different?" He wasn't sure he believed her story. He believed she saw someone, but a cop?

"I'm sure she told us the truth," I said.

"Sure she did," he said. "At least what she thought was the truth. But you have to remember she'd just seen her boyfriend get killed right before her eyes. With that kind of trauma, she might have imagined a police badge when it could have been something else."

"Like what?"

"Like a belt buckle or something."

"It wasn't just what she saw," I countered. "It was what she heard too."

"Okay...so what exactly did she hear?"

I sighed and thought back, trying to remember her exact words. "She heard him talk to someone on the phone about taking the cash and drugs. I think if she heard his voice again, she'd recognize it. Would you be willing to let her listen to their voices? She wouldn't have to be in the same room for that."

"Why? Didn't you understand when I told you it wasn't either of them? That they weren't anywhere near that house and their partners confirmed it?" He called me a few choice names in his mind and my temper flared.

"Shhh...keep it down will you?" I glanced around the room, but luckily, no one paid special attention to us. "Look, I don't care about that. A partner could just as easily be involved. Maybe that's who he was calling. The thing is...you don't know for sure, and if you'd waited for me when you talked to them, we wouldn't be having this argument." Now I was calling him names in my mind, and for once I wished he could hear what I was thinking.

"Yeah...right." His voice rose in anger. "Because you're never wrong about anything. You're the mighty Shelby Nichols with some kind of psychic power that tells you without a doubt what someone has done, and you don't even have to lift a finger to prove it. You just know. Well...I'm sorry, but there's no way in hell anyone can do that."

I took a step back, totally floored by his vehement outburst. That's when I noticed that everyone in the room had stopped what they were doing to listen, and they were all staring at us. I heard a few random thoughts that Bates had lost his cool, but he did have a point. What they'd seen me do was kind of freaky, but freaky cool.

I was grateful for that last thought, and the tension fell from my shoulders. Bates realized he'd caused a scene and sent a few icy glares at those still staring. That got them moving, and the moment passed, even though it still lingered in their minds.

Bates' animosity hit me like a tidal wave. He was thinking that I did something he couldn't explain and it scared the crap out of him. He tried to convince himself that there was a reasonable explanation for what I did, and I was just good at reading people's emotions. But he hated that I had the audacity to call it premonitions, like I was psychic or something.

It was preposterous...and put him on edge. I had to be working an angle. People who said they were psychics usually did it for the notoriety or the money. Maybe that's how I was building my reputation as a P.I. to get clients.

What if I was using my role with the police department as a pretense for something else? Maybe I was informing on them? He knew I had ties with Joey "The Knife" Manetto.

Maybe I fed him information. What he didn't understand was how I had fooled everyone in the department. They were all idiots to put their trust in a fraud. The chief even paid me to consult with them...and it made him so mad he could hardly stand it.

Anger, along with a touch of worry about Uncle Joey, sent my heart racing. "I don't care what you think," I said quietly, hearing enough to last me a lifetime. "I want Chloe to listen to their voices. She's an innocent kid, and she deserves that much."

"Well it's not up to you, is it? I'm the head of this investigation, and I don't take orders from you." He was thinking Chloe got herself into this mess, so she wasn't entirely blameless, and my little guilt trip wasn't going to work on him.

Could this get any worse? "Then what are you going to do about it?"

He was thinking he might have to let Chloe listen their voices, but he'd be damned if he told me that. "I'd like to talk to Chloe myself. Everything we know about this is second-hand from you. I want to hear what happened from her before I decide how to proceed."

Raw anger surged through me, tightening my hands into fists and thinning my lips. I inhaled through my nose, and my nostrils flared. He made it sound like I was making all of this up to get attention, and I couldn't possibly have anything worthwhile to add since I was a fake. It took all my effort to let out my breath and calm down enough to speak.

"Then by all means," I got out through clenched teeth, "let's go talk to her and clear this up. But Bates," I waited until his gaze locked with mine. "Once we do, I don't ever want to have this conversation again."

I stabbed daggers at him with my steely gaze. If looks could kill, he'd be so dead.

It didn't cow him one bit. In fact, he smirked just a little. "You're right. I think I should talk to her." He was thinking he should have insisted on talking to Chloe yesterday and saved himself all the trouble of dealing with me.

"Fine. I'll meet you there."

"Who said you were going?" he drawled.

I inhaled sharply. He couldn't possibly mean that, could he? "I'm going whether you like it or not."

He huffed out a breath. "Just kidding, Nichols. Geeze."

"And don't call me Nichols!"

He twisted his lips and pulled on his jacket, not about to give me the satisfaction of an answer. He also didn't want me to get there before he did and conspire with Chloe about what to tell him.

I gasped, and my heart raced with fury. What a grandstanding jerk! He was the biggest, brattiest bully I had ever known. How dare he? I brushed past him and hurried to my car, needing some space to get under control before I clobbered him.

I sat in my car and slammed the door shut, then closed my eyes and concentrated on breathing in and out until I calmed down. With my heart rate back to normal, I sent a quick text to Holly to let her know we were coming. I dreaded putting Chloe through this again, especially with Bates questioning her truthfulness. It had been bad enough for her to tell me. I could only hope that if I was there she wouldn't freak out.

I pulled up to Holly's house behind Bates, but hurried to the door to arrive ahead of him. Holly took one look at my face and raised her brows thinking something wasn't right. Was Bates causing me trouble? And where was Dimples?

She ushered us inside and glanced up and down the street before closing the door. "Please...have a seat. Chloe's downstairs."

I sat on the couch after Bates took the chair, grateful he wasn't sitting next to me since I couldn't trust myself not to strangle him.

"What's going on?" she asked, folding her arms and standing tall. She wasn't going to bring Chloe into this until she knew more. "What do you need to talk to Chloe about? Did you find the cop?"

I stared pointedly at Bates while my lips drew down into a disgusted frown.

"I just need to ask Chloe exactly what she saw," Bates explained, making his voice all smooth and nice. "We're having a hard time connecting any of the cops she pointed out. I thought maybe if I got the story straight from her mouth, something might click that Shelby forgot to mention."

"Really?" Holly asked, slightly offended that he didn't believe me. With wide eyes, she glanced at me for an explanation.

"Yeah, he wants to hear it firsthand," I answered, trying to sound like it didn't bother me. "Do you think Chloe will mind too much? You can tell her I'm here if that helps."

"Okay," she agreed, even though she didn't like it. "I'll get her."

"Thanks," I said, shooting Bates a stare since he wasn't going to say it.

A few minutes later, Chloe followed Holly into the room. Holly had obviously told her Bates wanted to hear what happened again, and her step faltered as she came in. I sent her a smile and nod, but it didn't do much to curb her anxiety, and she wondered if she was in trouble.

I almost blurted that she wasn't, but bit my lip instead. I didn't want to give Bates a reason to think I was interfering and kick me out. At least he picked up on her nervousness and spoke gently to reassure her that he was there to help.

As she recounted the events to him, her voice wavered with pain, and Holly quickly put an arm around her. Holly's solid presence was enough to help her past the part where Liam died, but talking about the cop worried her. She knew what she'd seen, but what if Bates didn't believe her?

"Go ahead and tell him what happened," I said. "He needs to know what you saw and heard." She nodded and took a deep breath, then finished telling Bates the rest of the story.

To Bates' credit, he listened attentively, then nodded and thanked her. "I know that wasn't easy, but I had to hear it for myself. I believe you. I'm just not sure about the badge. Could it have been anything else? Like a belt buckle or something?"

"No!" Chloe said. "I know what I saw, and it wasn't my imagination." She was thinking that this was exactly why she hadn't gone to the police in the first place.

"Okay," Bates said, wanting to placate her. "I'll do my best to find him."

"Do the cops you talked to have any idea that Chloe's been found?" I asked, suddenly nervous.

"No," he said. "I was discreet. They don't know a thing."

"That's good," I replied, "because I want to talk to them myself. I already have their names, but I need their phone numbers."

Bates couldn't believe I was going over his head, but he couldn't tell me no in front of Chloe or Holly. "Fine. I've got them on my desk. I'll call you when I get back to the precinct."

"Okay...good." Relief swept over me to finally get him to cooperate.

Bates stood, eager to leave, and said his goodbyes, promising to call me. Once he left, I told Holly and Chloe what had happened with the interviews, trying to leave out how angry and upset it had made me. "Don't worry, Chloe, I'll talk to them today, even if I have to track them down to do it. Okay?"

"Sure," she nodded, troubled by Bates' lack of trust in her story. At least I believed her.

"Good. I'd better get going then."

It was past one in the afternoon, so I stopped by my house for something to eat before Bates called. I was nearly finished with my sandwich when my phone rang, and I let out a relieved breath. I hadn't been sure he'd actually call. I glanced at the caller ID, and my relief turned into a groan. Why now?

"Hello," I said, hoping I didn't sound too unhappy.

"Shelby." Uncle Joey answered. "Is something wrong?"

"Oh...I'm okay, I guess." Since I didn't want him to think I was upset he'd called, I decided I'd better explain. "I'm just working on an important case and this detective who's supposed to be helping me is just...uh...um...well he's giving me a really hard time."

"Oh? The one with the dimples?"

"No...not him. He's great. It's the new one. His name is Bates."

"Hmm...does he have frizzy hair?"

"Yes, that's him," I answered, surprised he knew. "He doesn't like me much."

"Good to know. I'll see what I can do about it."

"Uh...wait...no. That's okay...I didn't...I don't mean...I was just complaining. You don't need to do anything...I can take care of Bates."

He snorted. "Right...well, let me know if you change your mind."

"Um...sure. But I'm fine...really." Part of me wanted to think he was just kidding around, but the other part knew he was dead serious, and I didn't want to be responsible for anything happening to Bates, no matter how much I disliked him.

"I was calling to see if you were available for breakfast in the morning...around eight-thirty?" he asked.

"Uh...I guess that would work. What's going on?"

"I found out that Blake is staying at the downtown Marriott, and he eats breakfast there every morning at eight-thirty. I thought maybe you and Ramos could eat breakfast there too and have a little chat with him."

"What kind of a chat?" I asked.

"Let's just say that Ramos will invite him to meet with me, and you can listen in to find out what he really thinks about that. Even if he refuses, you should be able to pick up on what he's doing here. If he accepts, you can accompany him back to the office and we'll find out what he's up to."

"Oh...okay. I can do that."

"Good. Ramos will pick you up at eight o'clock in the morning."

"Uh...wait." He'd already disconnected and I sighed. Just one more thing to add to my growing list of things to do. Would it ever end? Of course, it shouldn't be too bad. I got a free breakfast out of it. Plus, I'd be with Ramos. Only...I wasn't sure I wanted him to pick me up. What would my neighbors think?

My phone rang again, and this time it was Bates. He tersely rattled off the names and cell phone numbers of the two cops and disconnected. Hmm...maybe it wouldn't be so bad if something happened to him. Not like getting beat up...but if he got transferred somewhere else? I wouldn't feel too bad about making that happen. If I could be sure Uncle Joey would agree with me, I might suggest it.

I shook my head and moaned. How could I even think about doing something like that? I'd just have to get over it and not let him get to me. That's what I told my kids to do when they were in situations like this. It was the way life was, and I couldn't go around getting rid of people, just because I didn't like them.

Feeling fortified, I glanced at the numbers. Might as well get it over with and call. But what was I going to say? Besides the truth, what possible reason could I give them? I had no idea, but I wasn't about to let that stop me. I licked my lips and punched in the numbers, holding my breath until he picked up.

"Officer Bellini? This is Shelby Nichols. I'm a consultant with the police department?"

"Yeah?" he said sharply.

"I'm working on a case for the chief, and he gave me your number. Said you could help. Can I meet with you at the precinct? It'll only take a few minutes."

I heard him sigh. "Fine. I can be there in half an hour." He disconnected before I could say another word. Dang! It would take me twenty minutes to get there myself. I rushed out the door, deciding to call the other cop after I talked to this guy. With any luck, he'd be the one and I wouldn't have to make the second call.

I got to the police station with five minutes to spare and hurried inside. Since I had no idea where to meet with him, I wandered into the detective's office space and waited near the chief's door. Lucky for me, Bates was gone.

I noticed Bellini as soon as he came in, and he wasn't alone. His partner spotted me first and motioned Bellini toward me. He was thinking that this was the second time today Bellini had been summoned and wondered what was going on. Bellini was thinking the same thing.

He closed the distance between us, and I extended my hand with a smile. "Thank you for coming. I really appreciate it."

Bellini shrugged. "What's going on?"

"Let's go in here and I'll explain." I ushered him into the special room where friends and relatives of homicide cases were questioned. He sat on the couch, and I took the chair across from him. He had hoped he'd never have to meet me face to face, and there I was sitting right in front of him. Sweat popped out on his brow. If the chief had asked me to talk to him, did that mean he'd messed up somehow? He'd been so careful. He couldn't think of anything he'd done that could possibly give him away, so what was going on?

Whoa! This guy was hiding a big fat secret of some kind. I'd better find out what it was. "I guess you've heard of me...that I have premonitions?"

"Yeah," he shrugged again, trying to show that he didn't care. "So?"

"Well...sometimes I get impressions, and I thought you might be able to help." He nodded, but his mind was guarded, waiting to hear what I wanted.

Crap! That wasn't helping, so I plunged ahead. "It's about the missing girl, Chloe Peterson. Do you know anything that could help us find her? For some reason, one of my premonitions includes you...or someone who looks like you."

He sat back, confused. Maybe this wasn't what he thought at all. "Um...okay." He leaned forward with his elbows on his knees and thought about the case. "I know two of the three men were known drug dealers. The third was just a kid. If the girl saw something she shouldn't have, I think she'd be dead too. But that would mean another person was there, and all the evidence points to the three guys killing each other." His gaze caught mine. "Bates was asking me the same thing. So what do you know that you aren't telling the rest of us? Was someone else involved?"

He was so close to the truth that my breath caught. He noticed my reaction and knew he was right. Since it wouldn't do me any good to lie, I shrugged. "Yeah, that's what we think."

"And I'm here because..." he prompted. He was thinking, *you think I'm involved, or at least someone who looks like me.*

"Um...well...I'm hoping you might know something about it."

Relaxing, he sat back, relieved I didn't know about him. "I wish I did. With all the focus on finding the missing girl, I think we're missing something. We should be looking at the two drug dealers and who they worked for. It might lead us somewhere, especially if you think there was another person involved. But regardless of your premonitions...it's not me." He shook his head in perplexity. "I don't get it. Why did you think it was me?"

He was telling me the truth, and I had to give him something. "I don't know for sure. It's clearly not you, so I must have gotten it wrong." Oh boy...Bates would have a heyday if he ever found out I said that.

Bellini nodded and stood to leave, thinking that hadn't been so bad after all. He was also thanking his lucky stars that his secret was safe, but he might have to talk with Manetto. Maybe I was getting premonitions about him because he worked for Manetto, and it was messing things up. So far, he'd managed to stay away from me, but now that wasn't possible. Even though he knew I worked for Manetto, the last thing he needed was for me to know that he worked for him too.

Bellini left the office, casting a quick glance over his shoulder at me. I managed to close my mouth into a smile and give him a little wave. It must have been a sick-looking smile though, since he wondered if I was feeling all right, but he chalked it up to the fact that I had admitted I was wrong about something. That thought cheered him up, since it was kind of legendary that I was never wrong. It made me seem more normal, and he couldn't wait to tell his partner.

I watched helplessly as he did, and nearly choked to find Bates standing close enough to hear him. The ugly smile on Bates' face sent my blood boiling. He was thinking it was about time someone found me out, and he wouldn't let me or anyone else in the department forget it.

I stepped back into the room and shut the door. Damn! I hated that man! I might just have to take Uncle Joey up on his offer...or never help the police again. And now I knew something I wished I didn't. With a name like Bellini, I should have suspected something, but what the freak! Taking a deep breath, I tried to calm down and get back to business. I still had one more cop to call, and I'd better do it now before I lost my nerve.

This guy answered cheerfully and quickly agreed to meet with me. He told me to call him Pete and was so friendly that I didn't think it could possibly be him. He was downstairs in the evidence room and said he'd come right up.

I opened the door and peeked out, relieved to find Bates away from his desk. I stepped outside the door to wait and prayed Pete would get there before Bates came back. Less than a minute later, Pete entered the floor and made his way toward me.

"Nice to meet you, Shelby," he said. "I've heard a lot about you."

"All good, I hope," I said, shaking his hand. "Come on in."

"So is this your office now?" he asked, thinking I must have the chief wrapped around my little finger if he was letting me use this.

"Oh no. It wasn't his...I mean...I wish!" Crap! What was I doing? How could I be so stupid? I swallowed and let out a little laugh. "I mean, don't tell the chief...if he knew he'd probably kick me out."

Pete smiled and nodded, but his eyes held that look of incredulity, and he thought I was a little 'off,' or maybe I was just plain crazy. "So what can I help you with?"

"It's about the missing girl, Chloe Peterson. I was hoping you might know something about the case that could help."

"Um...really? Like what?" His mind flooded with suspicion. This was the second time today. First was with Bates, and now me. What was going on?

"I don't know for sure. You know I've helped out around here, right? I just had a feeling you might know something."

"Oh...you mean because of your premonitions?" He could hardly believe that the chief would go along with this, but he also knew I was working for the family, so maybe that had something to do with it. But why was I was talking to him? "I really don't know any more than what I've heard around here. Why would you think I did? That doesn't make any sense."

"I know...it doesn't always make sense to me either. I just had a feeling I needed to talk to you."

"Hmm...Bates talked to me this morning too, but I don't think he has premonitions." He smiled at his joke but was wondering what I was up to. Both of us talking to him was not a coincidence. "Something's happened with the case. You must think there's someone else involved. Did you find her?"

"No...I wouldn't be talking to you if we had." Wow...he was fast. I'd better come up with something quick. "If you must know, we've sort of hit a dead-end, so we're following up on everything we can think of that might be related."

His brows scrunched together as he connected the dots. "You think a cop is involved." He stood and started pacing. How had I come to that conclusion? "What made you think that?"

"Only my premonitions," I said. "Why? Am I right? Do you know who it might be?"

He stopped pacing and sat back down, thinking he'd like to find out what was going on, and what information we had to come to that conclusion. "How would a cop be involved? What do you think he did? Take the girl?"

I shrugged. "I don't know. Probably not. He'd probably just kill her."

His gaze flew to mine. "Why?"

"Maybe she saw something she wasn't supposed to."

Now he thought it made sense, but why was I talking to him? Why would I think he was involved? Did I know where the girl was? Had I talked to her? He nodded, thinking that must be it since he didn't believe in premonitions. The girl must have told me she'd seen a cop.

"So, I'm on the list," he said. "That explains why Bates was asking me about it. Is there anyone else?"

"Yes, a few others. I only wish we could find her, then we'd know who it was for sure."

"What I don't understand is why you would think I was involved."

I shrugged. "My premonitions. You probably don't believe it, but that's all we have to go on, so..." I took a deep breath. "I guess it's another dead end."

He nodded solemnly, but his lips turned into a frown. "To be honest, I'm not happy you thought I had something to do with it."

"Oh...yeah, please don't worry about it. Like I said, it's just a premonition...sometimes they don't always pan out. I'm sorry I bothered you with this."

"No...it's okay. There's a girl missing...you have to cover all your bases."

"I'm glad you understand."

He rubbed his chin. "Maybe you should check out the two drug dealers. That's where I'd start." He walked to the door, then sent a parting glance over his shoulder. "If you need anything else from me, let me know, I'm happy to help."

"Thanks."

The door closed behind him and I slumped back in my chair. That was intense. He was good, too. I didn't know if it was him or not. He was certainly upset about the cop part, but then wouldn't any cop be upset? There was no way I could tell if it was him, and that worried me. Because now he knew we suspected him, and he also had a pretty good idea I'd talked to Chloe.

Chapter 6

Discouraged and exhausted, I opened the door and peeked out, then ducked back in and quickly shut it. The chief was halfway across the room and walking toward his office. Right now, I didn't want to talk to him, or anyone else for that matter. I waited until I heard his door close and slipped out, making a beeline for the exit.

"Nichols!" Bates shouted. "Wait up."

I almost didn't turn around, especially since he'd called me Nichols, but he'd shouted so loud it would make me look bad if I didn't. I plastered a smile on my face and stopped so he could catch up with me.

"Make any progress?" he asked.

"Uh...yeah...some."

His brows rose in surprise. "Really? What?"

"I'm pretty sure it's not Bellini."

"That's it?"

"I think that's progress," I said, knowing I had to be vague about how my premonitions worked.

"Oh...yeah, right. I heard Bellini saying that your premonitions were wrong about him." I didn't answer, but he knew he'd hit a nerve. "What about the other one."

"Pete? Well...I didn't really get anything concrete off of him. So, at this point, I can't say for sure that he's the one."

Bates snorted, thinking I wasn't so high and mighty as I thought. "All right. I'll go have a chat with the parents tonight and see what they want to do."

"Have you checked out the drug dealers that were killed?" I asked. "Looked into their background? Maybe there's a clue there."

"Yeah. I have their rap sheets. Do you want to take a look?"

"Did anything stand out to you?" I asked, not wanting to take a look at all. Why couldn't he just tell me and get it over with so I could leave this place and go home?

"Actually it did. Come over to my desk and I'll show you."

I followed him back, and he shoved an open file into my hands. I didn't know what I was looking for, but since he wasn't in a talking mood, I scanned over them just the same. After a minute, I broke down. "So? What is it?"

He smirked and turned the page, pointing at a few lines in the center. "Right here it says they were both brought in on charges of aggravated assault and possession, but all the charges were dropped due to insufficient evidence."

"Hmm." When I didn't say anything else, he pursed his lips in annoyance.

"See who the arresting officer was? Right there."

He stabbed his finger on the tiny print at the bottom of the page and the name jumped out at me. "Detective Pete Royce?"

"Quite a coincidence, don't you think?" Bates asked.

"Yeah." A surge of frustration roared over me, and I turned to face Bates. "When were you going to share this with me?"

"I just did."

"It sure would have been nice to know a few minutes ago when I talked to him," I said, trying not to raise my voice. "So what's next?"

"I'll tell Harris when he comes in, and we'll go from there. In the meantime, I'll keep an eye on Pete."

"Okay. Let me know if you find out anything else."

"Sure," he said, thinking he'd already talked to Pete about his role as the arresting officer, since that was the reason he gave for talking to him this morning. Everything Pete said about the drug dealers made sense, and since he'd been working narcotics, arresting them probably wasn't a coincidence.

But of the two officers, Pete seemed the more likely candidate. Still, it made him wonder about Chloe, and if she'd made a mistake. Too bad I didn't pick up anything from Pete. It certainly would have helped, and he really thought I might, but now he knew I didn't always have the answers.

It was time to do some real police work, and let everyone in the department know I wasn't all I was cracked up to be. Maybe this was a good thing and, once everyone knew I didn't have all the answers, the whole department, including the chief, wouldn't rely on me so much. Even better, I wouldn't be sticking my nose into their business and getting paid for it too.

What the freak! How could he do that to me?

I headed toward the exit and shoved the door open. I couldn't get into my car fast enough. I managed to buckle my seat belt before the tears came, and I dropped my forehead onto the steering wheel for a good cry. That man would be the death of me. I didn't know if I could ever go back in there. Maybe I should stop helping the police. If this was what happened, it wasn't worth it.

A knock on my window startled me and I jerked up to find Dimples staring at me in concern. "Shelby? What's wrong? Are you all right?"

I sniffed and wiped my nose before nodding. "Yeah...I'm okay."

He frowned. "No you're not. Why don't you come in and tell me what happened?"

"No!"

His eyes widened. "Okay. I'll come sit by you."

I opened my mouth to tell him not to, but he'd already started walking around my car. I grabbed my purse and pulled out a tissue to wipe my face and nose. I didn't want him to see me crying like this, but I couldn't seem to stop the tears from running down my face. The fact that he was worried about me made my tears flow even harder.

"I'm sorry," I said, after he closed the car door. "I shouldn't be so upset, but it's just been kind of a hard day."

"That's okay," Dimples assured me. "I don't mind. Just tell me what's wrong."

"It's Bates," I blurted. "He doesn't believe me, and he's set me up to fail in front of everyone."

I told Dimples how Bates talked to the cops without me, and then how he had to hear Chloe's version of what happened from her because from me it was second-hand and not good enough.

"He acted like I'd left something out...on purpose!" I wiped my nose again before explaining how Bates kept Pete's involvement with the two drug dealers from me, and how that information could have helped me when I talked to Pete.

"He wants me to fail. I had to tell Bellini I'd made a mistake with my premonitions, since that was the only excuse I could come up with, and Bates found out. He was so happy I admitted to a mistake. It was humiliating! And he was thinking the worst things...like now I would be exposed for the fake I am and maybe it was all for the best. And worse...he'd make sure the chief and the whole department knows about it! He's trying to ruin me! I can't stand him, and I don't know if I can ever go back in there again!"

Dimples murmured consoling words, shocked by the intensity of my feelings. A growing desire to punch Bates in the face rose in him as well. He was thinking Bates was an idiot and didn't have an ounce of respect for me and all I did for them. Someone needed to set him straight, and he wasn't going to let it go until Bates apologized to me. How could he say those hurtful things to me? It made his blood boil.

Then it hit him that I'd said "thinking the worst things" not "saying the worst things." He glanced at me, and his eyes widened. My eyes widened too, and that made his eyes get even bigger. I glanced away and busily wiped my cheeks and nose.

"Shelby?" Dimples said. "What's going on?"

I sniffed, but still couldn't bring myself to look at him. "I don't know what you're talking about."

"Holy hell!" he shouted. "You...you just answered me. How did you do that?"

I jerked to catch his gaze, and my stomach clenched with dread. "Do what? What do you mean?"

"I said your name in my mind, and you heard me! You answered me!"

"I don't think so...you know that's not possible, right?"

His eyes narrowed, but he wasn't going to back down. "No it's not, but you can do it. You just did."

I let out my breath and closed my eyes. There was no way I could undo this, but I hated telling him the truth. "Um...there's a reasonable explanation."

"Like what?"

"It's complicated."

"No it's not. Just tell me the truth," he said. "I'm your friend. We've been through a lot together. I'm not going to tell anyone. I just need to know."

"But...I can't tell you. It will change things, and I'm not sure I'm ready for that." It freaked me out to have one more person know my secret, even if it was Dimples.

"Okay...fine. Don't tell me. But you know I know, right? Even if you won't say the words."

"Can't you just let it go?" I begged. "Pretend that what I have are premonitions...like you've always believed?"

He pursed his lips, not sure why it was so hard for me to admit. It was pretty damn awesome, and he wasn't going to act like he didn't know. He couldn't. "Sure...whatever you say...but now that I know, it all makes sense. I guess it does sound a little crazy, but now I finally get the whole premonitions thing. You've been reading minds. It's...really quite remarkable. When did it happen? Have you always been able to do it?"

He wasn't going to let it go, so I huffed out a breath and answered. "No. It started the day of the bank robbery in the grocery store. I got shot in the head, remember?"

"Oh...yeah...sure I remember."

"Right. Well, after the doctor finished stitching me up, I started to hear what people around me were thinking, but I didn't know that's what it was at first. I thought maybe I was imagining things. When you and Detective Williams came to the house the next morning, I heard everything you were thinking, and that's when I knew for sure. It was quite a shock."

"Yeah...I'll bet." Dimples began to think about all the times I'd helped him after that and, suddenly, it all fell into place. "Now it makes total sense. I don't know why I didn't figure it out before. There were a few times I thought about it...but I always brushed it off."

"That's easy to explain," I said. "Because reading minds isn't possible."

He nodded, a dazed look in his eyes. "Wow...this is incredible."

"Um...now that you know...there's something I have to ask you."

His gaze caught mine, and his eyes cleared. "You need me to keep this a secret."

I let out my breath and nodded. "No one can know. Not the police, not Billie, not anyone."

"What about Chris? Does he..."

"Yeah...he knows. It's not something I could keep from him. Believe me, it's been hard on our marriage, but we've managed."

"Yeah...I'll bet," Dimples said, thinking about how hard it would be to know your wife could read your every thought. "Wow. Un-freakin-believable."

"I hope this doesn't mean things will get awkward between us," I said. "Really...just keep thinking about it like I have premonitions, and it won't be too much different, right?"

"Okay...I'll try doing that."

"Good, that's great. It should work out fine. And be sure not to tell anyone. Okay?"

He glanced at me in awe and shook his head. "I wouldn't dream of it. They probably wouldn't believe me anyway." He thought about that for a minute then took a breath. "Well, I'd better get going. I was just stopping by to check on the investigation. So...you think Pete's the cop?"

"I don't know. Now that I know he knew the drug dealers, I'll have to take another shot at him. Maybe I'll hear something more useful next time."

"That makes sense. Okay...I'll let you know what we decide to do next."

"Okay. Oh...how's Billie doing?"

"Better. Her parents are here, so that's good. Her mom's a lot like her."

I snickered. "Pretty bossy huh?"

"Yeah," he said, smiling. He opened the door, then glanced back at me, marveling all over again. "Uh...see ya."

He shut the door, and I watched him walk into the station. I sat for a few more minutes in a worried daze. Dimples knew. I didn't know if it was good or bad. It might change things between us, more than I liked to admit, but he was my friend. I trusted him. He'd been there from the beginning of this whole mess. It should be fine. At least, I sure hoped so.

The drive home passed in a blur with me worrying about the whole debacle at the police department, and Dimples knowing my secret. The pull to get home, where I was safe and sound, ached in my chest. As I pulled into my driveway, relief poured over me. Maybe now I could relax.

I checked the time and found it was almost three-thirty. Dang! My kids would be walking in any minute now. I hurried into the bathroom to freshen up my face and gasped at the damage: streaks of mascara and red swollen eyes. I couldn't fix this. I'd just have to wash my face and start over.

The cool water felt amazing on my hot cheeks and lessened the swelling around my eyes. Inhaling the fresh scent of my moisturizer soothed me, and I decided to forget putting on more make-up. The day was nearly over anyway, and I wasn't going anywhere else tonight.

Downstairs, the door opened, and voices filled the house. From the noise, it sounded like lots more people than just Josh and Savannah. I frowned and hurried to the kitchen where they were congregating. Two of Josh's friends sat at the kitchen table while Josh got out the milk.

"Oh, hey mom," he said. "I thought we'd have a snack before we played some basketball." He glanced at me, and his brows drew together. I looked washed out and pale, like I was really tired or something. I usually looked lots better than this. Was something wrong?

"I got something in my eye, so I had to wash my face," I said.

Josh stilled, thinking I'd answered his question without him saying a word.

"There's some cookies I made in the freezer," I said. "Do you want some? We can thaw them out in the microwave. They're peanut butter."

Enthusiastic agreement came from everyone, and I quickly opened the freezer to pull them out. After a quick zap in the microwave, they were perfect for dipping in milk, and none of the boys gave me a second thought after that.

Whew! That was close. Thank goodness for cookies and milk. Of course, putting up my shields would have been much better...and smarter. Savannah walked in and blinked to find the boys at the table. She hesitated a moment before going over for a cookie. Her gaze lingered on Cole, and I caught the unmistakable surge of desire flickering over her. She liked him...a lot...as in a huge crush.

Holy cow! I did not want to know that, but now that I knew, I had to know if Cole looked at her like that too. I listened carefully, but only picked up that he noticed her, but as Josh's kid sister and nothing more...for now.

Relieved, I let out my breath and asked about her day. That seemed to break the spell, and soon the boys had gone outside to throw some hoops, and Savannah was talking a mile a minute. "So we're going to Aikido tonight, right?" she asked.

"Oh, that's right. I forgot. Yes we're going."

"Good." She smiled, thinking how great it was going to be. "I'd better get my homework done then."

I cleaned up the table and ate a cookie for courage since it was time to call Holly and let her know I'd failed to find the cop.

"Hey Holly," I began, trying to keep my voice upbeat. "How's it going?"

"Good. I think Chloe's going a little stir-crazy though. Did you find him?"

"Not yet. After we left your house, I went back to the precinct and managed to talk to both cops, but it wasn't as easy as I'd hoped. I mean...I know it's not one of them, but I don't know for sure if it's the other one. It could be, but I just don't know yet."

"Oh...that's not good."

"I know...I'm sorry. I think if I talk to him again, I might know more."

"Okay," she said slowly. "So...what happens next? You'll talk to him tomorrow?"

"Yeah. This time I'll be better prepared. I think if Bates hadn't left me out in the first place, this could have been resolved by now."

"Yeah...what's up with that guy? He's a real jerk."

I told her what happened with him after the interview and how mad it made me. Talking to Holly was always good therapy, but I had to be careful since Chloe was involved. "I left before Dimples got there, but I saw him in the parking lot. He was going to talk to Bates and decide what to do next. He should be calling Scott tonight. Scott might want to take Chloe home to his house."

"I'll give Scott a call and see what he thinks, but if you just need one more day, I'd feel better about keeping her here."

Now it was my turn to sigh. "I hope I can figure it out by then, but if I can't, maybe he should take her on a long trip or something."

"We'll see," she said. "I'll call you later and let you know what's going on...and...thanks for everything you're doing, Shelby. I don't know what we'd do without you. Really, I couldn't have a better friend."

"Oh...well, it goes both ways. You know I'd do anything for you. I just wish I had more, but I promise to keep at it until I find him," I said.

"I know you will," she agreed.

We disconnected, and my lips turned down. I hated not knowing more. With my skills, I should have solved this case by now. I knew Holly would keep Chloe at her house as long as she needed to, but I also knew the longer she stayed, the more risk there was of someone finding out. Maybe Scott should take her on a trip somewhere.

Later that night, I soaked in the bathtub with my aromatherapy bath salts. The soothing scent of spearmint and eucalyptus helped relieve the tension, and the hot water helped my sore muscles after my Aikido lesson. I had to admit that taking Aikido was great for me...probably because I got to throw people around. Also, Holly had called to tell me they were keeping Chloe at her house, which I thought was a good idea. So, at least for tonight, things were under control.

After we went to bed, I finally had time to tell Chris all the details about my horrible day, ending with Dimples finding out my secret.

"Oh no," he said. "How did that happen?"

"Well...I was kind of crying, and pretty upset when he got in the car. I guess I slipped up when I was explaining what was going through Bates' mind."

Chris' eyes widened that I could make such a huge mistake, and he couldn't constrain his disappointment that I had let Harris find out. I should have been more careful.

I tried not to feel bad, but after everything else, his censure hurt. "I know it's my fault, but it's not like I did it on purpose."

Chris sucked in a breath. "I never said...oh...yeah...sorry." He sighed and rubbed his chin, wishing I hadn't heard that. He certainly didn't want to dig a hole he couldn't get out of. Oops. Now I'd heard that too.

"Shelby...sweetheart...it will be fine. I'm sure you were upset and didn't mean for it to happen. I trust Harris. He was bound to find out sooner or later. Heck, I'm surprised he hadn't figured it out before now. So it's okay. He won't tell anyone. Don't beat yourself up about it."

"Really?"

"Yeah...it's okay."

"Thanks honey," I said and snuggled up next to him. "That makes me feel better."

He pulled me into his arms and kissed me soundly, thinking he knew of a great way get my mind off my troubles...and keep himself out of the doghouse.

"Chris!" I swatted him.

"Hey...you can't blame me. Besides, I think it's working pretty good."

He kissed me again, proving his point, and I relaxed into his arms. His love surrounded me in a protective cocoon and fed my growing desire. "Okay...I guess you're out of the doghouse."

He chuckled. "Oh baby, oh baby."

I blinked my eyes open the next morning and jolted up in panic. What time was it? I checked the clock. Seven-thirty? Damn! I jumped out of bed and threw on my bathrobe before running downstairs.

"Hey mom," Savannah said. "Dad and Josh already left. Dad said you needed to sleep in."

"Oh...well that was nice of him. Are you ready to go?"

"Sure." A car honked, and she grabbed her backpack. "See ya."

"Okay...have a good day! Love you!"

I watched her get into the car and then ran back upstairs. I had thirty minutes to make myself beautiful before Ramos was supposed to be here, but maybe it wasn't too late to change plans and have him meet me at the hotel.

I called his number, and he picked right up. "Babe."

I let out a sigh. "Hey Ramos. Uncle Joey said you were picking me up at home, but I was wondering if I could just meet you at the hotel. Will that work?"

He chuckled. "Don't want the neighbors talking?"

"Exactly," I agreed.

"Yeah, that makes sense. See you there."

At least I didn't have to shower since I'd taken a bath last night. I got my make-up on in record time and went for the wind-blown look with my hair since that's all I had time for. Satisfied, I hurried into my closet and stood there, hoping for inspiration to strike.

Blue jeans were off the list, but I had a nice pair of black straight-leg jeans and a new black-and-white blouse that should work. Along with my black boots and matching necklace and earrings, I'd look good enough for the Marriott.

I spritzed on some perfume and took one last look at my outfit before hurrying downstairs. I needed a black leather jacket for the best effect but, since I didn't have one, I decided to go without, even if it was chilly. I grabbed my purse and opened the door, shivering a little. It was supposed to get up to the sixties today, but right now it was only in the forties.

I arrived at exactly eight-thirty, so I let the valet park my car, and hurried inside. With all the hurrying I was doing, I couldn't wait to sit down and breathe for a minute. I hesitated in the lobby and glanced around. I'd never been inside the hotel before and didn't know where to go. Catching sight of a familiar set of shoulders, I smiled and headed in that direction.

Ramos glanced my way and stood with a grin. He wore a sports jacket over an open-collared shirt with jeans and looked delectable. As I approached him, thoughts from a woman wondering who I was halted me in my tracks. I caught a few more thoughts and relaxed to know they were coming from a lady who'd been admiring Ramos. She was disappointed to see him meeting me.

I smiled and glanced knowingly at Ramos, who wondered what was going on. "Not something you need to know," I said, reaching him. "So where's breakfast? I'm starved."

"Hmm...you know I have ways of making you talk."

I burst out laughing. He'd said that with a Russian accent, and it was hilarious. He grinned. "This way." But he was thinking, *you might be laughing now...but I wasn't exactly kidding.*

"I heard that...and you don't scare me."

"Really? I guess I'll have to sharpen my image."

Before I could respond, the hostess greeted us. Ramos took charge and asked if we could sit at the table by the window...right next to Blake Beauchaine. Ramos motioned me to take the seat closest to Blake, and he sat opposite. While I looked over the menu, I listened to Blake's thoughts.

Outwardly, he ignored us completely, but I registered his surprise that Ramos had found him. He was impressed. Manetto must have better resources than he'd thought. Given that, the timing couldn't be better. He just wished he had more information. He'd hit a wall in the investigation, and his window of opportunity was closing fast. But now that we were here, we presented him with a perfect break. He was going to eat his breakfast and observe me. *Shelby Nichols.*

He knew I worked for Manetto occasionally, and that I had my own consulting agency. But why did I come with Ramos? Manetto must want me here for a reason, but what could that be? It was a puzzle he aimed to figure out, along with the rest of Manetto's organization. Maybe I was part of the puzzle that he could use against Manetto. He'd have to learn more, but it gave him a place to start.

Yikes! I didn't like that one bit. Ramos took in my widened eyes and frowned, wondering what was going on. I swallowed and sent him a quick smile. The waiter came to our table and, since I hadn't looked at the menu, I blurted out the first thing that came to mind. "I think I'll have an omelet...and some juice...no make that chocolate milk...and some toast."

He nodded and turned to Ramos who quickly gave him his order. Just as our waiter left, another waiter came with Blake's food and I relaxed, knowing he wouldn't leave before I got to eat. I hoped.

"Did you see the paper this morning?" Ramos asked, wanting to start a conversation.

"No, I didn't get a chance. What did it say?"

"Oh...just the usual," he said. "I guess there was another shooting by the police. It seems like almost every day some cop kills someone."

"Yeah...I know. It's terrible. Must be all the guns. That reminds me...I want to get a black leather motorcycle jacket like yours...only one that fits me. Do you know of any good shops?"

Ramos' lips twitched. He was wondering how I got from police shootings to leather jackets. There must be a connection in there somewhere. Maybe it was the guns?

"Yeah...that could be it," I said. "I don't like guns much, so I think of other things. Like clothes and shoes and maybe some nice jewelry. Guns are just bad, and they kill people." Ramos lifted a brow in challenge, so I continued. "I know...there's that whole thing about how guns don't kill people, only people kill people, but I don't entirely agree. I mean...just two nights ago my friend got shot. She almost died! She walks into her apartment, and these two guys are in there, robbing her. But if they wouldn't have had a gun, instead of shooting her...well what could have happened?"

Ramos opened his mouth to answer, but I was on a roll. "I guess they could have attacked her, but she has mad Aikido skills...and she could have defended herself. And even if they got away, at least she wouldn't have been shot."

"I think I see what you're saying," Ramos said, but he was mostly being polite.

"You just think I'm nuts."

"Now you know that's not true," he said, holding my gaze until I smiled. "But I do have a question. Does your friend have a gun?" I nodded, and he continued. "So what's the difference?"

"She wouldn't have used it to kill them."

"Okay, that's fair." But he was thinking she might have used it if her life was in danger, so what was the difference?

He had a point, and I didn't add that she had pulled her gun out to stop them, and since they'd used it to shoot her, that pretty much blew a hole through my argument. But I wasn't ready to drop it yet.

"There's this other case I know about," I continued, brushing off his thoughts. "These two drug dealers decided to take out a couple of teenagers because they saw too much, but one of the teenagers had a gun and guess what happened?"

"What?" he asked.

"They ended up shooting each other. All three of them are dead. It's insane!"

Ramos quickly nodded his agreement, thinking I seemed more than a little upset over something I'd just heard about. Knowing me, there was probably a lot more to it. Had I been there? Quietly, so only I could hear, he took my hand and asked, "Did you see this?"

Pursing my lips together, I nodded. "I'm helping with an investigation, so...yeah. I was at the crime scene. The boy was only seventeen."

Ramos inhaled sharply and shook his head before catching my gaze. "Shelby...maybe you should stop helping the police." He was thinking the fact that I hated the sight of blood should be enough to convince me.

I pulled away and sat back in my chair. "I've been thinking that too, but not for the same reasons you're thinking, although ...there is that."

Just then our food arrived, and I tried to remember how hungry I was a few minutes ago. It smelled delicious, so that helped. In my tirade, I'd forgotten all about Blake, and I realized he'd been listening intently, gleaning the useful information that I helped the police. There was a lot more to me than he realized, and his curiosity ratcheted up a notch.

Oh great! What had I done? Instead of helping Uncle Joey, I was helping his enemy. Crap!

"How's your omelet?" Ramos asked, concerned that I hadn't taken a bite, but instead had managed to mangle it into a mess with my fork. "Want some ketchup with that?" He cursed in his mind, thinking that was probably not the best thing to ask since it might remind me of the teenage boy and the blood. Then his eyes widened as he realized I'd probably just heard that. "Damn! Sorry."

My lips twisted into a smile. "It's okay. Here...give me some of that." I held out my hand for the ketchup, and he passed it to me. Then he worried that I might just squirt it all over him to get revenge. I smiled. "Gee Ramos, I hadn't even thought of that. Maybe I should."

He didn't even flinch, but his eyes narrowed and one brow lifted. Did I really want to go there? I looked damn good in my outfit. It would be a shame to have it ruined with ketchup stains.

This time I laughed out loud. "Wow...you're good...and...thanks for the compliment." With a flourish, I tipped the ketchup bottle and squirted some onto my omelet, then set it back down. I took a bite and sighed. "Hmm...this is really good."

I turned my attention to Blake and caught him thinking that our conversation didn't make any sense. It was like I was talking to myself, even though Ramos was sitting right there. It was weird. He shook his head and finished his coffee. It seemed like we had forgotten him. Maybe it was time to leave.

I caught Ramos' gaze and nodded my head toward Blake. Ramos quickly rose from his chair and loomed over Blake with a threatening lift of his brow. "Mr. Beauchaine. Would you care to join us?" It wasn't a request, and Blake knew it.

He sighed. "I was wondering when you were going to ask." He placed his napkin on his plate and picked up his coffee cup, then moved into the empty chair beside me.

"Ms. Nichols," he said with a nod. I nodded back but couldn't say anything because my mouth was full of food. "Please...don't let me interrupt. Enjoy your breakfast." He turned his attention back to Ramos. "I take it Joe found my envelope?"

"He would like to know what you're doing here," Ramos said.

"I'm sure he would." Blake kept his gaze on Ramos, refusing to say anything else. He didn't want to look like a pushover, so he needed to do some pushing back of his own.

Ramos knew how to play this game. "You can meet with him at his office now or worry about your health for the rest of the day."

Blake's nostrils flared, but that was the only thing that gave him away. "As much as I'd like to take you up on your kind offer, I can't. I have work to do today that can't wait. But I could meet with Manetto later tonight over drinks...like old friends. How does that sound?"

Ramos took his time answering, taking a sip of juice while keeping his gaze trained on Blake. He'd expected Blake to suggest something like that, but he didn't want to seem too eager. "All right. I think we can agree to that. Nine p.m. at the Comet Club." Ramos stood, signaling the discussion was over and he was in charge.

Blake pushed back his chair but, before standing, glanced at me. "Nice to meet you, my dear." He stood straight and tall, catching Ramos' gaze with a penetrating one of his own. I knew what he was going to say, and my heart sank. "I'll be there on one condition."

"What's that?"

"She comes." Blake motioned at me with a tilt of his head.

Ramos held back his grin. This was too easy. Blake had no idea what he was getting into, and having me there was perfect. He glanced at me with apology in his eyes, then turned back to Blake. "Agreed."

Blake nodded, then left the table, thinking that went better than he'd expected. Now all he had to do was dig up some dirt on me. Or find out if I was helping Joe willingly, and if I could be enticed to come over to his side. He had his work cut out for him but, with his resources, it should be a walk in the park. Without a backward glance, he rounded the corner and was gone.

Ramos sat back down and grimaced. "Sorry about that. I know Manetto would want you there whether I agreed or not, so it just made sense to go along with it. Can you come?"

"I think so," I said. "But does it have to be the Comet Club? Last time I was there didn't turn out so good for me." I didn't like that place much, mostly because I'd gotten shot there.

Ramos' brows drew together, remembering how I'd nearly died in the basement. "This is different. No one's trying to kill you. You'll be perfectly safe, I promise." He was thinking, *I'd never let anything happen to you. You know that, right?*

I let out a breath and glanced up at him. "Okay...I'll come."

"Good," Ramos said, his lips quirked into a smile. "Don't forget it's also where you won a lot of money in a little poker match. That was fun, right?"

"Yeah...it was." How could I forget about beating Uncle Joey out of his money? It was awesome!

"Did you pick up anything from Blake that we need to know?"

"Not really...except that he's hoping I'm the weakest link and he can buy me off or something. I have no idea why he'd do that, although he was thinking about connecting Uncle Joey to some investigation he's working on...or at least that's what it sounded like."

"Investigation?" Ramos asked.

"Yeah. What did he mean by that? Do you know what Blake does?" Ramos sighed, but decided he might as well tell me.

"We think he's a spy."

Chapter 7

"Seriously?" I asked, surprised. "You mean like a real spying-for-your-country-kind-of-spy, or more of a corporate-espionage-kind-of-spy?"

Ramos shrugged. "I'm not sure. That's something you'll have to ask Manetto. But now that you know, don't let on that you know. I'm not even sure Manetto wanted you to know that, but he can blame me if he doesn't like it."

"Um...yeah...okay."

"You done?"

"Yeah." I'd only eaten half of my breakfast, but I wasn't hungry anymore.

Ramos stuffed some cash into the black bill folder and stood. I followed him out to the lobby and we handed our tickets to the valet parking attendant. "I'm not sure I've been much help," I said, chewing my bottom lip.

"Of course you have," he assured me.

"Hmm...I don't know. Blake had a lot of thoughts, but most were about me. He picked up that I helped the police, which could be bad, and he already knew I had my own consulting agency." I finally had the courage to glance into

Ramos' eyes. "He wondered what Uncle Joey had on me and if I could be bought or used against him."

The attendant pulled my car to a stop and ran toward me with my keys. Ramos intercepted him, took the keys, and deftly slipped him some money. He turned to me and placed the keys in my hand. Giving my hand a warm squeeze, he gazed into my eyes with a sweet tenderness that took my breath away. "Babe. Don't worry so much. You did fine. I'm sure Manetto will be grateful."

Taking my arm, he walked me to my car and opened the door. He waited for me to sit down and then leaned in close enough to send my heart racing. I caught the spicy scent of his aftershave and, without thinking, I closed my eyes and inhaled deeply through my nose.

With dawning realization at what I was doing, I jerked them open to find him regarding me with a lopsided grin. "We'll pick you up tonight at eight-thirty. Sound good?"

"Okay," I said, breathlessly. He took a step back and closed the door. I sucked in air like I'd forgotten how to breathe, which was pretty much true, and started my car. Wowza.

As I drove away, I rolled down the window to let the cool air knock some sense into my brain. A few seconds later, I was in control, although it kind of freaked me out that he had such an effect on me. I pushed that unsettling thought aside and focused on where I was going next.

I should probably head over to the precinct and talk to Pete again, but just thinking about seeing Bates filled me with dread. Maybe I should see how Billie was doing first, and then go over there. She'd want to know about the thumb-drive, and since I hadn't given it to Dimples yet, she wouldn't be mad at me about that. Plus, it would be nice to see how she was doing. With that happy thought, I turned on the radio and sang along with the tunes.

I knocked before entering Billie's room and found her sitting up in bed. "Wow...you look so much better today," I exclaimed.

"Thanks," she said. "I'm feeling better too, but I'm stuck in here for a few more days, which is probably a good thing since my parents are here and they're cleaning up my apartment. Did Drew tell you? He met them yesterday...and I haven't seen him since." She was worried that they'd scared him off, since her mom could be a little overbearing. She hadn't planned on introducing him to her parents this way.

"Yes he told me."

"What did he say about them?"

"He said they were great." I wasn't about to tell her that he thought she was a lot like her mom, since she might equate it with the overbearing part. "I think he's glad they're here watching over you so he can do his job and figure out who attacked you."

"Oh...yeah. That's probably right."

"Did you tell him who you think may have stolen the original thumb-drive from your desk at work? That might be a good place for him to start."

"No. I hadn't thought of that." She was thinking she couldn't remember telling me either. "Did I tell you that?"

"Who you thought it was?" I asked, buying time for a response.

"Yes." She raised her brow, thinking that was just what she'd said.

"No. You didn't tell me a thing, but I'm sure you've got someone in mind. Don't you?"

"Yes."

"Anyway...I'm glad you're doing better. Don't worry about the thumb-drive. It's safe and sound."

"That's a relief," she said. "Please don't tell Drew you have it. I don't think he'd let me keep it if he knew."

"How about I make him a copy?"

She stilled. From my tone of voice, it sounded like I'd already done that. "Did you tell him?"

I let out a big sigh. "Yes. But he figured it out, and I think it's for the best. I haven't given it to him yet, but I think I should." At her raised eyebrows, I continued, "Look, Billie, you were nearly killed over this. It's not worth your life. You need his help. If it will make you feel better, I'll make another copy for you. Then you'll both have one."

She knew that I was right and she was being stubborn. "Okay...that should work."

"And tell him who you think took the original too," I said, since she was being amenable. "We need to get to the bottom of this before anyone else gets hurt."

She nodded. "Okay, I'll do it."

"Good," I said, smiling. "I guess I'd better go. Is there anything else you need?"

"Drew," she said. "Can you tell him to come see me?" She missed him and worried he'd give up on her because of her secrets.

"Yes of course. I'm headed over to the precinct right now, so I'll let him know."

"Thanks, Shelby," she said, closing her eyes. She hated to admit it, but now that she didn't have to keep it from him, she could finally rest, and she realized she should have done it long before now.

Since I couldn't put it off any longer, I got in my car and headed for the precinct. Just as I put the car into drive, an announcer on the radio said they had breaking news and it looked like the missing girl had been found alive and well. My mouth went dry and my heart raced. Were they talking about Chloe?

A second later my fears were confirmed with the announcement that Chloe Peterson had been found safe and unharmed, and was being held at an undisclosed location.

What the freak?! This was terrible. I grabbed my phone and called Holly. She picked up, and I blurted, "What's going on? I just heard the news on the radio!"

"I know," she answered. "I just got a call from Scott."

"What happened? Did he let it out?"

"No, it was Kira. Apparently she'd had enough of the media hounding her every move. I guess this morning one of the reporters told Kira that she didn't seem upset enough for a mother with a daughter who'd been missing for three days, so what was she hiding? Kira lost it and told the whole bunch that Chloe had been found and was safe so they'd leave her alone."

"Oh man! So what did Scott tell you to do?" I asked.

"He said to hang tight, and he'd call me back after he talked to the police."

"Okay. Well, at least no one knows where she is, right?"

"Yeah," Holly agreed. "Kira didn't go that far, thank goodness."

"Do you want me to come over? I was just heading to the precinct when I heard the news on the radio. I was going to see if I could get anything else out of the other cop, but I could come to your place if you want."

"No. I think you should go to the precinct. Chloe's fine for now, and I'd rather have you find the cop."

"Okay," I said. "Call if you need me for anything." She agreed, and we disconnected.

This was bad. I probably should have gone straight to the precinct instead of visiting Billie. I could have been there when the news broke out and listened to Pete's thoughts. I would have known if it was him or not. Now I wouldn't have that advantage. I vowed then and there not to let Bates get in the way of my better judgment.

A few minutes later, I pulled into the parking lot and found several news people getting out of their vans. I hurried inside where the reporters were gathering. One of the police officers told them that the chief had scheduled a press conference in half an hour, so they needed to be patient and wait.

I ducked around them and through the door to the detective's offices, finding everyone crowded outside the chief's office, listening to his plans for the press conference. Dimples caught sight of me and motioned me over.

"I guess you heard?" he asked, his voice low.

"Yeah, on the radio. It was quite a shock. Did you know?"

"We had no idea. So now it looks like we're doing damage control."

"What's the chief telling everyone?" I asked.

"Just that she's safe, and we're keeping her off the grid until we know more about where she's been. That sort of thing."

I nodded and glanced around to see if Pete was there. I sure wanted to know what he was thinking, but I couldn't find him in the crowd. I caught a few thoughts about Chloe. Most were glad she was okay, but a few were wondering why all the secrecy, and that there must be more to it.

The meeting broke up, and everyone headed back to their desks. The chief caught sight of me with Dimples and motioned us, along with Bates, into his office. "Shut the door and have a seat," he said.

I tried not to cringe when Bates sat beside me, and I gamely greeted him with a smile. He ignored me and began to talk. "I just got off the phone with her father, and he wants Chloe to stay at his sister's house. I'm not sure that's a good idea, but as long as it stays in this room, it should be all right."

"What do you think Shelby?" the chief asked.

"I think that's the best place for her."

The chief glanced at Dimples. "You?"

"I agree with Shelby," Dimples answered. "We need to keep her secure until we find out who's involved."

"All right, we'll leave that option open," the chief agreed. "But how close are we to solving this?" He glanced at me for an answer.

I cleared my throat. "I'm hoping I'll know soon."

"What have you done so far?"

"Questioned the officers Chloe picked out," I answered. "From what I could pick up, I'm pretty sure it's not Bellini, but I'm not sure about the other one. I need to talk with him again."

"Who's that?"

"Uh...Pete Royce."

The chief's brows drew together. "He's a good cop. Been working narcotics, but he seems solid."

I shrugged, since I couldn't be more specific about my premonitions.

"Yeah...well, he was connected to the two drug dealers," Bates said, surprising me. "He arrested them a few months ago, but the charges were dropped. So there might be something to it."

Chief Winder stood, then placed his hands on his desk and leaned his imposing bulk toward us, barely restraining his frustration. "Well...figure it out! Do some real investigating. I've got the press and Chloe's parents breathing down my neck. This needs to be solved yesterday."

He glanced at me with disappointment, thinking that, normally, I'd have solved this case...yesterday. Maybe my premonitions didn't always work, and they were relying on me too much.

He let out a breath and straightened. "It's time for the press conference. I want the three of you in the room with me. Let's go."

I dutifully followed behind him, a stab of pain in my heart that the chief thought I'd let him down. Of course Bates had told him I hadn't come through, so naturally he had doubts, but it still hurt. We turned into the large conference room, and I flinched when someone snapped a photo. Most of the reporters wondered what I was doing there and who I was, but there were a few who knew my name.

I didn't like being in the limelight much, so I stayed back by the door while the chief took his place at the podium with Dimples and Bates standing behind him. The room quieted except for the clicking of cameras.

"Chloe Peterson was found safe yesterday," the chief began. "Due to extenuating circumstances, we are keeping her location private but, let me assure you, she is unharmed and doing well. I can tell you that she was not kidnapped or taken against her will and has returned of her own accord. Her family asks that you allow them space to deal with this experience and the consequences of her actions. Thank you."

"Why didn't you tell us this yesterday?" someone shouted. "Was she involved in something illegal? Was she alone? Where has she been?"

The chief held up his hands, and the questions subsided. "Because this is an ongoing investigation, I am not at liberty to tell you the details. Just know that she is safe and unharmed."

"Do you know where she is?" The low voice caught me off-guard, and I glanced over my shoulder to find Pete Royce standing close, his gaze scanning the crowd. I didn't answer right away, and he frowned, thinking I must know, or I would have denied it by now.

"I have my ideas," I said. "But no one's talking, so I don't know for sure." He finally looked at me, trying to determine if I was telling the truth. "Do you?" I countered.

His eyes crinkled at the corners with a barely perceived smile. I'd turned the tables on him...good for me. "I have my ideas too."

He motioned with his head to exit the room, and I followed him out, stopping in a corner of the hall away from the crowd. "Look...I knew those guys at the house, and I've been working narcotics for a long time. I can probably help you, but I need to know what's going on."

"Why?"

"Let's just say...word on the street is there might be some people interested in finding her."

I inhaled sharply and caught his gaze. "I think you'd better tell the chief what you know."

"I can't right now...there's something I need to take care of first. But tell him to keep her safe...and don't let anyone know where she is. Okay?"

"Sure," I agreed. He was worried about her safety, but he was also concerned about something else. Something he had no control over, and he was thinking it was time he took care of it.

Noise coming from the room with the press conference signaled it was over, and he nodded his thanks before joining the crowd coming down the hall. He was thinking that, with the way things were going, it was time for him to make some hard choices and see if he could do something about this mess...

I lost him in the shuffle and turned to follow. What did he mean by hard choices? I took a couple of steps, but someone grabbed my wrist to stop me. Without thinking, I used my Aikido technique to break his hold and bend his wrist back, sending him crashing into the wall.

"Oww," Dimples said.

"Oh...sorry." I dropped his wrist. "I didn't know it was you...and..." I glanced at the crowd, but Pete was long gone. "I was trying to follow Pete..."

He rubbed his wrist and frowned. "Pete was here?"

"Yeah."

Dimples groaned. "Oh...I thought you were leaving, and I wanted to talk to you. Did you hear anything from him?"

My eyes widened, and I glanced at the people standing nearby. "Hey...not so loud."

He sighed, thinking no one would have known what he was talking about. "Okay...let's go somewhere else." He turned down the hall in the opposite direction, and I hesitated before following, knowing the dead files room was not a place I wanted to be. Apparently Dimples thought it was perfect.

As he opened the door and flipped on the light, a cold chill rushed over me, but I followed him inside anyway. Rubbing my arms, I leaned against the door. "Okay...this is what I picked up, but it doesn't make a lot of sense. In fact, Pete asked me if I knew where Chloe was, but then he told me to tell the chief to keep her safe and not let anyone know where she was. See what I mean?"

"Yeah...I wonder why he'd say that if he was after her."

"He was also thinking that he needed to make some hard choices and do something about the mess. What does that mean?"

Dimples let out a long breath. "I'm not sure. Maybe he's been doing some kind of undercover work or something. If he is, the chief should know. I'll ask him about it."

"Good idea. So what about Chloe? Still planning to let her stay at Holly's?"

"I don't know. That's next on the list of decisions to make. I think as long as her mother doesn't tell anyone, it should be okay, but who knows? Her parents are coming in to discuss it right now. But before we go back up there, I need to ask you something."

"Okay," I said.

"It's about Billie." His lips turned down, and his brows drew together. "I got a text from her that said she'd asked you to tell me something." He glanced up at me, worry in his eyes that it was something he wouldn't want to hear, and that's why she was making me tell him.

"Oh yeah. I went to the hospital this morning. She's looking a lot better, so that's good. Anyway, she told me I could give you the thumb-drive, and she wants your help."

"Oh," his face brightened. "That's great. So...did you bring it?"

"Uh...no. It's at my house, but I can get it for you...after I make a copy for her."

"Fine," he said, thinking he'd pretend he didn't know that part.

"She misses you," I said. "Maybe you could stop by later."

"Yeah...I'll do that." He didn't think he'd have time, but he'd try.

"I can help with that investigation too, you know. If there's someone you want to question, I can go with you...so be sure to let me know."

"Thanks Shelby. That could make all the difference. We know it's all tied up with the A.G.'s office, and once I see what's on the thumb-drive, that will help." He was thinking that he wouldn't mind going over to the A.G.'s office right now and ruffling some feathers, but he didn't want to show his hand until he knew more. But with me reading their minds...it was like an ace in the hole.

His gaze caught mine, and he shook his head in wonder. "I still can't get over it...what you do, I mean. Well...we'd better get back upstairs."

He opened the door for me, and I nearly plowed into Bates. How long had he been standing there? His eyes narrowed, and he wondered what kind of hanky-panky was going on between me and Harris. He'd seen us go into the room together and was waiting for this moment to catch us. Too bad he couldn't hear anything through the door.

"There you are," he drawled. "Something you want to share with me?"

"No!" I brushed past him, nearly biting my tongue off to keep from calling him a tubby pervert.

"What do you want?" Dimples asked, his voice hard.

"Chloe's parents are here. The chief wants you and Nichols in his office while he talks to them."

Since I was halfway up the stairs, I led the way back to the chief's office, determined not to let Bates get to me, even though he'd purposely called me Nichols.

Scott and Kira waited inside the office, each sitting on opposite sides of the couch. Since I didn't want to be any closer to Bates than I had to, I sat between them and hoped for the best. Scott was furious with Kira, and Kira was mad at me. Hmm...maybe this wasn't the best place to sit after all.

They both started talking at once, each blaming the other, before Kira pounced on me and included the police at the same time. "This wouldn't have happened if you were doing your jobs. What's so hard about finding the cop Chloe identified? You should know who it is by now. I want to bring Chloe in so she can identify him in a line-up and you can arrest him. This could be over and done with today, and Chloe could go back to school, and we could get our lives back."

It sounded so simple when she put it that way. Was it my fault? I'd told them I could figure it out, and I hadn't, and now look where we were. The chief glanced at me, thinking he could easily get the two officers into a line-up for Chloe to look at.

"I understand your frustration," he said. "And we can certainly do a line-up for Chloe, but that doesn't mean we can make an arrest. From what I understand, she didn't get a good look at him, so that might not work. But I want you to know, I've got my best people working on it, and we have narrowed it down. I think leaving her at your sister's house is still a good idea, but if you want to bring her home, I understand. I just can't guarantee her safety, so it's up to you to do that."

"I think she's better off at Holly's for now, but we can't leave her there for long," Scott said. "She's missing a lot of school, and it's hard for her to be cooped up like that.

"Scott's right," Kira agreed. "And we won't tell anyone where she is, but you've got to do something soon."

"We'll get this resolved as soon as we can," the chief said. "Just give me a few more days."

After Scott and Kira left, I wanted to leave too, but Dimples told the chief and Bates that I had some news about Pete. I told them most of it, along with Pete's reluctance to speak to the chief himself. "Does he do any kind of undercover work with narcotics?"

Chief Winder rubbed his chin. "I know he did in the past, but I thought he was done with that. We can check with the narcotics division and see, but he can't just rush off like that without telling me what's going on. Bates...you call him and get him back here. Harris...you check with narcotics. Shelby..." He glanced at me, thinking I'd helped some, but maybe it was time to cut me loose and let his detectives handle this. "You're free to go."

Ouch. It didn't help that Bates was snickering with glee in his mind, and even Dimples felt a little embarrassed for me. I nodded and walked out of the office with Dimples trailing behind. He was trying to think of something to say to make me feel better but was afraid he'd only make it worse.

I stopped at his desk and turned to face him. "I guess I'll head home now. Let me know if you need anything."

"Uh...sure. I will. And Shelby, don't feel too bad. I'll keep you in the loop. You're a valuable asset, they just don't know it."

"Right," I said, trying not to let my disappointment show. "Listen...I'll get a copy of that thumb-drive for you."

"Great," he said, then sucked in a breath as a thought occurred to him. "Just don't do anything about it on your own, all right?"

"Of course not," I said, lying through my teeth.

Chapter 8

I got into my car and slammed the door, realizing today hadn't gone much better than yesterday. Maybe I really should quit helping the police. I was relying on them too much, when I should be doing my own investigating. I had Pete's number. I could call him and set up a time to talk away from the precinct. If he wasn't surrounded by his co-workers, maybe he'd be more forthcoming.

I also needed to take a look at that thumb-drive. Looking at it didn't mean I'd have to do anything about it, but it might help me know who to talk to. That reminded me of Billie's thoughts about who might have taken the original thumb-drive. I could go to her office and talk to that person right now. If he felt guilty that Billie had been shot over this, he might be thinking about who sent him after the thumb-drive in the first place.

Her office wasn't far, so I turned in that direction. Might as well talk to him now and look at the thumb-drive when I got home. After that, I'd give Pete a call and set something up. Who knew? By the end of the day, I could have the information to solve both cases. That would show the chief, and maybe even shut Bates up.

With that happy thought, I drove to the newspaper's offices and parked in the visitor space. I added some lipstick and touched up my hair, grateful I looked 'damn good' in my outfit. Now came the tricky part. Since I only knew Billie was thinking about 'the intern,' I didn't have a name and, for all I knew, it could be a girl just as easily as a guy. That meant I'd have to come up with a reason to talk to the intern. I could say I was from the University and was there to ask the intern some questions, but that might get tricky.

I sighed and rubbed my forehead, glancing down at my lap. That's when I noticed my police ID badge around my neck, and optimism swept over me. Telling them I was working on a case for the police and needed to talk to the intern would be the perfect cover...and mostly true.

With my stomach a bundle of nerves, I hurried inside and smiled at the receptionist. "Hi, I'm Shelby Nichols, a private investigator, and I need to talk to your intern about a case I'm working on with the police."

"Okay," she said. "Which one?"

Oh crap! There was more than one? "Um...let's start with all of them, and I'll take it from there. Do you have a meeting room I could use?"

"Well...let me see." She checked her computer. "We usually keep the room right over there open for interviews, and it looks like nothing's scheduled for today, so that should work. But I'm not sure how many of the interns are here."

I held my breath as she looked through her lists. "Oh...you're in luck. It looks like they're all here."

"Great," I said, relieved.

"I'll put in a call to their departments and have them sent right down."

"Thank you so much." I turned toward the room she indicated and slipped inside. It was small, with a rectangular desk and six chairs. But since she was thinking three interns, it should work. Now all I had to do was figure out which of the interns Billie had been thinking about.

Sitting on the edge of my seat, I watched through the glass partition as a young man exited the elevator and stood by the receptionist's desk waiting for the others to arrive. Two young women soon joined him and they started toward me. From their puzzled expressions, I knew they were asking each other what was going on.

With a deep breath, I opened the door and gave them my best smile. "Hi, I'm Shelby Nichols, a private investigator with the police. Please come in and sit down. This won't take long."

Now that they were properly intimidated, I began. "I'm sure you're wondering what's going on, so let me get right to the point. Which one of you has worked with Billie Payne?"

The two girls glanced at each other, then at the boy. They knew her, but hadn't worked with her personally. The boy glanced at both of the girls, then settled his gaze on me and shrugged. "We've all worked with her at some point," he lied, hoping I'd take the bait, and thinking there was no way I knew anything. He'd been careful; this was just a fluke.

"What's your name?" I asked.

"Uh...Corey."

"Okay," I said. "You girls can leave. Thanks for coming, but it's Corey I need to talk to." He inhaled sharply, and his eyes got big. That was quick. How had I done that? He could hardly believe he'd given himself away so fast unless...did I already know something?

The two girls were curious, but not surprised. They thought Corey was full of himself, and they were sure he'd done something he probably shouldn't have.

Well...that was easy. Now I just had to make him talk. Too bad Ramos wasn't here, but maybe I could project some of that intimidation into my voice. After the door snapped shut, I studied him for a moment to make him sweat before I began. That tactic was something I'd picked up from Uncle Joey, and I knew first-hand how great it worked.

"I'm a friend of Billie's," I said, keeping my voice low. "And right now I'm helping the police as part of an ongoing investigation. You heard that Billie got shot, right? And she nearly died?"

"Yeah, I heard that. I also heard that she's going to be all right." He clasped his hands together, thinking he had to play it cool.

"Do you know what happened?"

"Uh...yeah. I heard someone broke into her apartment and she surprised them." He swallowed, hoping it didn't have anything to do with the thumb-drive he'd lifted from her desk.

Hot resentment swept over me. No doubt about it now. It was him. I clenched my fists together and leaned forward. "Corey...I know what you did. You stole that thumb-drive from Billie's desk."

His nostrils flared, and he flinched with guilt. "I don't know what you're talking about."

"Yes you do. Someone put you up to it. Who was it?"

"I didn't do it," he insisted. "You have no proof." He'd been careful. No one saw him do it. He'd made sure. The money was even safely hidden under his mattress. Five thousand dollars was just sitting there because he'd been afraid to deposit it in his bank.

"Five thousand dollars, huh? That's your price?"

He gasped in surprise. How did I know that? He hadn't told anyone. Unless...did Devon talk? Did he say something? Devon was the only one who knew. It had to be him...but

Devon had also been adamant about not telling a soul or they could both get in a lot of trouble...so it didn't make any sense. Something wasn't right about all this. I had to be bluffing. Beads of sweat popped out on his forehead, and he nervously swallowed the fear creeping up his spine.

"Do you even know what was on the thumb-drive?" I asked.

He clamped his mouth shut, but doubt crept over him. Devon had assured him it was nothing that would get him in trouble. Just something Devon's boss didn't want leaked because it was embarrassing. He figured it was compromising pictures of him with a woman or something...but nothing illegal.

"You sold Billie out," I said, laying it on as heavy as I could. "That thumb-drive was evidence on a case she was working on. You stole the thumb-drive, but it didn't stop there. Someone tried to kill her because of what you did."

"What?" he sputtered. "Why would someone do that if they already had the thumb-drive?"

"She had a copy at home. She's a great reporter and had a back-up plan. You could have learned a lot from her, but what did you do? You sold her out. And now...your career is over."

"But...it wasn't like that. I swear I didn't know." He was thinking that Devon had said it was easy money as long as he kept his mouth shut. He knew he was taking a risk, but how was he supposed to know it was all a big lie? "Look...you can't tell anyone. I swear...the money wasn't worth it, but I didn't know it was serious. He said it wasn't anything illegal. I didn't know that someone could get hurt over it."

I narrowed my eyes and crossed my arms, giving him my best tough-guy impression. "Okay, then help me. Tell me why Devon put you up to this and who he works for. If you tell me the truth, I might even forget we had this conversation."

He paled. I knew about Devon? But wait...I didn't know who Devon worked for...maybe he could still salvage this mess. His gaze flew to mine, and I leveled him with a cold stare Uncle Joey would be proud of. It wasn't hard, since I wasn't feeling so warm and fuzzy at the moment.

He looked away, guilt and despair washing over him. Why had he ever agreed to take the thumb-drive in the first place? He'd told himself nothing bad would happen for taking a stupid thumb-drive, and the five grand was just a bonus. He'd never thought it could ruin him. Now I knew. At least I had thrown him a bone. Maybe he'd better take it.

"I'll...I'll tell you everything I know...I'll even help you if I can. But we have to keep a lid on it until we know more. And Devon can't find out that I talked to you."

"Fine," I agreed. "I suppose I can live with that. So spill."

"Devon is an intern for the Attorney General's office, but he mostly works for Anthony Kerby, one of Grayson Sharp's assistant state's attorneys. Since we're in the same class, we've been going to lunch together and comparing notes about our internships. One day, Anthony Kerby saw us at lunch, and Devon introduced me to him. It wasn't long before Devon said he had a proposition for me from his boss that could make me a lot of money.

"All I had to do was keep an eye on Billie and let him know if she kept anything under lock and key, like a notebook or something. Well, one day I saw her put a thumb-drive in her desk drawer which she took extra pains to lock up tight. I thought it might be significant, so I passed the info along to Devon.

"The next day Devon told me it was worth five grand if I took it from her desk and gave it to him. I wasn't even sure I could do it, but I figured it was worth a try. Anyway, a couple of days later, she left her keys on her desk while she went to a meeting, and I saw my chance." He sighed and hung his head, thinking the thrill of being a spy had worn off fast. "I'm sorry. I didn't know it would hurt her."

"Fine," I said. "I'll try to keep you out of this if I can. Don't tell anyone else what you've told me. If Devon or his boss approach you again, roll with it, just be sure to let me know what they want, and we'll figure out how to handle it together."

"Sure," he agreed, rubbing his hands over his face with relief.

"Here's my card, please call me if anything else comes up. You're my inside guy now...got it?" He swallowed and nodded. "Good. Now you'd better get back to work."

"Right." He tucked my card into his pants pocket and left without a backward glance.

I waited a moment, relieved and happy that I'd found out what was going on. This was huge. I thanked the receptionist for her help and walked out the door. Back in my car, I took a cleansing breath and started for home. It was time to dig in and take a look at that thumb-drive. I needed to find out exactly what was on it.

I arrived at home, took off my boots, and changed my blouse for a comfortable tee shirt. Then I got a diet soda out of the fridge, filled a glass with crushed ice, and took a couple of swallows. Feeling better, I took my drink into the computer room and booted up my computer.

I'd left the thumb-drive in the box under my bed and hurried to retrieve it. After plugging it into my computer, I opened the files and glanced through them. One file held a list of campaign donations with the money amount and the person or company donating.

I clicked on another file and found a list of names and monetary amounts linked to cases investigated by the A.G.'s office. Another file listed deposits of money into four different businesses, but I didn't recognize any of the names. The last file had several people's names with money amounts beside them. Some were positive amounts and others were negative. I wasn't sure what that meant, but it looked like there was some kind of racket going on.

Out of curiosity, I glanced through the campaign contributors and caught my breath to find Thrasher Development as one of them. Of course, that didn't mean anything illegal was going on. Still, I glanced through the investigations file to see if anything showed up. Thrasher wasn't listed anywhere, or Joe Manetto either, and I sighed with relief.

Now I could turn this over to Dimples without worrying about Uncle Joey. But it made me wonder. What if Uncle Joey had been on that list...what would I do then? I shuddered, grateful I didn't have to worry about that...mostly since I didn't think I could erase that info for him, even though he would want me to.

I copied the information onto another thumb-drive for Billie, and slipped the first one into my purse for Dimples. With that done, I put the copied thumb-drive back in the box and slipped it under my bed.

From the information on the thumb-drive, it shouldn't be too hard for Dimples to piece things together. I could also give him the assistant state's attorney, Anthony Kerby, as the main perpetrator behind Billie's break-in. Not bad for a couple hours of work.

With that out of the way, it was time to switch gears to Chloe's investigation and put a call through to Pete. For some reason, he didn't quite fit the mold of the bad guy here, but there was definitely something going on with him, and I intended to get to the bottom of it.

Before my courage failed, I put the call through and nervously chewed on my fingernails. It went straight to voice mail, so I left a message to call me and disconnected. The stress of it all was getting to me, and I hoped he'd call back soon while I still had some fingernails left.

As I carried my empty glass to the kitchen sink, a loud knocking on the glass of my sliding door startled me. Cautiously, I pulled back the curtain to find Chloe standing there shivering and wide-eyed. Unlocking the door, I quickly pushed it open and ushered her inside. "What's happened? Are you okay?"

"Yeah...I'm okay now." Her small frame shook. "He came to the house...but I got away before he saw me."

Dread tightened my stomach. "Who came?"

"The cop! He was there at the house!"

"What? Where's Holly? Is she all right?" My heart pounded with fear that something bad had happened to her.

"She left...the school called. She said she'd be right back, but I got nervous...and then..." She swallowed, and her eyes filled with tears.

"It's okay," I said, rubbing her arms. "You're safe now. Come in and sit down, and start from the beginning." I grabbed a blanket off my chair and wrapped it around her, then ushered her into the living room and got her comfortable on the couch. I got some tissues out of the box and handed them to her and waited while she blew her nose. "Better?" I asked.

"Yeah," she said. "Thanks." She took a moment to compose herself and began. "Holly got a call from the school asking her to come. I don't know why, but it sounded like an emergency.

"I watched her drive off and, as soon as she left, a man got out of a car that was parked down the street. His jacket collar was up around his neck, and he kept his face down, but when he looked toward the house...I knew it was the cop. I got a better look at him this time, so I know for sure which cop it is."

"That's good," I said. "So what happened?"

"I had all the doors bolted, but I was afraid if he broke through a window or something, I was a sitting duck, so I watched him to see where he'd go. He came right up to the front door and rang the bell!"

"What?" I exclaimed. "Did he think he could just waltz in and grab you?"

"I don't know," she said. "But I didn't wait around to find out. I ran out the back door and climbed the fence. Then I went through the neighbor's yard to your street and made my way around to your backyard. I don't think he ever saw me."

"Oh Chloe! I'm so sorry that happened. But you did great. Leaving like that was really smart. I think I've still got that book around here somewhere. Do you mind taking a look at the pictures again and showing me which one it is?"

She nodded, and I ran to the office to get it, grateful I hadn't turned it back into the chief. I grabbed it and hurried back to Chloe. I'd marked the page with Pete's photo and pulled it open. "Here's the first one. What do you think?"

Chloe glanced at the photo and nodded. "Yes...that's him." She swallowed and closed her eyes. "I'm sure it was him this time."

"That's a huge help. Now we can stop him." I closed the book and set it aside. "I should probably call Holly first and tell her you're here, or she'll freak out when she gets home."

"Yeah, that's a good idea. Um...is it okay if I use your bathroom?"

"Sure, go on upstairs and use Savannah's." I pulled my phone out, but before I could call Holly, it started ringing. I expected to see Holly's picture, but the number wasn't readily familiar.

"Hello?"

"Shelby, this is Pete. I got your message, and I think we need to talk."

My heart started to race, and I could barely get my mouth to work. "Um...yeah...okay. When?"

"Are you at home?" he asked. "I'm not too far away. I could stop by your house."

"Oh...uh...not at the moment," I said, my stomach clenching with alarm. "I'm...at the hospital visiting a friend, but I could meet you. In fact...there's a diner right across the street. How about that? Say...in about twenty minutes to half an hour?"

He sighed, pausing to think about it. "Yeah...okay. What's the name of the place?"

"Uh...the Dragon Diner...just on thirteenth and forty-fifth."

"Right...I know the place," he said. "Okay. I'll meet you there. See you soon."

We disconnected, and I took a deep breath. What had I just done? Was this a trap? Was he watching my house? Was he really the bad guy? I had my doubts before he'd showed up at Holly's, but now I didn't know what to expect. I glanced up and down the street from my living room window, but there wasn't any sign of a strange car that I could see. Still, I locked all the doors just in case.

Meeting him was taking a risk, but it would help me know what was going on. As long as Chloe was safe, it should work. Besides, it was a public place. Nothing would happen to me, and I needed to find out what he was thinking. This might be my only chance.

My phone rang again. This time it was Holly.

"Chloe's gone!" she shouted. "I had to leave for a minute and she's not here!"

"Stop! It's okay. She's here at my house and she's fine. I was just going to call you, but you beat me to it. Listen, she went out your back door and climbed the fence, then went through the block to my house. So nothing's wrong. She's fine."

Holly made some strangled choking sounds before she got under control. "What the hell! Why did she do that?"

"Someone came to the door and it scared her, so she ran." I didn't want to freak her out too much, so I tried to break it to her slow. "Uh...it might have been the cop. Look...I think she should stay here for a bit just in case. Is that okay?"

"What? Oh my gosh! Really? It was him?"

"I think so...but I have a plan. What happened anyway?"

"Oh no," she groaned. "This is bad. He must have found out she was here. How did that happen? Who could have told him? This is terrible."

"Holly...what happened? Why did you leave?"

"Now it all makes sense," she continued. "I got a phone call from the principal at the school saying Isabell had been hurt and I should come and take a look. When I got to the school, the secretary said she didn't know anything about it. The principal had left for the day, which seemed a little strange, so we checked with the teacher to see if Isabell was okay.

"I guess she had scraped her knee on the playground, so they thought the principal must have called me before he left. I didn't think anything of it until I got home and realized Chloe wasn't here." She took a few deep breaths, clearly struggling with the situation. "What's going on? Should we call the police?"

"I'll call Dimples and let him know," I said, checking the time. "Josh should be home from school anytime now, so he can keep Chloe company while I...um...check something out."

"Should I call Scott and Kira and tell them what happened?"

"No. I don't want anyone to know until I've talked with Dimples. Someone leaked her location, and I want to find out who it was before we tell anyone where she is now. Okay?"

"Sure," she said, subdued. "What are you checking out?"

Dang! I was hoping she'd forgotten that part. "Uh...I'll explain it all later...oh...there's Josh now. I'll call you back." I disconnected, cringing a little that I'd cut her off, but at least the carpool had just dropped Josh off, so I hadn't told a lie. Besides, she'd probably want to go with me, and that wasn't an option. I quickly unlocked the door and pulled it open.

"Hey mom," Josh said, surprised I'd opened the door for him. "Sup?"

His happy nature, and the fact that he was so darn cute, always brought a smile to my face. "Well...there is something... Chloe's here. Can you keep her company for a while? I have to meet someone, and I don't want to leave her here alone."

"Sure," he said, shrugging like it was no big deal, even though I knew he was pleased. "Why is she here?"

I took a deep breath and told him the truth. "The cop came by Holly's house to pay her a visit, but she ran out the back door and climbed the fence."

"Whoa! That's sick."

"Yeah...she's pretty smart." I hoped that was what he'd meant.

Chloe came into the kitchen, timing her entrance perfectly. She'd freshened up in Savannah's bathroom and even borrowed a little make-up. The haunted look was gone from her eyes, especially when she glanced at Josh. Did I really want to leave those two alone? Nah. They'd be fine. Especially since Savannah would be arriving soon. Plus, they were still a little awkward around each other, so it was all good.

"Okay...well. I'll be back soon. Keep the doors locked...and don't let anyone in except for Savannah. Call me if something comes up, okay?"

"Sure," Josh said.

I grabbed my purse and got in my car, hoping I wasn't making a big mistake by leaving them alone at the house. I pulled to the end of the driveway, looking both ways for any sign of an unfamiliar car. I couldn't see anything, but I decided to drive around the block just to make sure.

Passing my house a second time reassured me that everything was okay, so I began the drive to the hospital. The closer I got to the diner, the more my stomach hurt, and I worried that I might be giving myself ulcers. Maybe this wasn't such a good idea. Finally arriving, I pulled into the parking lot and tried to get my nerves under control, checking my purse to make sure my stun flashlight was handy.

With no reason left to stall, I got out and hurried inside the diner. A quick glance let me know Pete wasn't there yet, and my shoulders sagged in relief. It was late afternoon, so the place was nearly empty, and I had my choice of spots. Naturally, I chose the booth in the far corner where I could watch for Pete.

The waitress brought a menu and some water. I sipped it while I waited, and tried not to fidget too much. After ten minutes, I called home. Josh answered and said they were fine, so I tried not to worry. The waitress came back and, since I hadn't eaten lunch, I ordered some wontons and a diet soda. I checked my watch and calculated that it had been about thirty minutes since my chat with Pete, so there was still time for him to make it.

I called home again, this time to Savannah's cell. She assured me they were fine and, from her voice, I could tell she thought I was going overboard with the phone calls. With no sign of Pete, I called his cell phone, but it went straight to voicemail, so I left a message that I was at the diner waiting for him.

Twenty long minutes later, I called Josh again.

"Mom...we're fine. You don't have to keep calling."

"Okay...good. Um...you'd tell me if that cop was there, right? You'd say something like 'pick up a pizza'...if he was there, right?"

"Mom...he's not here. It's just me, Chloe and Savannah. You don't have to pick up a pizza...but...I wouldn't complain if you wanted to anyway."

I sighed. "So he's not there?"

"Yes," he said.

"Yes he's there?" I squeaked.

"No! Yes he's not here...that was your question...you asked if he was not here."

"Okay, okay...I get it...Sorry...I'm just feeling a little paranoid. I'll be home soon."

"Okay. Don't forget the pizza!" he chuckled.

Shaking my head, I disconnected and tried Pete again, but with no answer from his cell, it was time to call Dimples and let him know what was going on.

"Hey Shelby, what's up?" he asked. Before I could answer, I heard someone in the background say my name. "Uh...Billie says hello. I'm at the hospital visiting for a minute."

"Oh...that's great. I'm not far. Is it okay if I swing by?"

"Sure," he said.

I paid for my food and drove across the street to the hospital, wondering why Pete hadn't shown up. Had he changed his mind, or had something happened to him? From the sound of his voice, I thought for sure he was anxious to talk to me, so it made no sense that he wouldn't show up.

Unless he was luring me away like he did Holly, but every time I'd called home, Josh had assured me they were fine, and I knew from our last conversation that he was telling the truth. Something must have happened to change his mind. Maybe Dimples would know what it was.

I knocked on Billie's door, and then pushed it open. Billie smiled a greeting. Her cheeks were flushed with color, and she looked even better than she had this morning. But the fact that Dimples stood next to her, holding her hand, made it easy to understand why.

"Hey Shelby," Billie drawled. "Twice in one day. I'm honored." She knew I was there to talk to Dimples and had decided to tease me about it.

"This is perfect timing since I have something to tell you both." That caught her by surprise. "I had a little chat with your intern. He's the one who took the thumb-drive from your desk...and you'll never guess who he gave it to."

"Who?" she asked.

"Anthony Kerby, an assistant state's attorney under Grayson Sharp."

"Son of a gun!" she exclaimed. "But...wait. I don't remember telling you about the intern."

"Yes, you did," I said, realizing my mistake. "You were pretty out of it though, so I'm not surprised you don't remember."

"Yeah, that must be it. So what happened?"

I quickly described my interview with the intern and ended by giving Dimples the copy of the thumb-drive I'd made.

"Don't worry," I assured Billie. "I still have your copy."

"I certainly hope so," she said, then glanced at Dimples. "So what are you going to do now?"

"My job." His gaze caught mine. "Do you think Anthony is behind the attack on Billie?"

"Yes, but I don't know how we can prove it. I'm not sure his intern knows anything more, but I might be able to find out if I get a chance to talk to him."

"Hmm...yes, I can see how that might work," Dimples said, with a gleam in his eyes since he knew my secret. "Or we can just talk to Anthony."

I nodded. "Why don't you take a look at the thumb-drive and let me know what you want to do."

"Sure."

"There's something else," I said, taking a deep breath. "It's about Chloe. Pete showed up at Holly's house a couple of hours ago. Did you or Bates tell him where she was?"

"What? Hell no. At least I didn't. What happened?"

I explained how she got away and was now at my house. "This time Chloe positively identified the cop as Pete. I talked to Holly, and she's okay with leaving Chloe at my house, but I made her promise not to tell Scott or Kira until I'd talked to you."

Dimples took out his phone to call Bates, but I stopped him. "Wait. There's more. I called Pete to see if he'd talk to me and we set up a meeting at the diner just across the street. That's where I was when I called you."

"What did he say?"

"That's just it. He never showed."

Dimples swore under his breath, thinking it was nuts for me to try and meet with Pete anyway, so it was just as well he hadn't shown up. He pushed in the numbers for Bates and put him on speaker phone so I could tell him what had happened. Of course, I left out the part where I was supposed to meet Pete.

Bates swore a few times, then said he hadn't been able to contact Pete like the chief had wanted him to. "I can't see how Pete found out where Chloe was. Are you sure Shelby didn't let it slip somehow?"

I gasped, and my mouth dropped open in outrage.

"Yes. I'm sure," Dimples answered, shushing me before I could say anything. "We need to let Chloe's parents know. Since I'm not too far from their house, why don't I talk to them? Chloe is at Shelby's house right now, so she should be fine, but her parents need to decide what to do next."

"Fine," Bates said. "Talk to them and let me know what they want to do. I'll let the chief know what's happened."

Dimples disconnected and shook his head. "I'm sorry for what Bates said, Shelby. He was way out of line. You'd think he'd be over it by now."

"Ha...I doubt that will ever happen."

"Probably not," he conceded. "But I'm glad you didn't tell him off." He turned to Billie to say goodbye, which I knew would involve some tender words and a kiss or two if I wasn't around.

"Okay...well, I'm going home. Let me know what the plan is, and be sure to tell Chloe's parents that she's welcome to stay at my house for as long as she needs to. Bye Billie."

Aside from Bates being such a big jerk, my mood was a little lighter as I left. It was good to share that information and leave things in Dimples' capable hands. I only wished I knew where Pete was. Why had he changed his mind? Had he made new plans? Whatever it was, I had a feeling something bad was about to happen, and it tied my stomach in knots.

Chapter 9

Since it was on the way home and close to five-thirty, I got a couple of pizzas. Mostly for Josh, but also for me, since I didn't have anything planned for dinner, and I was too worn out to cook. The smell permeated my car, and my stomach growled in anticipation. I pulled into the garage and brought them into the kitchen.

Expecting to hear the sounds of excited chatter from Chloe and my kids, I froze to hear nothing but dead silence. Oh no! Had something happened to them? Did Pete come and take them all? A giggle erupted from the basement, followed by shouts of laughter, and I let out a huge sigh.

"I'm back," I shouted. "And I brought pizza."

With footsteps pounding up the stairs like a herd of elephants, they burst into the kitchen, and I opened the boxes with enthusiasm and got out paper plates and napkins. It wasn't quite dinner time, but we were all hungry, and I hoped Chris wouldn't mind too much if we ate without him. Besides, he'd probably be late...again.

"Hey...why don't we take this downstairs and watch an episode of *Castle*?" I asked. They didn't seem so eager about that so I added, "Or maybe *The Flash*?"

"Yeah," Chloe said. "I love that show."

We grabbed the pizzas and plates and headed downstairs. In a few short minutes, we were watching the latest episode and eating to our hearts' content. Or at least Josh was shoveling it in, and I hoped Chloe didn't get too grossed out. Just in case, I listened in and caught that she thought I was the coolest mom ever.

I smiled, even as a wisp of guilt fluttered inside me. I should be a better example but, for now, it was good to unwind and forget about all my troubles.

The show was just reaching its exciting conclusion when my cell phone rang. "Pause!" I yelled. Amid grumblings, Josh pushed the pause button and I quickly answered my phone.

"Hey Shelby, it's Harris. I talked to Kira and Scott, and they've decided to have Chloe stay with Scott for now. He should be coming over to get her in about half an hour. Just wanted to let you know."

"Okay...thanks. Did you find out any more about Pete?"

"No. He's still not answering his cell, but Scott's sure he wants Chloe with him, and I think it's a good idea."

"Yeah, you're probably right. Will you let me know if you hear anything from Pete?"

"Of course," Dimples agreed. "As long as you do the same."

"You bet," I said, and we disconnected.

Now I had to break the news to Chloe. I hoped she was okay with it. "Um...Chloe, your dad's coming to get you soon. He wants you to stay with him for now."

"Okay," she answered. She was relieved to go home to his house, but also slightly disappointed she couldn't stay here with Josh. "Do we have time to finish the show?"

"You bet."

I picked up that Josh was a little disappointed she was leaving too, so I was grateful for the distraction.

After the show, the kids helped clean up the pizza and, right after that, Scott came by. He hugged Chloe tight and thanked me for my help. "Your police friend, Harris, told me you'd tried to meet with the cop, but he never showed. I just wanted you to know how much I appreciate what you've done."

"Well, I wish I could tell you more. It's such a worry with him still out there, but I'll be sure and let you know if I hear anything. At least the police are looking for him now, so that's good."

"That's true, and they're keeping a patrol car outside my house for the night," he said, determined to keep Chloe safe. "I'm taking some time off work for the next few days, so I'll be working directly with the police until they find out what's going on."

"Oh...that's great news, and I'm sure they will. Please call me if you need anything. And Chloe," I said to her. "You're welcome to come over anytime."

"Thanks, Shelby...thanks for everything." She gave me a quick hug, thinking she wanted to be just like me when she grew up. That melted my heart a little, and I squeezed her back. She said her goodbyes to Josh and Savannah, telling Josh she could use his help with all the homework she'd missed. He readily agreed, and I knew we'd be seeing more of her.

Things quieted down after they left and, at a little after seven, Chris got home. I gave him a big hug and felt the stress of the last few hours drain away. "I'm so glad you're home. It's been a stressful day."

"Yeah...I can tell." He was thinking I usually only bought pizza when something bad had happened, and worry tightened the muscles around his eyes. "So what's going on?"

"Oh...everything's fine now. Here..." I pulled out a chair at the kitchen table. "Sit down and have some pizza, and I'll tell you all about it." I waited until his mouth was full before I started, mostly because I didn't want him to interrupt me for details I might not want to share.

"I visited with Billie this morning about the thumb-drive," I began, purposely leaving the breakfast part for later. "The news broke that Chloe had been found, so I drove over to the precinct." I explained the press conference and my conversation with Pete. Then the visit with Chloe's parents and how the chief told me they didn't need me anymore. "That was mostly because of Bates," I added. "But it still hurt my feelings."

Next, I told him of my visit to the newspaper and my interview with the intern. "So at least now we have a lead on who was behind Billie's break-in."

"Wow...that's huge," Chris said. "You've been busy. No wonder you got the pizza."

"Yeah...well, there's more." I told him how Chloe showed up at our house and all of the events that happened after that, ending with Scott coming to get Chloe.

Chris shook his head, barely taking it all in. He didn't like that I'd tried to meet with Pete, mostly because I could have gotten hurt. That was a huge risk. What was I thinking?

"I can't imagine how he found out where Chloe was staying," I said, hoping to take his mind off the risky part. "Do you have any ideas?"

"Well...he might have overheard someone talking about it. Or maybe even you and Bates? Maybe he was listening outside the door or something when you were discussing it.

At least now you know it's him. I wonder what he wanted to talk to you about."

"I know," I agreed. "I can't figure out what he would have told me. He was thinking something that seemed strange after the press conference."

"What was that?" he asked.

"He thought he was facing some hard choices and needed to do something about the mess."

"Hmm...maybe he's working for someone and wants out."

"That actually makes sense," I agreed, then sighed with discouragement. "I hope we figure it out soon. I hate to think of Chloe being afraid for her life, but at least she's with her dad, and the police are looking for Pete."

Chris was thinking that if anything like that ever happened to Savannah, he'd do whatever it took to keep her safe. "Yeah, she's better off with him."

"Although I think Chloe was a little disappointed to leave." I lowered my voice. "But that's because she likes Josh."

"Yeah...I caught that," Chris agreed, then glanced at me with a frown. "Were you listening to them? I'm not sure that's such a good idea."

"Oh...no. I mean, maybe a little, but...not like you think. I only picked up bits and pieces, but I'm really careful not to intrude. At least I'm trying to be careful...but I did hear something from Savannah's thoughts...that she has a crush on Josh's friend."

"Which one?" Chris asked, his eyes narrowing. He didn't like the 'older boy' part of that revelation.

"Uh...Cole. But...don't worry, he doesn't look at her like that...so it's all good."

Chris sighed, thinking that maybe it was okay that I listened in. Then he wondered how other parents managed without the mind-reading skills I had.

"Hey...relax," I said. "Our kids are great, you don't need to be so concerned. We've got this."

"Yeah...you're right," he agreed, taking me in his arms. "And we've got each other to rely on."

My phone bleeped at me with a text message. "I wonder who that could be?" I checked it and gasped. "Oh my gosh! I totally forgot!"

"What?" Chris asked.

"I'm supposed to go to Uncle Joey's club tonight, and meet with him and Blake Beauchaine. They'll be here in fifteen minutes! I've got to get ready."

Chris' brows drew together in confusion. "When did you schedule this?"

"Uh...he asked me just this morning. With everything else going on, I totally spaced it."

Chris followed me into our bedroom, thinking there was a lot more to my story than that. I had obviously met with Manetto and hadn't told him a thing about it.

He was right since I'd left out my appointment with Uncle Joey yesterday, and the breakfast-with-Ramos part of my day today.

"So who's Blake Beauchaine?"

"He's the one who left the note at Uncle Joey's wake...in Seattle?" At Chris' nod, I continued. "He's here in town for some reason, which is why I'm going tonight. To find out...you know...what he's doing here."

"Is he dangerous?"

"I'm not sure," I said, quickly throwing on my sexy red dress. "But I'm sure I'll be fine..." I was about to say that Ramos would be there, but I didn't since Chris had already figured that out. He didn't like Ramos much, although he couldn't say a whole lot against the man since he'd saved my life a few times.

"I'm sorry," I said, turning toward him. "I should have told you, and I'm sure I would have if I hadn't been so distracted with Chloe, and then the whole thing with Billie...it's been a rough day. Please don't be mad." I turned around. "Could you zip me up?"

He sighed, thinking I drove him crazy, and he was a saint to put up with me. Especially right now, when I was dressed like this and going to a club...without him. Again. And Ramos would be there. I'd have to do something really nice for him to make up for it...

"I will, I promise." I hurried into the bathroom and freshened up my make-up. Then I applied an ample amount of my reddest lipstick and spritzed on some perfume. Tousling my hair, I ran back to my closet and grabbed my black stilettos. "I shouldn't be too late. How about I call you as soon as I'm done helping Uncle Joey. If he's not ready to leave, maybe you could pick me up?"

Chris shook his head, clearly unhappy. He knew I was trying to calm him, and he wasn't sure he wanted to be calmed.

"I love you," I said. "I'll tell you all about it when I get home." My phone chirped again. They were here. "Okay...they're here. Wish me luck?"

Chris struggled to get over the fact that I hadn't told him about this before now. I was afraid I'd have to leave him like this. Then he closed his eyes and pulled me into his arms. "Just...be careful Shelby, no crazy risks...and come back to me."

"Of course." I kissed him passionately, then pulled away, grimacing to see his lips covered in red lipstick. "Um..." I pointed to his mouth. "You might want to fix that before the kids think you've gone off the deep end."

He shook his head and wiped at his lips, smiling in spite of himself.

I hurried out the door to Uncle Joey's car, where Ramos waited. As he opened the door, he glanced at my lips and his brows scrunched together. "You might want to fix that."

Alarmed, I quickly sat down inside the car and pulled open my purse, taking out the mirror. "Yikes!" After that kiss I looked a little bit like the joker on steroids.

Uncle Joey chuckled. "How are you, Shelby?"

"I'm good," I said, grabbing a tissue and dabbing at my mouth. "It's been a crazy day...but so far I've survived." I got my lips mostly repaired and added some lip gloss that helped tone them down. "That's better." I glanced at Uncle Joey and realized I'd just said that out loud. "So how are you doing?"

"Doing well," he said, his lips turned up in a broad smile. "I'm looking forward to our little meeting." He was thinking that knowing what Blake was doing here would certainly help him sleep tonight. "Thanks for coming...I hope it wasn't an inconvenience."

"Oh...no...I just forgot." At Uncle Joey's raised eyebrows, I hurried to explain. "I've been really busy. Anyway, I'm glad Ramos texted to remind me."

Uncle Joey nodded in agreement. "So tell me what you've been doing."

I didn't think it could hurt, so I told him about Chloe and the bad cop and how she had come to my house to get away from him. "Before that, I was looking at a thumb-drive from the attorney general's office. He's as crooked as they come. You wouldn't believe who's on his list."

"Really?" Uncle Joey said, his tone low and sly.

Oops. Maybe I shouldn't have said that part. "Not that I studied the list all that well. But...at least your name wasn't on there." Oh crap. I swallowed and licked my lips, tasting coconut lip gloss.

"Hmm...that's nice." He was wondering what I would have done if it was.

"Um...I'm really glad it wasn't," I answered. "Anyway...it looks like the authorities will probably investigate the attorney general's office now. With the evidence on the thumb-drive, they should have a pretty good case."

"I see," he said. "Good to know."

I nodded, deciding to change the subject before it got any worse. "So...you and Blake are old friends. Didn't you say you were roommates in college?"

"No. I never said that," he responded.

"Huh! Right...good one." This was not going well, and I hoped he'd let it go. I closed my eyes as my brain automatically began singing, *let it go, let it go, can't hold it back anymore.*

Luckily, we pulled up in front of the club and Ramos jumped out to open the door. He had a lopsided grin on his face and was thinking that I just didn't know when to shut up. His thoughts would have upset me if they weren't so true.

He took my hand to help me out and noticed my stricken expression. As I came beside him, he leaned against my ear and whispered. "Cheer up...it's not so bad." He thought it was highly entertaining, and he loved it.

Well...at least someone thought it was funny, but I wasn't so sure Uncle Joey would agree.

Uncle Joey came to my side and ushered me into the club while Ramos drove the car around back. The large man at the door lowered his head and greeted us. "Mr. Manetto. Good to see you. I have your private room ready. Your guest has already arrived."

"Thank you," he answered, not surprised in the least that Blake was already there.

I remembered how to get to Uncle Joey's private room from the last time I'd been there, so I led the way. It brought back memories of how much fun I'd had winning all that money from Uncle Joey and his poker friends. "Do you still play poker with the guys?" I asked him.

He smiled. "Yes. In fact, the boys have asked about you and how well you did in Vegas."

"Really? What did you tell them?"

"The truth. That you haven't gone yet. We'll have to remedy that sometime...if you'd like," he added. "We could take my jet. It'd be fun and make us some good money."

"Well...I do owe Chris a favor. Could he come?"

"Certainly." He was thinking Ramos and Chris both looking out for me on a trip to Vegas would be extremely amusing.

"Um...maybe I'd better think about that."

Uncle Joey chuckled, and we turned the corner to the back room. Inside, a waitress set a drink in front of Blake who glanced at us with a quick nod. She waited for us to join him and asked for our drink orders. After she left, Uncle Joey began. "It's nice to see you Blake. It's been a long time."

"Yes, it has," Blake answered. "I didn't think we'd ever cross paths again, but things change. I take it you're still in the business?" There was a definite undertone of disapproval in his voice.

"Of course," Uncle Joey answered. "You knew that wasn't going to change."

Blake shrugged. "But things do change...all the time."

"And some don't," Uncle Joey countered. "You still working for the government?"

Blake tilted his head. "Touché." His thoughts turned to the past, and guilt struck again for what he'd done to Joe. After all this time, he realized they weren't so different after all. In fact, he'd probably been the reason for more people's deaths than Manetto ever was. Sure, he'd taken the high ground, but in the end he was a bigger bully than any crime lord. The fact that he did it on the side of the law was supposed to make it okay, but now he wasn't so sure.

"I'm sure you're wondering why I'm here in your life again," Blake began, then glanced at me. "And I'm wondering why you keep Shelby so close." He smiled apologetically, hoping Joe would explain his reasons for my proximity.

"I thought you wanted her here," Uncle Joey countered. "That's what Ramos told me."

"That's not what I meant," he said, pausing to give Uncle Joey a chance to respond. When he didn't, Blake sighed dramatically. "Fine. Maybe someday you'll tell me."

Uncle Joey chuckled. "Don't count on it."

Blake nodded and took another sip of his drink. He'd checked up on me after breakfast, when he'd heard that I helped the police, and found my website. He'd also found out that the FBI had a file on me. It was small, but I'd helped them with a gang problem a while back. In big letters it said I was a psychic, or more accurately, that I had premonitions.

That came up in the police files he'd studied as well. So he concluded that there must be something to it, or Manetto wouldn't value my services...and, more importantly, keep me so close. It also made perfect sense that Joe wouldn't want him to know any of that.

His thoughts swirled with speculation about me, going from disbelief to hope that I was the real deal. If so...he could use someone like me and hoped there was a way he could work out a deal for my services. He thought there was a pretty good chance it could happen, given his investigation.

I swallowed and felt the blood drain from my head, making me a little dizzy. This guy had connections...and knew way too much about me. I took a sip of my drink with a wish that I'd never come. This was awful. Maybe he really was a spy.

Breathing a little too fast, I took a deep cleansing breath and let it out slowly to get under control. Now, more than ever in my life, I needed to keep my wits about me and not slip up. There was too much at stake if he ever found out my secret.

"I might as well get right to the point," Blake said, thinking that with his silence and unruffled stare, Joe was a master at getting people to talk. "I heard some things about your trip to Mexico. From what I've gathered through the intelligence agency, I think I know why you were there and, as far as I'm concerned, you did nothing wrong. In fact, you defeated el puño de hierro, The Iron Fist. Not something many could do. Even Inspector Salazar was under his thumb...and...you almost got away with it."

Oh crap! Did he say intelligence agency...meaning CIA? I'd had a visit from them while Uncle Joey was in Mexico. Did that mean they had a file on me too?

"What do you mean?" Uncle Joey asked.

"His father...he's an old man now, but he vowed revenge on the man who killed his son and destroyed his family business. With his last penny, he sent an assassin after you. I was on my way to warn you when you "died" on that boat. I thought I was too late. In retrospect, that little stunt might have saved your life. I followed the assassin's trail to Seattle, but lost him after your 'death.'"

Uncle Joey raised his brows. He wasn't sure he believed any of it. "So what brings you here now?"

"I got word that he's back in the country." Blake read the skepticism in Uncle Joey's eyes and smiled. "I didn't think you'd take my word for it, so I brought some proof." He reached into his inside jacket pocket, and Ramos was on him in an instant. He huffed out a breath and raised his hands. "Go ahead and take it out yourself."

Ramos reached into Blake's pocket and pulled out a folded manila envelope, which he placed on the table, and stepped back. Blake opened it and drew out a few grainy photos of someone with black scraggly hair and a big mustache. With all that hair, it was hard to tell what he looked like. "That's him arriving at the airport. See the date and time stamp?"

Uncle Joey frowned. "How can you tell it's him?"

"Without the hair and mustache...the computer images fit the descriptions we have of him." No one had ever taken a photograph of him without a disguise, but he'd had his computer experts work on this image for a possible match to other photos they had of him, and it had come back positive.

"That's the same day you sent me that little package."

"Yes," Blake said. "I knew that if I left that package for you, you'd find me, thereby allowing me to keep our association under wraps. As I'm sure you know, there are some people who wouldn't approve of my reaching out to you."

He was thinking that he was also here for another reason entirely, but that was not something we needed to know. "I'm being upfront about this because of our past...and that unfortunate incident."

Uncle Joey considered his sincerity. What Blake had done to him was bad, but he'd gotten his revenge and thought they were even. When I'd given him Blake's note, he'd had a foolish hope that they could let bygones be bygones. But now he wasn't so sure. Why did Blake bring it up now? Was there some other reason he was here, and this was just a front?

"So where's this assassin?" Uncle Joey asked.

"I'm not sure," Blake shrugged. "I know he's here and I might be able to tell you more if you agree to help me with something."

Uncle Joey smiled. "Now that's more like the Blake I know. What do you want?"

Blake's lips twisted into a smile as well. He knew Joe would see through this and, for some reason, it brought him immense satisfaction. He'd always admired Joe...hell, he still did. "Do you still have connections with PLM Investments?"

Uncle Joey's smile fled, and his brows furrowed. "No. In fact, I dissolved that company a few years ago."

"Hmm...well...it's recently come up in something I've been looking into." Blake thought, from Joe's response, that he was telling the truth. Joe had no idea what was happening.

"You're serious," Uncle Joey said. "What's going on?"

"If you don't know...my guess is someone's using your old company as a front, either to frame you, or as a safeguard for themselves if they ever get caught. Naturally, you'd be the first to get the blame for any illegal activity."

"I don't know anything about it. But I will certainly look into it. Is that what you wanted?"

"Yes," Blake said.

"And what about this assassin? Is he real?"

"Oh yes, he's very real, and he's here. They call him the 'chameleon' because he's good with disguises and blends in so well with his surroundings. We've been trying to track him down for years, but he's always one step ahead of us. I hoped we could help each other and get rid of him once and for all."

"How did you plan on doing that?" Uncle Joey asked. Blake didn't answer right away, and Uncle Joey nodded. "I see...you want to use me as bait."

Blake shrugged. "To be honest, I don't know of any better way. He's coming for you whether you like it or not but, this way, you'll be prepared."

"And how would you help me?"

"I can assign a couple of my men to keep tabs on your movements. Once they spot him, they can relay that information directly to you."

"You mean they can follow me wherever I go? No. I don't think so." Uncle Joey was thinking there was no way he'd ever give an agent permission to follow him. That was like asking to be arrested.

"Just think about it," Blake said. "And...as a show of good faith, we think he may have come to your building today as a delivery person with a package. Did you get a package today?"

"I...don't know." He turned to Ramos. "Did we?"

Ramos remembered how excited Jackie was over a delivery that came late this afternoon. "Yeah...we got a delivery...after you left for your meeting. It was a floral arrangement."

"From whom?" Uncle Joey asked.

"Uh...I think Jackie said it was from you. There might have been a card...but I don't know."

Uncle Joey whipped out his cell phone and called Jackie. "Hi dear...did you get the flowers?" He listened to her response, then closed his eyes. "Good...I'll be home in a little bit. Could you do me a favor and lock the doors and turn on the security system? I want to make sure it's working when I get home. Good. I'll see you soon."

Uncle Joey slipped his cell phone into his pocket and glanced at Blake. "You think he might have killed me if I'd been there?"

Blake lifted a brow. "Maybe, but I doubt it. He might have put some kind of bug on the vase, so he'll know when you're in the office and what your schedule is like. It would give him a better opportunity to kill you while no one's looking."

Blake could tell that Uncle Joey still didn't want his help. "Check the vase...if there's a bug on it, then you'll know I'm telling the truth, and you'll let me help you."

"All right, I'll check it out, along with the investment company," Uncle Joey agreed.

"Good. I just have one more request. If you do get a shot at the assassin, I would deem it a great favor if you could take him alive. I'd be happy to take him off your hands."

"Is that all?"

I thought that was a great question and listened closely to Blake's thoughts. He was thinking *not by a long shot,* but he smiled agreeably. "For now...yes, but I'm hoping that if our paths cross again in the future, we can become allies if conditions warrant it. You never know when you might need someone like me on your side." He was thinking, *maybe even sooner than you think.*

Uncle Joey raised a brow but knew he couldn't turn down an offer like that. There were times in the past when he could have used Blake and his connections. Of course he'd be a fool to turn this opportunity down. But he knew he could never trust him again.

Blake took a card out of his pocket, wrote something on the back, and handed it to Uncle Joey. "Here's a phone number you can use to reach me...it's untraceable."

He turned to Ramos. "Be sure and take extra precautions for Joe's safety tonight. I wouldn't want anything to spoil our agreement."

Blake stood and glanced at me, holding out his hand for me to take. Naturally, I placed mine in his, and he raised it to his lips for a quick kiss. "My dear, it has been a pleasure. I hope you'll warn Joe if you see anything threatening him in the near future."

Wow. I couldn't help being impressed, and a genuine smile came to my lips. He was a master at taking control of a situation, and he had the southern charm to show it. "Thanks Blake, but the only thing I see threatening him right now is you."

That startled a laugh out of him, and he let go of my hand and inclined his head. He turned to Uncle Joey. "Joe...maybe when this is over, we can spend some time talking about the good old days. We had some fun times, didn't we? I'll never forget that stunt we pulled on Professor Blackwell and his T.A. Remember that?"

"Of course," Uncle Joey answered. "It was brilliant, and the best part was that we got away with it."

Blake smiled and nodded. "Goodbye old friend. Let's chat tomorrow." He walked out of the room, thinking that he didn't want Joe to die, and he sincerely hoped Joe wouldn't be hard-headed about taking his offer of help. Then he turned the corner and was gone.

Uncle Joey glanced at Ramos, who made sure we were alone, then turned to me. "Well? Is he telling the truth?"

"Yes, believe it or not, he is. He doesn't want you killed by this assassin. So that part is true. But there's also something he's hiding about that company. Unfortunately, I can't tell what it is...just that he needs your cooperation; and he's hoping by sharing this, it will enhance his odds of getting it."

"So the assassin is real?"

"Yes. Blake wants him captured in the worst way. The assassin's killed a lot of innocent people. So...I think you can trust him on that point."

"All right," he said. "Did you pick up anything else?"

"Well...the only thing that really stood out to me was when he was talking about you needing his help in the future. He was thinking it might be sooner than you think...but I have no idea what that's about."

Uncle Joey's eyes narrowed. "Hmm...Well, I guess we'll have to ride this one out and see what happens."

"There is one more thing," I said. "He's done some research on me. I guess the FBI and maybe even the CIA have files on me, and he's convinced that I must be a real psychic. He's hoping to bargain for my services in the future."

"Then that might be his ulterior motive."

"I don't think so. I wasn't on his radar until this morning when Ramos and I talked to him at breakfast. He heard me talking about how I helped the police, and I think that's what got his attention. So we know that besides you, there's another reason he's here in town that probably has to do with that company he mentioned, but since he didn't think about it, I don't know what it is."

Uncle Joey nodded, thinking that this was one hell of a challenge. Not only did he have the assassin to worry about, there was me and whatever else Blake was hiding. But instead of feeling intimidated, it made him feel young again. It surprised him that he actually looked forward to sparring with Blake. Just like the good old days.

"That's totally twisted," I said. "Blake has ulterior motives we know nothing about. You should stay away from him...uh...once you get the assassin."

Uncle Joey glanced at me, not liking that I'd read his mind. His forceful gaze trapped mine with such displeasure that my stomach twisted into knots. Yikes! "Or not," I added, "totally your call."

"Shelby," he said. "You shouldn't worry about me. I've always been the one to best him, not the other way around." Except for that one time when Blake so utterly betrayed him. But something like that would never happen again.

He glanced at me, thinking I'd probably just heard that, but he hoped I had the smarts to keep my mouth shut this time.

I raised my brows, but that was the only response he got from me. I was proud that I didn't roll my eyes or ask what the heck Blake had done. I kept it to myself for once...yay me. I hoped maybe someday I'd find out all the juicy details, just so I'd have some leverage against Blake for future references. But now was not the time to ask.

"All righty then," I said. "If that's all you need me for, I guess I should go home."

"Wait Shelby...I don't like to talk about it, but you should probably know what happened with Blake. You need to know what kind of man he is, especially if he ever asks you to help him."

"Okay," I said, a bead of apprehension running down my spine.

"As you know, we were roommates in college. I had my own money, but he was there on a scholarship. He wasn't a privileged, spoiled brat like most of my friends, and when they bullied him for it, I stood up to them. It wasn't long before we became fast friends, and I invited him home for the holidays and other special occasions.

"My father had expectations of me taking over the business at some point, but I wasn't sure that was what I wanted to do. I made the mistake of confiding this to Blake, and he pushed me to stand up to my father and tell him what I really wanted.

"The only problem with that was I didn't know what I really wanted. I was good at the business, and I enjoyed it. I was just going through a rebellious stage. Anyway, my confession to Blake got him thinking of how to bring my father down. I guess he didn't want me to follow in his footsteps.

"In the end, he used our friendship to spy on me and my family. My father's number-one guy went down for something Blake told the cops, and he died in prison."

Uncle Joey sat back in his chair and inhaled deeply. "Right before it happened, Blake warned me, or it would have been my father in prison. I think Blake must have felt guilty." He was also thinking that he'd held a gun to Blake's head when he'd found out, but let him go. To this day he didn't know if sparing his life had been the right thing. "So you can see why I wanted to know why he was here."

"So is he really an undercover agent or something?"

Uncle Joey nodded. "I think they recruited him in college because we were roommates. I've tried to keep track of him, but it's been a while." He was thinking that his contact in the FBI had retired a few years back, and the fact that Blake knew about his exploits in Mexico suggested he was still involved.

"Okay...uh...thanks for telling me." I wasn't sure how much to tell Uncle Joey, but I decided to go for it. "Blake was thinking that you and he were a lot alike. The things he'd done were on the side of the law, but he wasn't sure that made him any different. I don't know if that helps, but there it is..."

"Thanks for telling me."

"Although I'm totally with you on the not-trusting-him part, I don't think he means you any harm. But who's to say...it could change."

"No doubt," Uncle Joey agreed. "Well...let's get you home."

Now that Ramos knew there was a real threat to Uncle Joey's life, he wasn't taking any chances. His initial surprise that Uncle Joey had told me that story was eclipsed by his desire to protect him at all costs. He made us wait while he called in his men and coordinated our movements with precision timing.

A different man drove the car with another riding in the front seat beside him, and Ramos sat in the back with us, watchful and alert. I also picked up a few thoughts that this reminded him of the first time he'd met Uncle Joey, and how he'd saved his life from a killer.

Wow...that sounded interesting. I hoped someday I'd hear the whole story, but his thoughts had already moved on to getting Uncle Joey home safely, and then how to keep him safe through the night. It was nearly eleven p.m. when we pulled into my driveway, and Uncle Joey thanked me for my help.

"I'll be in touch," he said.

"Okay...be careful." The man in the front passenger seat opened my door and walked me to the house. At the door, I thanked him and hurried inside.

I locked and bolted the door, flipping off the lights Chris had left on, and headed to my bedroom. Everyone was in bed, including Chris. He'd left my bedside lamp on, and I could tell he'd tried to stay awake but had lost the battle. I changed and washed my face, then climbed into bed and turned out the light. Chris stirred and turned toward me.

"Glad you're home," he mumbled. "How did it go?"

"Good. I'll tell you all about it tomorrow."

"No way...you're telling me tonight. Even if I am half asleep, I want to hear it." He was thinking that he didn't want me to think I could 'forget' to tell him things and get away with it. "So start talking."

He didn't interrupt while I gave him the basics, but was sound asleep before I finished, so I quit mid-sentence.

"You're not done are you?" he asked, surprising me.

"Oh...I thought you were asleep."

"Not a chance...well maybe a little. Come here." He pulled me into his arms. "I'm glad you're home."

I rested my head on his shoulder and let out a deep sigh. Feeling safe in his strong arms, the weariness of the day overcame me, and I promptly fell asleep.

Chapter 10

The ringtone on my cell phone woke me from a deep sleep, and I felt for it on my nightstand. I found it by the fifth ring and, with my eyes half-shut, managed to say a raspy hello.

"Shelby? This is Harris. Did I wake you?"

"Um...yeah. What time is it?"

"Oh...uh...it's about six-fifteen. I'm sorry I woke you, but we found Pete, and I thought you should know."

"Oh...that's good. I'd like to talk to him. Should I come down to the station?"

"Well...that's just it. You can't talk to him. He's dead."

"What?" That news jolted me awake, and I sat up. "Did you just say he's dead?"

"Yes."

I pushed the hair out of my face and blinked the sleep from my eyes. "How? When?"

"He was shot in the chest, close range. From what we can tell, the Medical Examiner says it happened between midnight and three a.m."

"Do you have any suspects?"

"Not right now, but there's more. Can you come down to the crime scene? I want you to take a look at something."

"Really? Are you sure I can get past the crime scene tape?" I did not want to see another dead body, so I hoped this was a good reason to stay away.

"Sure. Just wear your ID badge. But don't take too long, we're almost done here."

"Okay," I said with a sigh. "I'll be there soon...wait...where is there?"

"I'll send you a text with the address." He disconnected and, almost immediately, the text came through.

"Who's dead?" Chris asked, pushing to sit up next to me.

"Pete."

"Whoa, that was unexpected."

"Yeah, and Dimples wants me to meet him at the crime scene, so I'd better get going."

Just then Chris' alarm went off. He groaned before reaching to switch it off. "Want to shower with me?"

I chuckled and got out of bed. "I wish...but I don't have time. I'll just throw something on and go. Can you make sure the kids get off to school?"

"All right," he agreed. "But be careful."

A few minutes later, I put the address into the GPS in my car and started driving. As I got closer to the scene, something kept niggling at me, but I didn't know what it was. Then it hit me. I'd seen this address before, but I had no idea where.

As I followed the directions, worry tightened my stomach. Instead of a house like I was expecting, the road took me back under the freeway into a bad part of town. It wasn't far from the homeless shelter, and garbage and shopping carts littered the street. Mounds of clothing were heaped up in doorways and, with dawning horror, I realized they were people either asleep or trying to stay warm.

Further down the road, I caught sight of red and blue flashing lights and sighed with relief. I'd never been to this part of town, although it did remind me of the house where Chloe was taken. What was Pete doing down here? Had he met with someone from the narcotics unit? It had to have something to do with Chloe, but what?

I parked close to the police cars and hurried over to the group of cops near the huge round pillars beneath the freeway. Two police officers talked near the crime scene tape, but quit when I got close. I held up my ID card, and one of them waved me through.

About thirty feet away, Dimples stood with several other officers surrounding the body and I hesitated. As far as I was concerned, I was as close to the dead body as I wanted to get. I waited for Dimples to notice me, but he was too involved to look up. Still, I couldn't seem to get my legs to move any closer.

"What's the matter Nichols? Afraid of a little blood?"

I sucked in my breath to hear Bates' voice. He'd come up from behind and now stood at my side. I glanced at him and decided to be honest. "Yes I am. It's hard for me to see anyone like that. Especially someone I know."

He was thinking that it was hard for everyone, but you just had to get over it, otherwise you couldn't do your job...and... what the hell was I doing there anyway? I shouldn't be looking at dead bodies. I wasn't one of them. I shouldn't be here...seeing this.

"Dimp...uh...Harris asked me to come," I explained. Oops...I hoped saying that out loud didn't seem suspicious.

Thankfully, Bates didn't think anything of it, although he couldn't understand why Harris would do that. "Harris!" he yelled, taking pity on me, and motioning Dimples over. "Shelby's here."

While I marveled that Bates had called me Shelby instead of Nichols, Dimples hurried to my side. "Sorry! I didn't see you. Thanks for coming."

"Sure. What did you want me to see?"

"The body," he said. "I need you to take a look and tell me what you think."

Damn! I was going to have to go over there after all. Dimples didn't wait for me, so after taking a deep breath for courage, I followed him over. Bates trailed behind, hoping I wasn't going to puke, or worse, faint, and wondered what Dimples was up to.

I kept my gaze down until Dimples stopped in front of me. "Do you see it?" he asked.

I finally raised my gaze to the body, and my breath caught. "Oh my gosh! He's sitting there just like Tom...the cold case you gave me."

"Exactly," Dimples said, nodding with grim satisfaction.

"But...so does this mean he was killed by the same person?"

"I believe so, yes. They're too much alike to be a coincidence." He was thinking that whoever did this got away with it once, and figured he could do it again.

"I see what you mean," I said.

"Uh...yeah." Dimples didn't know if I was answering his thoughts or what he'd said, but figured it didn't matter...as long as it made sense.

I glanced at him and smiled. He smiled back thinking this was totally cool.

"I obviously missed something," Bates said. "Tell me about the cold case."

"There's not much to tell," Dimples began. "But a man helping at the food kitchen ended up dead right here about a year ago. The remarkable thing is that he was positioned exactly like Pete...against this same pillar. It makes me think that if we can find a link between that man and Pete, we'll find our killer."

Bates shrugged, thinking it might be better to focus on Pete and let the chips fall where they may. "I get that," he said. "But let's focus on what we know about Pete for now."

As they discussed his death and what could have happened, I glanced at Pete's body. Thankfully, someone had closed his eyes, but seeing him like that still got to me. I'd just talked to him yesterday and now he was gone. I turned away, glancing at the view of bare concrete slabs and piles of garbage. Sadness flowed over me to think that this was the last thing both he and Tom had seen before they died.

A soft breeze blew into my face, surprising me with its warmth on this chilly November day. I caught the faint scent of Irish Spring and fresh cut grass. What in the world? Puzzled, I looked for a house or laundromat, anything that would explain the smell, but there was nothing like that anywhere.

It came again, and this time I closed my eyes and deeply inhaled. Somewhere in the recesses of my mind, recognition burst to the surface and my pulse raced. Was it real? I inhaled again and caught the elusive scent I hadn't smelled since high school and the last time I'd seen Tom.

My eyes flew open and I swallowed. This was just like that other case. It had to be him. I licked my lips, trying not to panic and, in my mind, asked, *Tom, is that you? Can you hear me? Help me figure out what happened.*

The breeze tugged a few strands of my hair back toward the body, and my eyes widened. Oh boy...this was real. Taking tentative steps, I let the breeze direct me around the body to a few feet beyond the other side of the pillar. All at once, my hair fell and the breeze was gone, taking the mysterious scent with it.

Okay...that was freaky. I took a few deep breaths to get under control and glanced around. Some clue had to be here, right? I bent down and went over every inch of the ground, finding only a few rusty nails and bolts, along with plastic water bottles and bags.

I turned my attention to the pillar and examined it, but nothing stood out. I glanced up at the underside of the freeway, taking in the vast expanse of concrete, but couldn't see anything out of the ordinary. The loud chatter on a police radio cut through my concentration, and I glanced back to find the crime scene unit putting Pete's body into a body bag.

I could hear Dimples and the other officers still talking, but I knew they were ready to wrap it up, and I didn't have much time. Heaving a sigh, I stepped back to the spot where the breeze had stopped and faced forward, looking beyond my immediate vicinity.

A chain-link fence separated this side of the freeway from several buildings on the other side of the road. A large, square building sat directly across from where I stood. I stared at it, taking in the surrounding area, and hoped for something...anything, to make sense.

Maybe I needed to find out who owned that building? The only other thing I could see was a billboard. I could barely make out what it said, but it had a picture of a newer looking home with a for sale sign on it, so I struggled to make out the logo.

"Shelby?" Dimples asked, touching my shoulder.

I nearly jumped a foot. "Sheesh! You scared me to death!"

"Sorry." His brows drew together, and he was thinking I looked kind of pale and frazzled, like something had spooked me. "What's going on? Are you okay?"

"Yeah...I'm fine. I was just looking for clues."

"Back here?" His brows rose, and he wondered if the shock was getting to me.

"Uh...can you see that billboard over there?" I pointed at it, hoping to distract him.

"Sure."

"What's the name of the realtor company? I can't make it out."

"Uh...it's...Countrywide Homes."

"Oh, right. Thanks." I had no idea if that meant anything or not, so I pointed out the buildings across the way. "I think we should check out those buildings. I have a feeling that something over there will tie into the case."

Dimples' face went blank, then he barked out a laugh. "Shelby...you don't have to pretend with the premonitions thing. Nobody can hear us over here. Just tell me what you heard."

Oh crap! Now what? I laughed and he joined in with me, mostly to be polite. He stopped first and looked at me expectantly, sending me into another fit of laughter. I finally calmed down enough to talk. "Um...can I tell you later?"

That was not what Dimples expected, and he glanced around to see if someone was listening. Finding no one nearby, he decided I must know something he didn't, and he'd just better go with it. "Sure...I guess."

"Great, thanks. I think I'll go home and get cleaned up...since I didn't have time to get ready this morning. I can come into the precinct after that if you like. Maybe we can go over a few things then."

"Okay." He didn't know if the chief wanted me involved, but he figured he could run interference if he had to. "Bring the file I gave you on that other case too. Maybe we'll find someone, or something, that both victims have in common."

"I will for sure," I agreed. "See you soon."

I hurried to my car and gratefully sank into the seat. My stomach growled, and weakness washed over my entire body. What was going on? I'd just had another psychic experience...and it was totally freaking me out. I thought after the last one I was done, and now this? I didn't think I could take it.

Of course, if I hadn't picked up that scent, I never would have known it was coming from my old flame, right? I would have thought someone was just doing their laundry and the breeze was blowing the smell my way. In fact...maybe that's what really happened, and I was reading too much into it.

Besides, where was the clue? Did I even have one? Maybe the wind was just blowing my hair that way, and that explained it. If it weren't for that special scent, I might believe it. That scent was different from anything I'd ever smelled before or since...so it had to be him.

The only thing I could do now was check out those clues. If neither of them panned out, I'd just have to come back here and look again. Maybe I'd missed it?

I started up the car and decided that I might as well drive over to those buildings across the way and at least get an address. They might even have an owner's name on the outside. Wouldn't it be great if it was the name of the killer? Ha! Even I knew it couldn't be that easy.

Several minutes later, I pulled my car to the side of the road and glanced at the buildings. From this side I could see that the buildings housed several businesses. One was a plumbing supply store, another looked like a window business, and the third was a garage door place.

I found some paper in my purse and wrote down their names so I could check them out on the Internet. Maybe one of the owners knew Tom? But how would that link them to his murder? Or Pete's? Maybe one of the employees was the killer and would recognize his name when I asked about him.

I glanced at the clock. It was close to eight in the morning, but it didn't look like any of the businesses were open yet. I might as well go home and come back later with Tom's picture. Besides...I was starving and needed to take a shower.

Taking one last look at the building, I noticed an alleyway between the businesses. Looking straight down the alley, a well-used path led to the fence I'd seen on the other side of the freeway. Curious, I got out of my car and walked to the entrance.

Finding nothing but asphalt and grass, I continued between the buildings to the back and followed the path through the dirt to the fence. As I got closer, an advertisement across the bottom of the fence came into view. Because of the tall grass, it couldn't be seen from my crime scene vantage point. It looked like the wind had blown it against the fence some time ago, since the photo and words were faded.

As I made out the words, my breath caught, and a chill ran up my spine. The poster said, "A Vote for Grayson Sharp is a Vote for You," with an image of a confident, smiling Grayson Sharp in the background. Holy crap! Was this just a coincidence, or did it mean he had something to do with Tom's death? Was this the clue?

I continued to the fence and noticed the chain links had been cut apart just high enough for a person to crawl through, with the tall grass on the other side covering it up. It made a quick escape from the crime scene across the street. Maybe I should crawl under the fence to the pillar and look back this way. Maybe I'd see something I'd missed.

"Hey! You! What do you think you're doing?"

My heart thumped, and I jerked around. A man came toward me from the buildings with an angry frown. I debated crawling under the fence to the other side before I picked up that he was trying to scare me off his property.

He was tired of people passing through here, mostly because of the drug deals that went on under the freeway. Just last night, his building alarm had gone off, and he'd had to come down to re-set it and make sure the building hadn't been broken into. So what the hell was I doing there?

I waited for him to stop a few feet away and put on my nicest smile. "Hello. I'm Shelby Nichols and I'm with the police." Luckily, I still had on my badge, so I waved it in front of his face. "I'm sorry I didn't check with you before I came out here, but it didn't look like you were open yet."

"Hmph," he grunted.

"I'm investigating a murder that happened sometime last night. A police officer was killed just down there, under the freeway. I was checking out the surrounding buildings and wanted to see if anyone could have come this way. Did you know there's a gap in this fence?"

"Uh...no," he said, all the fight gone out of him. "Where?"

"Right there." I pointed it out. "Have you seen many people use this to come through your property?"

"I thought they just climbed the fence. I didn't know the wires were clipped. But...yeah, when I saw you, I came out here to see what you were doing. I'll have to get it fixed."

"That might help with your problem," I agreed. "So what time did your alarm go off during the night?"

His startled gaze flew to mine. "How did you know...?"

"Just answer the question, please," I said, channeling my best detective voice.

"I got the call at about one-thirty in the morning."

"When did you get here?" I asked.

"Fifteen minutes later. I checked the building and everything was secure, so I re-set the alarm and called the security company. Then I went home."

"Was there anything out of place? Why do you think your alarm went off?"

"I don't know, sometimes a door doesn't get shut right. Or the sensors get tripped. I've only had one real break-in, and that was about a year ago."

"A year? Do you remember the date?" Tom's murder was a year ago. It was a long shot, but maybe there was a connection.

"Uh...not off the top of my head," he said. "But I could look it up for you."

"That would be helpful. Thanks."

We walked back to the buildings, and I realized I didn't even know which shop was his. He strode to the back entrance of the plumbing supply store and pulled the door open, holding it for me to go ahead of him. He went into a side office and sat behind a desk, motioning me to sit on a chair.

"I should have it on my insurance claims file here." He opened his filing cabinet and pulled out a manila folder. "Yeah...here it is...November fourth."

From what I could remember, the date seemed about right, and my heart raced. "Did they catch the guy who broke in?"

"No. The police thought the thief was looking for drug money, but I don't keep cash here, so they were in and out pretty fast. They broke a few windows, but that was the only damage."

"Okay. Well, thanks. You've been a huge help."

"Sure."

"I might be back. And I hope you'll call if you remember anything else." I handed him one of my business cards and left.

I got home, unsure if I'd made progress or not. The fence looked like a way for the killer to escape, but I wasn't sure that helped much. The poster of Grayson Sharp could mean something, but I had no clue how drug-dealing cops and innocent bystanders had anything to do with an attorney general who took bribes.

While I cooked an egg for breakfast, I made a quick call to Holly. "Did you hear the news about the cop?"

"Yeah, Scott called me a few hours ago. What a crazy way for this to end. Why was he killed?"

"I think he might have wanted out of the whole business."

"Yeah, and maybe his partner killed him because Chloe could identify him. Rather than kill Chloe, who really didn't know much anyway, he must have decided to get rid of the cop she saw and not worry about the cop telling anyone who he was."

"Exactly," I agreed.

"So how do you find his partner now?"

"I don't know, but we're working on it. Do you think I should call Scott and tell him what I know?"

"Yes, that's a good idea. I'm not sure the police will fill him in on everything. Besides, he's your client, so it makes sense that you'd call him."

"Okay. Thanks, Holly. I'll call him right now." Scott answered right away and I told him what I knew. "With him gone, Chloe's probably safe now."

"Maybe," Scott agreed. "But I'm not sure I can let her out of the house yet. I mean, what if the dead cop told his partner, or a bunch of other people about her?"

"Yes, but even if he did, they have no reason to come after her. Pete was the only one she could identify, and he's gone. That's probably why he was killed."

"Yeah, I suppose that's true."

"So now Chloe can get back to school and not have to look over her shoulder or be scared." He didn't respond right away. "You still don't seem real happy about that."

"Oh...I'm relieved...it's just that it's been kind of nice to know where she is and who she's with all the time. I felt so helpless to find out she was with some older kid at a drug house. I mean...I had no idea, and look what happened to her. She almost got killed. How can I let her out of my sight now?"

"I totally understand," I agreed. "But you have to remember that what happened to her was very traumatic. She witnessed someone's death and could have died herself. That's going to take time to get over and she'll need you now more than ever."

"Yeah, that's true. Thanks, Shelby. How much do I owe you?"

"Oh...nothing...just consider it a favor for a friend. I was glad to help Chloe, so we're even."

"Huh," Scott replied. "I don't think so, but maybe Chloe and I can have your family over for dinner sometime. If you won't let me pay you, at least I can feed you."

"Now that sounds great. We'll look forward to it. Uh...one more thing," I paused. "Would you like me to call Kira and let her know?"

"No...that won't be necessary. I'll give her a call right after I tell Chloe the news."

"Okay...listen...tell Chloe she can call me if she needs to talk. She'll know what I mean, all right?" I wasn't sure how she'd feel about one more person getting killed because of this mess, but at least it was over for her.

"Sure," he agreed, thanking me again before we disconnected.

I showered and put on some make-up, then did my hair. Besides going to the precinct, I needed to figure out if there was anything else I needed to do. With so much going on, I couldn't keep it all straight in my head, so I got out a legal notepad and sat down at the desk in the office.

First, I wrote down Chloe's name then, under it, Pete's and Tom's with an arrow to drugs. The only clue I had was the buildings and the fence, and that was only because of that freaky incident at the crime scene. I could tell Dimples about my meeting with the plumbing guy, and we could talk to the other people who worked there, but it seemed like a waste of time to involve him. Maybe I should just go back with the pictures and question them on my own.

Next I wrote down Billie's name and, under it, Grayson Sharp and Anthony Kerby. If I could talk to Anthony Kerby, I might pick up something about Billie and whether he'd hired someone to ransack her place for the thumb-drive, or did it himself. At least I could make some progress there.

I couldn't see how these cases were connected, but I also couldn't explain the poster of Grayson Sharp on the fence, so I added a question mark and a link to Tom and Pete. Which also linked them to Chloe? Dang! This was nuts. They couldn't be related, especially if the only clue I had came from a dead man and was probably just a figment of my imagination.

I sighed and shook my head to clear it. There was one more thing on my mind that I was worried about, and that was Uncle Joey and the assassin. I figured I might as well add him to my list. I wrote down his name and put Blake Beauchaine and the assassin underneath. At least this was totally separate from Billie and Chloe. Plus, I didn't think I had to worry that Uncle Joey and Ramos would take care of the problem, although Blake worried me. What was his other reason for being here?

I hoped it had nothing to do with me, but I couldn't get over the fact that he had retrieved a file about me from the FBI. It was enough to make my stomach clench with dread. Now that he knew I had 'premonitions' and helped Uncle Joey, he might get it into his mind that I needed to help him. That would be a disaster. Maybe I'd better get a diet soda out of the fridge and try and forget that part. No use borrowing trouble, right?

As I poured my soda into a glass with crushed ice, my cell phone rang, and I was seriously tempted not to answer it. Writing down everything I had on my plate overwhelmed me, and I wasn't sure I could handle one more thing.

I sighed and checked the caller ID. It was Dimples, so I answered, hoping he had something good to tell me.

"Hi Shelby," he began. "Good news. The chief wants you back on the case. Can you come down to the precinct? Oh...and bring that other file with you?"

Hmm...not exactly what I wanted to hear. And I wasn't so sure I liked the chief anymore either, but what could I say? "All right, I'll come, but there's something else I'd like to do."

"What's that?"

"Talk to Anthony Kerby. Could we fit that in today?"

Dimples let out a breath. "Uh...yeah...sure. That will probably work."

"Okay...see you soon."

I got out my to-go mug and poured in another can of Diet Coke to take with me, knowing I needed all the fortification I could get. While I was at it, I grabbed a couple of cookies and stuffed them in my purse along with a granola bar. Now that I was fully prepared, I could leave.

With my ID badge around my neck, I entered the precinct, fully expecting Bates to harass me. He sat at his desk and quickly stood after spotting me. I braced for the onslaught, but he surprised me with a smile.

"Hey Nichols, glad you're back." He actually meant it, but I also picked up that he liked having me around since it gave him someone to blame when things didn't go right.

"Yeah...sure," I said. Some people never changed. Dimples waved me over to his desk, so I hurried in that direction, hoping Bates wouldn't follow.

"Glad you're here," Dimples said, ushering me into the seat beside his desk. Bates stayed where he was, and Dimples sighed with relief, thinking he wanted this to stay between the two of us.

"This is what we've got so far. Pete's phone is missing, along with his gun, ID, and wallet. The chief thinks he was involved with some kind of drug ring. It makes sense...he worked narcotics and got to know some of the major drug dealers. The worst of it is, he also had access to the drugs locked up in evidence. The chief thinks the books may have been doctored and Pete took some of them."

"If he was involved, then why was he killed?" I asked.

"Maybe he wanted out." Dimples shrugged.

"Yeah...and the fact that Chloe saw him changed everything. Maybe they wanted him to kill Chloe and he couldn't do it, so they killed him instead. But I hate to think of him as a bad cop."

"Yeah...tell me about it." Dimples was thinking that the whole thing could be connected to organized crime. Maybe Pete was working with Joe "The Knife" Manetto, and feeding him information. His concerned gaze caught mine. Did I still work for Manetto? Did I know what was going on? His breath caught, and his eyes clenched shut.

"You just heard all that, right?" he asked.

"Uh-huh," I nodded. "But don't worry, it's not that. I'm sure I would know." I was lying through my teeth, since I knew Uncle Joey had an inside cop and I knew exactly who it was, but I also knew Uncle Joey didn't have anything to do with Pete, so I tried not to feel too guilty about it.

"Uh...good, good," he said, but he was thinking, *does she still work for him?*

Just then, Chief Winder stuck his head out of his office. "Harris, I need you and Shelby in my office. Now."

I glanced at Dimples, and he shrugged. He didn't know what was going on, but he obediently stood and walked into the office with me following behind.

"Shut the door," the chief said.

I did as I was told and turned back to face Chief Winder. He was hoping he'd made the right decision in telling us what was going on. "I just got a call from the FBI. They're investigating our department and taking over the investigation into Pete's death. So...we're out. I don't know any more than that, but if you have any information to share with me, now's the time to do it."

"Can we keep looking on our own?" I asked.

"Officially...no. Some big shot's running the investigation and wants our full cooperation. That means they'll take over all of the records Pete was involved with. They should be walking in here in the next hour, so I wanted you to know." He caught Dimples' gaze. "But that doesn't mean you can't continue to look on your own, as long as you do it discreetly."

"Got it," Dimples said.

"Good. You may go."

As we left his office, the chief was thinking that, if nothing else, he could tell the FBI about me, and maybe they'd have better luck using my skills.

My breath caught. I did not want to be involved with the FBI. I followed Dimples back to his desk, but all I wanted to do was get out of there before the FBI showed up.

"I have a new lead," I blurted, then proceeded to tell him about my run-in with the plumber near the crime scene. "We have pictures of both Tom and Pete we could show around at those businesses. Maybe someone who works there knows something about who killed them. Even if they didn't admit it, I'd know."

"That's right," Dimples said, smiling. His dimples grew into big tornados right before my eyes.

I grinned back at him. "And we can stop by Anthony Kerby's office while we're out. I'd sure like to know what he's thinking."

Dimples chuckled and stood. "Sounds like a plan. Let's go."

Chapter 11

We took Dimples' car and, once on the road, I asked him about Pete and the FBI investigation. "Why would they take over Pete's murder investigation?"

"Well, the chief said there was an internal investigation going on," he answered. "So they must have suspected Pete was crooked before all this went down."

"Yeah, I guess that makes sense." I knew Officer Bellini might be crooked too, but I wasn't going to touch that with a ten foot pole.

"So it has to have something to do with the drugs and whatever it was Chloe overheard," he continued.

"That's true. So who was Pete working with? If we can figure that out, then we'll get some answers."

"I agree. Maybe the FBI knows. Too bad they're not talking to us."

"Right. Unless we know someone who will talk to us, we're pretty much in the dark." I didn't know anyone with the FBI, but I did know Blake Beauchaine. Since he'd seen the file the FBI had on me, he could be an FBI agent...or at least have some connections. Maybe I could ask him?

Dimples was also thinking about who he knew at the FBI, and who he could ask, but he was hoping I would pick up a clue first, so he didn't have to. That made me smile and I was about to agree with him, but since it didn't occur to him that I had just heard that thought, I didn't want to remind him.

We pulled into the plumbing supply store's parking lot and went inside. No one recognized the photos of Pete or Tom at the plumbing store or any of the other businesses, so I showed Dimples the path to the fence and the cut chain links. I glanced to the place where the attorney general's sign had been when I was there earlier, but it was gone. That was weird. Had I even seen it there in the first place?

"Can we go down to the crime scene from here?" I asked. "It might be helpful to look around once more while no one's there."

"Sure," Dimples agreed.

Slipping through the fence wasn't as easy as it looked, and I managed to get dirt all over me. Disgusted, I brushed it off and followed Dimples across the street to the scene. Not much had changed since this morning, and I wondered if I'd imagined that elusive scent on the breeze. I went back to the spot behind the pillar and glanced around again, hoping I'd see something new.

"What are you doing?" Dimples asked.

"I'm just looking around," I said. "I want to make sure I didn't miss anything."

Dimples shrugged and joined in the search. I was just about to give up when I spotted something shining in a crack between the concrete slabs. The sun hit it just right, making the light reflect into my eyes. I knelt beside the crack. "Look at this. It looks like a tie clip."

"Oh yeah?" Curious, Dimples came to my side and watched while I took a fingernail file out of my purse and popped the tie clip out of the wedge. The long, flat part was gold, and mounted in the center was the shape of an eagle with the initials, F.O.E. set below.

The cool scent of Irish Spring and green grass touched my nose, and I inhaled sharply. "Can you smell that?" My heart rate spiked with panic.

"Smell what?" Dimples sniffed. "You mean the car exhaust?"

"Uh...yeah. It's pretty bad, huh?" I agreed, not wanting him to think I'd totally lost my mind. As the scent slowly faded away, I cleared my throat. "Anyway...what do you think of this? Are those someone's initials?"

"I don't think so," Dimples said. "But I've seen this before. Yeah...I remember now. With the eagle on there, I think the F.O.E. stands for The Fraternal Order of Eagles."

"What's that?"

"It's a charity organization of some kind, and I think you have to get sponsored and approved to be part of the group."

"Oh. Then this could be a clue." I examined it closely. The edges seemed worn, like it had been stuck in the crack a long time. "Is it okay if I keep it?"

"Sure," Dimples said. "But I doubt it has anything to do with the murders. I mean...linking a lost tie clip to the murderer would be great, but it looks like it's been there quite a while, so it's not likely."

"Yeah...I know," I said, shrugging like it didn't matter. But inside I knew there was more to it because of that elusive smell. This was the clue I was supposed to find. Whoever owned this pin was Tom's murderer.

I turned it over and found the words *Love, Mom* engraved on the back, with an October date from about ten years ago.

"You still want to stop by Anthony Kerby's office?" Dimples asked, ready to move on.

"Oh yes, of course." I followed Dimples back through the fence to the car, clutching the tie pin in my palm. Even though I'd found this clue, it would take some kind of a miracle to find out who it belonged to, and I tried not to get discouraged.

Back at the car, I carefully placed the tie pin inside the loose change part of my purse where it wouldn't be hard to find. Dimples watched, thinking I was making too big of a deal out of it, but he didn't want to burst my bubble, so he kept his mouth shut.

"How's Billie doing?" I asked, wanting to change the subject.

"Much better. They'll probably send her home tomorrow or the next day, as long as she has someone there to help her out."

"That's great. So are her parents still in town? Are they going to help her?"

"Her mom is. I think her dad had to get back home for work. But they got the apartment all straightened out and put back together, so that's good." He was thinking with how busy he was, it was a good thing they'd come, since he never would have found time to clean the apartment. But he was also looking forward to when they left so he could have her all to himself. He sighed, realizing how crazy that sounded, and knew he had it bad.

"It is," I agreed. "Hey...did you get a chance to look at that thumb-drive?" I hated eavesdropping, so I hoped this change of subject wouldn't seem too abrupt.

"Yeah...last night, but I was too tired to understand everything that was on there. Some of it made sense, and some of it didn't."

"I got that too. Maybe Billie knows more about it."

"Maybe."

We pulled into the parking garage at the attorney general's office and made our way to Kerby's floor. As we approached the receptionist, my stomach fluttered with nerves. Talking to him might just solve the case, and I didn't want to screw it up.

Dimples showed the receptionist his badge, and she put the call through to Anthony, then told us that he was on a conference call and would see us in about fifteen to twenty minutes.

"Is his intern here today?" I asked. "His name is Devon." I figured since we had to wait, we might as well talk to him too.

"Let me check...yes...it looks like he is. Just a minute, and I'll call him." She placed the call, telling him a detective with the police was here, and I couldn't help the jolt of satisfaction that ran through me. I could just imagine how that could scare the crap out of him. Devon came to the reception area with his head held high, but I knew his heart was pounding with fear.

As he approached, he was thinking he'd done nothing wrong, so there was no need to be afraid. He couldn't figure out what we wanted though, unless we found out, and it made him sweat.

"I'm Detective Harris, and this is Shelby Nichols. We have a few questions we'd like to ask you. Is there someplace we can talk in private?"

"What's this about?" he asked, stalling for time.

"You want to do this out here?" Dimples asked, his voice not so friendly anymore.

"Um...no, I guess not. I have a small office, but I think we can all fit." He led the way down a long hall and opened a door at the end. He wasn't kidding about it being small. It looked like a refurbished closet, fitted specifically for an intern who worked for free. At least there was enough room for two chairs, but I wasn't sure we could get a third one in there.

"I'll go find another chair," Devon mumbled.

"That's not necessary. I'll stand." Dimples said. "Please, sit down. This won't take long. We're here to see Anthony Kerby, but since there was a wait, we thought we'd chat with you for a minute."

Devon swallowed and sat, then licked his lips. "Sure...okay. What's going on?"

"We have reason to believe you were given money to take something that didn't belong to you," Dimples began.

"What? No way." Devon broke in. "You must have the wrong guy. I don't know what you're talking about. I've never taken anything."

"That's true," I said. "But you asked your friend, Corey, to do it, and then you gave him five thousand dollars." His eyes got big, and he swallowed again. How did we know? Did Corey tell us?

"Look," I said. "We don't care about that so much...and we know Anthony Kerby asked you to do it. He's the one who gave you the money. We just want to know if anyone else was involved."

He glanced between the two of us before caving in. "No, not that I know of."

"Do you know what was on the thumb-drive?" Dimples asked.

"Not exactly. Only that it's not illegal." He was thinking it was probably illegal as hell, but he never saw it, so he was telling the truth.

"Did he ask you to do anything else?" Dimples asked. "Like break into someone's apartment?"

"No way. Mr. Kerby would never do that and, even if he asked, I wouldn't do it. That's all I know, I swear."

Dimples glanced at me, and I nodded to let him know Devon was mostly telling the truth. Sure, he didn't break into her apartment, but for another five grand, he would have.

"All right. That will be all for now." Dimples opened the door, then turned back to face Devon. "But we might be back later." Devon paled and was thinking this was a disaster, and he hoped it didn't get him in trouble. Hopefully, he could keep the internship until the semester was over, since he needed the hours to graduate.

As we walked back to the reception area, Dimples whispered, "I was hoping it was him. But that would have been too easy. I guess we'll just have to see what Anthony has to say."

"I'm sure he'll deny it. But I'll see what I can find out." I sent him a wry smile, and Dimples smiled back, thinking what I did was the coolest thing in the world.

We approached the front desk, and the receptionist told us that Anthony was free and would see us now. We followed her to his office where she knocked and then opened the door.

"Detectives," Anthony greeted us, standing and shaking our hands. He wore a blue shirt with a dark tie and suit. His welcoming smile exuded wholesome charm and goodness. "What can I do for you?"

I had no idea what to say, but I knew Dimples had been thinking about it, so I glanced at him.

"We're following some leads on a thumb-drive that was stolen from a reporter's desk at the local newspaper," he began. "And one of them led us straight to you. What can you tell us about it?"

Anthony's brows creased together, and he recoiled in shock. "A stolen thumb-drive? I don't know what you mean. Who told you I had something to do with it?"

Dimples waited, wanting to give me time to read his mind, but all I could pick up was a sense of hostility toward us, along with righteous outrage. Then I picked up Anthony's disgust toward Devon for letting it slip, but he wasn't worried.

Sure, he'd suggested Devon ask his friend to get the thumb-drive since he was such a suck-up, but there was no way that money could be traced back to him. He hadn't given the money to Devon directly, so no one could prove it came from him in the first place.

"A source," Dimples answered, inserting some menace in his tone to intimidate Anthony. "There was also a break-in at the same reporter's apartment. She was shot and nearly died. Do you know anything about that?"

Anthony took a deep breath and shook his head. His lips thinned, and his eyes narrowed with indignation. "I don't mind helping the police out, detective. We're on the same side, but you're crossing a line to come to me with these sorts of accusations. Unless you have some kind of evidence, I suggest you use your time more wisely. The real criminals are out there, not in this office."

"I'm sure you're right," I agreed, smiling to appease him. "The people who broke into her apartment are the ones we should be looking for. I'm sure that had nothing to do with you. I mean, how would you even know who these people are or how to contact them? It's absurd."

He turned his full attention to me, trying to decide if I was being sincere or had the nerve to openly mock him. "If you'll excuse me, I have to get back to work."

"Sure," I said, standing. "Thanks so much for your time. Sorry to have bothered you."

Dimples opened the door with a questioning brow at my audacity and followed me out to the car. We didn't say another word until we were both sitting in the car with the doors closed.

"Well?" he asked. "What did you find out?"

"Okay...here's what I got. Anthony doesn't think the money can be traced back to him, but he did hire a couple of thugs to break into Billie's apartment to search for thumb-drives and grab her computer. He also regretted that Billie got shot...so I guess that wasn't part of the plan."

"So how do we find these guys?"

"Well..." I said, shrugging. "I got their names."

"Glory hallelujah!" Dimples shouted, surprising me with his enthusiasm. "You are the most awesome, wonderful, fantastic partner ever!"

"Wow...thanks," I said. "But before you go overboard, I only got their last names...so I hope we can still find them. It was Kramer and Haws. You ever heard of those guys?"

"No, but once we get back to the station, I can look them up."

"Great."

As soon as we arrived, Dimples checked the police records and found files on both Aaron Kramer and Jason Haws. Even better, they were the only Kramer and Haws in the system, so it had to be them. He handed Haws' file to me while he studied Kramer's.

"Hmm...there's a charge of disorderly conduct and harassment," Dimples said. "And there's another for petty theft and vandalism. Drug possession was implied, but dropped for insufficient evidence."

"That looks similar to this file," I said. "Can you bring them in for questioning?"

"Sure can." He smiled. "I'll call it in right now."

While Dimples took care of that, I took Tom Souvall's file out of my bag and studied it for anything I might have missed. The crime scene photos were so much like Pete's that it took my breath away. Dimples got off the phone, and I handed the pictures to him. "Do you think Tom was positioned like that after he was shot? Or was he standing against the pillar and slid down. It seems to me like he would have fallen forward."

"I know," Dimples agreed. "With Tom's case, the forensic evidence pointed to him being shot at close range against the pillar, like he was grappling with his assailant when he was shot. The assailant then let him sink to the ground in a sitting position in front of the pillar and shot him once more."

"Is that what you think happened to Pete?"

"No. With Pete, the blood spatters indicated he was moved into the sitting position after he was killed."

I studied the photo again, noting that Tom was wearing jeans and a button-up shirt. With no tie in sight, it confirmed that he could have pulled the tie-clip from the killer after he was shot. But why put Pete in the same position?

My stomach growled, and I realized I'd missed lunch. "When do you think Haws and Kramer will get here?"

"Probably not for an hour or so," Dimples answered.

"Then I think I'll go grab some food. Can you call me when they get here, and I'll come right back?"

"Sure," Dimples agreed.

As I passed Bates' desk, I caught him wondering what we were doing. He knew we weren't supposed to be looking into Pete's death, but he had a pretty good idea we were still checking it out on our own. I picked up my pace, hoping to get out of there before he tried anything.

"Hey Nichols, wait up," he said.

Damn! Did I really have to stop? I slowed my steps, but kept moving. If he wanted to talk to me, he'd have to follow me out the door. "Uh...I'm in a hurry."

"Just hold on a sec," he said.

My shoulders slumped, and I turned to face him. "What?"

"I just wanted you to know that I called Chloe's parents and explained everything we know about the case."

"Yeah, I called them too. Right after I got home this morning." I smiled and started backing away.

"Oh." His lips twisted into a frown.

"See you." I rushed out before he could tell me calling them was police business and I was overstepping my bounds. He also wanted to ask what Dimples and I were working on, but I pushed through the door before he could. Yay...score one for team Shelby!

I made it to my car and tried to decide where to go for a soda refill. Chris' office wasn't far, but neither was Thrasher Development. I chewed on my bottom lip. What I really wanted to do was check up on Uncle Joey and see how things were going with the assassin, so I headed in that direction.

A wave of guilt rushed over me that I was choosing Uncle Joey over my husband, but Uncle Joey was in a tight spot and needed me more, so it was natural that I'd want to help him, right?

I pulled into the parking garage and hurried to the elevator, stopping for just a moment to check around the corner and see if Ramos' motorcycle was there. Yup. For some reason that made me grin with happiness.

Oh a whim, I stepped beside it and ran my fingers along the sleek handle-bars, then down the black chrome to the leather seat. I imagined sitting on that seat behind Ramos, and sudden guilt sparked inside me like an electric shock, snapping at the tips of my fingers. What was I doing fawning over a motorcycle? That was just silly.

Sighing with dismay, since deep down I knew it was a combination of Ramos and the motorcycle, I turned toward the elevator, but stopped short before rounding the corner. The soft shuffle of footsteps echoed in the distance, so I peeked around the edge and caught sight of a man leaning over Uncle Joey's car. With something in his hand, he knelt down at the side of the car. Then, glancing beneath it, he stretched his arm under the car, like he was attaching something there. What was he doing? Was he planting a bomb? Was he the assassin?

Keeping my gaze on the man, I blindly reached into my purse and pulled out my phone. Using my camera, I zoomed in as close as it would go and snapped a few pictures. All at once, he stood up and glanced in my direction, giving me a glimpse of his face, so I snapped another one before pulling back to hide. I didn't think he'd seen me, but it was hard to know.

With my heart pounding to beat the devil, I waited for him to leave but couldn't hear a thing. No footsteps, no car starting, nothing. I straightened from the wall and glanced out at the car, but he wasn't there anymore. I glanced through the whole parking garage but couldn't see a sign of him anywhere.

He must be gone. But what if he wasn't? I didn't want to wait around for him sneak up on me, so I darted toward the elevators and pushed the call button repeatedly. It seemed like it took at least ten times longer than normal for the elevator to reach me. The doors finally swooshed open, and I jumped inside, then stabbed at the button for the twenty-sixth floor.

Just before the doors closed, a man stepped into view. He wore a hoodie, and his face was shadowed, but his hard gaze caught mine, and his eyes narrowed with suspicion. Was that me he'd seen? Had I taken his picture? All at once, he sped towards me. My eyes widened in shock, and I cringed to the back of the elevator. He reached out to stop the doors with his hand, but they snapped to a close before he could make it.

Trembling at my narrow escape, I could hardly catch my breath. That was him! The assassin. And he was planting a bomb under Uncle Joey's car. I swallowed, fighting for control of my panic.

The elevator doors opened on Uncle Joey's floor, and I staggered out, the adrenalin rush playing havoc with my legs. After a couple of steps, I could finally walk again, but jerked to a stop in front of Thrasher Development.

Two burly men stood on either side of the door, their faces a mask of solid stone. Before I could move, Ramos burst through the door. "Shelby? Are you all right? What are you doing here?"

"I came to check on Uncle Joey," I said. "Did you know the assassin was downstairs?"

"Yes." He brought a radio to his mouth and spoke. "Did you get him?"

"No," a man answered. "I'm afraid we've lost him, sir. I'll check with my men in the stairwells, but I don't think he's in the building anymore."

"Damn! Did he see any of you?" Ramos asked.

"I'm afraid so, sir," he responded.

"Do what you have to...but find him."

"Yes, sir."

Oops. Did I just ruin their plans to take down the assassin? Ramos glanced at me, but I couldn't hear a thing he was thinking. My stomach clenched with dread. It must be pretty bad if he was blocking his thoughts like that.

I opened my mouth to apologize, but Ramos surprised me by shaking his head and breaking into a sardonic grin. "You kind of messed things up down there."

"Yeah...I got that. Sorry."

"It's okay. I'm just glad he didn't make it onto the elevator."

"How did you...? So you saw that part?"

"Yeah. The surveillance cameras," he explained. "I saw the whole thing."

"You did?" My brows shot up in alarm. "Everything?"

"Uh-huh." He grinned, thinking it was a bonus to catch me drooling over his motorcycle like that. "I didn't know you liked the bike so much."

"Huh! Well..." I shrugged with embarrassment and didn't know what to say.

He took pity on me and dropped the subject. "Come on. Manetto wants to see you."

"Is he mad?"

"Probably, but he'll get over it."

He ushered me past the two goons and down the hall to Uncle Joey's office. He was thinking that he'd been so distracted watching me and his motorcycle that he'd missed the assassin planting the bomb under Manetto's car until I started taking photos with my camera.

He'd sent the team down, but they were too late. Thankfully, the assassin didn't get to me. He didn't even want to think about that. But now the assassin knew they were on to him, and it was going to be harder to catch the guy. He'd probably have to reach out to Blake for his help now, even though Manetto didn't want to.

Uncle Joey sat at his desk, talking on the phone. He held up a hand for us not to interrupt him, then finished the call and hung up. "Did we lose him?"

"Yes," Ramos said. "It looks like he left the building, but he might be back. I'll check with the team and take care of the bomb on your car."

"Fine," Uncle Joey said.

Ramos winked at me, then left me standing there to face Uncle Joey alone. How could he do that? I glanced at Uncle Joey. His mouth turned into a frown, and he was thinking it was lousy timing or a twist of fate that I'd showed up just then. Now he'd have to call Blake.

"So, Shelby, what brings you here?" He was thinking that he couldn't be too upset with me, even though I'd ruined everything.

"Um...I just wanted to see how things were going. I had no idea you were in the middle of something, or I wouldn't have come."

"Well. I'm sure you didn't know."

"That's right." I grimaced with guilt. "So...is there anything I can do to help you?"

"Yes," he said, his expression clearing. "I'm going to have to talk to Blake, and I don't trust him. But if you're there, I'd feel better about it."

"Yeah, sure. I can do that." My shoulders drooped, and I let out a breath, suddenly exhausted. That adrenaline rush left me shaky and out of sorts.

"Good. I'll give him a call."

"Okay. Do you mind if I get a Diet Coke?"

"Sure. Jackie's not here, but you can help yourself."

"Thanks." I made my way down the hall toward the apartment, passing the two bodyguards, who thought I was in a lot of trouble, and another person watching the cameras in the surveillance room. That guy glanced at me with a raised brow and wondered what I did for Uncle Joey.

I opened the door and closed it softly behind me, relieved to shut out those prying thoughts, then wandered into the kitchen and plopped my purse on the counter. I filled a glass with crushed ice and got out two cans of soda.

A pastry box sat beside the fridge, so naturally I had to see what was inside. The delectable smell of glazed donuts, along with apple fritters and frosted maple bars, assaulted my senses. My mouth watered as I grabbed a napkin and a maple bar. I knew it wasn't good for me but, after the day I'd had, I deserved to indulge myself.

I took a bite on my way to the table and groaned with pleasure. Maybe coming here wasn't a total loss after all. Once I'd consumed the pastry, I poured my soda and took it into the living room to sip while I relaxed on the couch. Now this was more like it. I rested my head on the back of the sofa and closed my eyes to get more comfortable, taking advantage of this rare moment.

My cell phone's ring-tone sounded, and I sighed long and hard before hurrying over to my purse and digging it out. "Hello?"

"Hi Shelby," Dimples said. "They're here."

"Oh...right. I'll be there soon. Don't start without me."

"Don't worry," he chuckled. "I won't."

Reassured, I finished off my soda and visited the bathroom before leaving. I walked down the hall and paused. Ramos and Uncle Joey stood inside the surveillance room and motioned me inside. They'd been watching the footage of me in the parking garage, and my face turned red to see myself in the act of caressing a motorcycle.

Ramos pointed out the assassin on another camera, explaining that he'd come in through an outside staircase. We watched him plant the bomb then turn to look in my direction before ducking between the cars.

It gave me chills to see him spot me as I ran for the elevator. The next clip showed him in front of the elevator, right before the doors closed. Ramos paused the clip and zoomed in, but his hoodie hid the top half of his face so it was hard to see what he looked like. "Too bad we didn't get a clear shot, but I'll print out some copies anyway."

"Do you want to see the pictures I got? Maybe they're better."

"Sure."

I found them on my phone and pulled them up, but my hopes were dashed to find them grainy and unfocused. "Oh well."

Ramos smiled at me. "It's okay. We'll find him."

I smiled back, but my heart wasn't in it. "Good. Um...I have to go. Do you need me to come back?"

"I'll walk you out," Uncle Joey said. Once we were out of earshot, he continued. "I talked with Blake. I don't know what he's up to, but he said he'd be in touch. When I know more, I'll call you." He was thinking that Blake had specifically asked if I'd be involved, like he wanted me there or he wouldn't agree, and it bothered him.

"He did?" I asked. "What does he want with me?"

"I don't know, but I don't like it."

"Me neither."

"Don't worry, Shelby. We might not need him after all and, even if we do, I won't let anything happen to you."

"Okay," I said. We got to the elevators, and I hesitated. "Is it safe to go back down there?"

He was thinking that with all the surveillance cameras I'd just seen, how could I ask that? But then he thought of how the assassin had nearly jumped onto the elevator with me. "You'd better wait, and I'll have Ramos go with you." I opened my mouth to proclaim that I could take care of myself, but then I remembered the assassin's hard, cold eyes and snapped it shut. Just then, Ramos joined us.

"Oh good, you haven't left yet," he said. "I'll walk Shelby to her car." He was thinking that even though they had lost the assassin's trail, that didn't mean he wasn't hiding out somewhere in the building, and he didn't want to take any chances with my safety.

"Really? You think he might be down there somewhere?" I asked.

"It's a possibility," he said. "But not likely."

Uncle Joey said goodbye, and we got on the elevator. Still feeling bad, I apologized to Ramos again. "I'm sorry I messed things up for you."

"Don't worry about it. I'll think of another way to catch him."

The bell dinged, and the doors opened into the parking garage. Without thinking, I immediately stepped behind Ramos and held my breath. Finding the garage empty, it was still hard to step out of the elevator into the unknown.

Ramos chuckled. "Don't worry. It's not you he wants to kill. But you can walk behind me if you want."

"Okay," I said. He was half-joking, but I thought it was a good idea.

We made it to my car without mishap, and I heaved a sigh of relief. "Thanks Ramos. Don't let him shoot you, okay?"

"I won't," he said. Then his brows drew together. "Did you steal a donut?"

"What?" My gaze flew to his. How did he know?

"Frosting...right there..." He pointed to a spot above my lip. I licked it with my tongue, but he shook his head. "Here..." He rubbed his thumb gently across my lip. "There. Got it."

"Uh...thanks." My breath hitched, and I seemed frozen in place.

"Maple bars."

"Huh?"

"Are they your favorite?" he asked.

"Yeah...well...no, but I like them a lot." Ramos chuckled and stepped back, giving me the room I needed to breathe again. "Uh...see you. Be careful."

"Count on it." He closed the door and watched while I backed out of my parking space. I waved once more and drove out of the parking lot, shaking my head to clear it, and get my breathing under control. Sheesh! Get a grip Shelby. I turned up the radio and started singing along, "radio-active...radio-active." Yup, that definitely fit.

A few minutes later, I hurried into the precinct to find Dimples waiting for me at his desk. "Sorry. I hope I didn't keep you waiting long."

"No...it's fine. I've got them in separate interrogation rooms. Let's talk to Kramer first."

"Sounds good," I agreed.

I followed Dimples into the room and got my first look at Kramer. He wore jeans and a tee shirt, and looked kind of scruffy with long straggly hair and a beard. His glance held defiance, and in his thoughts, he was madder than hell that the police had picked him up. This wasn't supposed to happen.

"I'm sure you're wondering what you're doing here," Dimples began. "But we just have a few questions for you, and you'll be free to go."

Kramer shook his head and huffed out a breath, thinking he wasn't going to get bulldozed into anything this time.

"Where were you last Tuesday night?"

His brows shot up in surprise. How did we know about that? "Tuesday? That's easy. I was helping my mom move some furniture. What's this all about?"

"And can she verify that?"

"Yes," he said. "I was there all night."

"Do you know Jason Haws?" Dimples asked.

"Yeah, sure," Kramer said. "But I haven't seen him for a while."

"Did you see him Tuesday night?"

"No. I told you I haven't seen him." Kramer was starting to sweat. He didn't know how we could think he was involved, but there was no way we could tie him to that break-in. They'd done everything by the book, and he was sure they'd left nothing behind.

If that broad hadn't surprised them, he could have been more thorough, but he knew there was nothing to tie him or Haws to that fiasco. They wore masks and gloves. No one could identify them, coming or going. They were professionals. So what happened? Haws would cut his tongue out before he'd roll. So who else would talk?

"We just want to know who hired you," I said.

He stilled, and his gaze cut to mine. "I don't know what you're talking about, and that's all I'm going to say."

"Fine," Dimples said. "We'll be back."

I followed Dimples out to the hall. "Did you get anything?" he asked.

"Yeah. I'm pretty sure it was him and Haws, but proving it might be difficult. I don't think he'll admit to anything. We need to find out who they're working for."

"Maybe we'll have more luck with Haws."

Dimples opened the door to the next interrogation room, and I followed him in, catching my breath at the sight of the big man seated at the table. He wasn't someone I wanted to meet in a dark alley. His hair was cut military short, and his tee shirt showed off his muscles and tattoos. He reminded me of the men I'd met in Uncle Joey's office earlier, and my pulse raced. Had I seen him before? My heart sank. I didn't think he'd ever worked for Uncle Joey, but how did I know?

Dimples began with the same questions he'd asked Kramer, but Haws didn't even blink. He wasn't worried about anything. He was good at his job, and nothing could tie him to that break-in. Unless Kramer talked, but Kramer was smarter than that.

"So, are you like a paid mercenary?" I asked. "Or maybe I should call it security, like a bodyguard or something."

He glanced at me with speculation, since I was right on the money. "I'm a bouncer...among other things."

"So if I wanted to hire you, I could?"

"As long as it was nothing illegal," he said, his lips turning sideways in a smirk.

"So who hired you to break into that apartment and steal the thumb-drive?" I asked.

A thin smile of respect spread over his lips. Asking about the thumb-drive could easily throw someone off their game. But not him. "I don't know what you're talking about." Dismissing me, he glanced at Dimples. "Are you going to charge me with anything?"

"Uh..." Dimples glanced at me and raised his brows. "Are you done?"

"Yes."

He nodded and turned back to Haws. "I guess we're done here."

Haws pushed his chair back and, without a backward glance, walked out the door.

"Do we need to talk to Kramer again?" Dimples asked.

"No. Cut him loose. I got the name. It was Anthony Kerby."

"I knew it," Dimples said.

"Yeah, but knowing it and proving it are two different things. There is absolutely no evidence to link them to Billie's apartment. So what do we do now?"

Dimples sighed. "I don't know. We can't bring charges, so I guess nothing's changed."

"Maybe, but since Anthony hired them, where did he find them? From cases he's found in his office? Is he working with someone else? Maybe we need to go back and talk to him, only with different questions this time."

Dimples nodded, but his heart wasn't in it. "You sure you don't want to talk to Kramer again?"

"Yeah, I'm sure, but I'd like to take a look at their files one more time."

While he took care of Kramer, I hurried to his desk and opened both files side-by-side. I shuffled through each page and looked at the officers involved in making the arrests, but none of them were Pete like I was hoping. That's when I noticed that both files had several pages missing. That was it...the link had to be in those missing pages.

"Shelby?"

I glanced up to find Chief Winder motioning me to his office. Puzzled, I hurried toward him, noticing that the blinds over his windows were shut. Who was he hiding in there?

"There's someone who'd like to meet you," he said, moving to usher me inside.

Curious, I stepped through the door and stopped short in surprise.

"Shelby," the chief said, closing the door behind me. "This is Special Agent Blake Beauchaine."

Chapter 12

"Nice to meet you." Blake stood and offered his hand, hoping I'd follow his lead.

"Yeah. You too," I said.

"Blake is the lead investigator on Pete Royce's death," Chief Winder explained. "He wanted to compare notes with you."

"Oh...he's with the FBI? The one you were telling us about?"

"Yes," he said, frowning at me. He turned to Blake. "Do you need to talk to Harris and Bates too?"

"In a moment," Blake answered. "I'd like to talk with Shelby first." He turned his gaze to the chief and smiled. "Thanks for letting me use your office."

"No problem." It soon became evident that Blake was not going to continue until the chief left. "Uh...I'll leave you to it."

"Thank you," Blake said again. As soon as the door shut, Blake let out a breath and smiled. "Thanks for not giving me away."

"Sure," I said, regaining my composure. "So you're the big shot with the FBI?"

He chuckled. "Right now I am."

"What's that supposed to mean?"

"It means I go where I'm needed, and right now it's here, with this investigation, although to be honest, I didn't expect to find you in the middle of it." He didn't think my involvement with the police was all for Joe's benefit, but it certainly didn't hurt Joe to have me snooping around the department either.

"I work as a consultant for the police, and it has nothing to do with Uncle Joey," I said. "In fact, I don't think he likes it much."

Blake nodded. "I'm beginning to see that. I just can't figure out why you help Joe in the first place. He's not really your uncle, so there must be another reason."

"That's no concern of yours," I said, wanting to put him in his place. "So is this why you're really here...I mean...besides this business with the assassin? To investigate the police department?"

"It's a little more complicated than that, but, yes...that's part of it." Thoughts about the attorney general's office popped into his mind, but he pushed them away. "Could you tell me about Chloe Peterson?"

Whoa...was he investigating the attorney general's office? Was that why he was here?

"Shelby?"

"Um...right. Chloe Peterson. She's my client. She saw a cop at a drug house and heard him talking on the phone making a deal with someone. She managed to get away, but he saw her. We kept her in hiding until we figured out who the cop was. It turned out to be Pete, but before we could question him, he turned up dead."

Blake nodded. "Do you have any ideas about who killed him?"

"Yeah...logically it's his partner in crime. Since Chloe could identify Pete, I think the partner got rid of him. Does that sound about right to you?"

"Yes. But there's more to it than that," he said. "I think Pete was supposed to kill Chloe and couldn't go through with it. I know this because my office got a call from him last night. He told one of my agents that he wanted to turn state's evidence against the man running this drug ring. The agent told him to come in and we'd talk but, for some reason, Pete refused. Next thing I know, he's dead." He shook his head. "We were so close."

"That's too bad," I agreed. "Your agent really messed up, huh?" Since he was thinking about firing him, I knew it was a good guess. His sharp gaze caught mine, and I shrugged. "So what do you need from me?"

"I'd like to know what you and Detective Harris have been up to," he said, leaning forward.

"Well...we've been trying to figure out who Pete was working with."

"No," Blake interrupted. "Not that. You visited the attorney general's office this morning and talked with Anthony Kerby. What was that about?"

"You mean...why did we talk to him?"

"Yes," Blake said. "And not just Anthony, but his intern and the two men you just finished questioning."

Crap! How did he know all that? Had he been watching me? Did he also know I'd been to Uncle Joey's office? What should I tell him? Blake was the good guy, right? So I should probably tell him everything. But could I trust him? I thought he had it in for Uncle Joey, but with all this going on, did it matter? Still, I couldn't be too careful.

Blake cleared his throat. "Uh...anytime now."

"Okay...fine. I'll tell you what I know, and maybe we can work together on this. Sound good?"

He sat back. Why was I making a deal with him? What did I want in return?

"I just want to know what's going on with the investigation. Once you tell me everything, there's a good chance that I can help you."

Blake's eyes narrowed. He knew he had a great poker face, but I'd read him like a book. Maybe there was something to those reports that I had psychic abilities...or I was just good at reading people.

"Sure," he agreed. He suddenly wanted to work with me in the worst way, so he could see for himself if I was anything like the reports said. If it was true, it certainly made sense that Joe would want to keep me around. The only problem with that was why would I work with a mob-boss? Joe must have some kind of hold over me. That's the only thing that made sense. But whatever it was, he hoped to find out. Maybe he could do something about it.

What the freak! Maybe I should stay out of this. But now it was too late. Why did I do stuff like this? Now I had to be careful with what I said and, with all the stress, I was bound to break out in hives at any moment.

"So...go ahead," he prompted. "Tell me what's going on."

I blinked. "Right. Okay. I think it all started when my friend Billy Jo Payne started looking into the Attorney General's Office." I started at the beginning, then told him about the thumb-drive and how it had been stolen from her desk. "But of course, she made a copy." That caught Blake's interest especially when I told him that her apartment had been ransacked and she'd been shot.

"Did they take it?" he asked.

"No. I went back later and found it."

His brows lifted, and he thought *that was you?* "You did?" he said.

"Uh...yeah." So he was the person I'd seen in the parking lot? The one who'd watched me leave Billie's apartment? "What were you doing there?" Oops. That just kind of slipped out. I held my breath, hoping he'd think I saw him and that's why I'd asked.

"What makes you say that?" He thought there was no way I could have known it was him. We hadn't even met yet.

"Oh, well...there was someone there. As I was leaving, I spotted him, and went down the other staircase to avoid him. There was something familiar about him, and now it just clicked in my mind that it was you."

"You put it together just now?" he asked, astounded. He could hardly believe it. How could I tell it was him from that moment to now? He'd stayed in the shadows and worn a hat and bulky jacket. Even if I'd spotted him, there was no way in hell I should have recognized him.

"Well...um...not really. It was just a hunch." I shrugged. "Guess I was right."

He let out a breath, dropping all pretense. "Is this your psychic powers at work?"

"Uh...yeah."

"Hmm..." He studied me, thinking I wasn't being entirely truthful. He was good at spotting lies, so what was I hiding?

"Anyway," I continued. "I gave the thumb-drive to Dimp...uh...Harris."

"Did you look at it?" he asked, wondering what I'd seen. I nodded, and he continued. "Did it have anything incriminating on it?

"I think so, but I didn't understand it very well."

"This is good, Shelby. This could be the break we need. I need that thumb-drive."

"Well...I'm sure Harris will be happy to turn it over. You might need to keep him in the loop though. So, is there anything else?"

He let out a sigh and glanced down at his notes. "Yes. You haven't finished telling me about Anthony."

"Right." I gave him the shortened version of events, telling him that we thought Anthony hired the two thugs to get the thumb-drive from Billie's apartment. "But without proof, we can't tie any of them together."

"We may not need to. That thumb-drive might have everything we need on it."

"So what does this have to do with Pete and the drugs?" I asked.

"I'm not sure. But I think there's a connection to the A.G.'s office somewhere, I just don't know where."

"I checked out those files on Kramer and Haws. There are pages missing. Maybe finding the missing pages will tell us what we want to know."

Blake wrote something down on a piece of paper. "I'll check into it."

"Good. So are we done here?" I worried that I'd said too much and also that I'd missed something...mostly that this was all somehow connected to Uncle Joey, and I'd just sentenced him to his doom.

"Yes...but there is one more thing. I got a call from Joe about the assassin. Did you see him?"

"Yeah, I did. I took his picture with my phone."

"Let me see."

I showed him the blurry snapshots, and he was relieved that I hadn't gotten a good look at his face. "Okay, good. I'll see what I can do to help Joe. Thanks Shelby, I'll be in touch. Will you send Harris in now?"

"Yeah...uh...sure." My heart raced with sudden fear from what I'd just picked up, but I managed to walk out of the office and shut the door behind me. I found my way to Dimples' desk and sat down heavily.

"Hey Shelby...what's going on?" Dimples asked.

"The FBI guy wants to talk to you in the chief's office," I told him.

"Are you okay?" Dimples asked, thinking I looked a little pale.

"Oh...sure," I said. He didn't believe me, but he kept his mouth shut and hurried into the chief's office.

I took a deep breath and tried to swallow past the sudden dryness in my mouth. Blake was thinking I might be in a lot of trouble, but it was lots worse than that. He'd been thinking that the assassin usually wore a disguise, since he didn't like anyone to see his face. Those that did were marked for death. The 'chameleon' lived by certain rules. Anyone who'd seen his face as the assassin...never lived to tell about it.

He wasn't wearing a disguise when I saw him. I'd seen his face under the hoodie. Did that mean he'd come after me now? Damn! I was in so much trouble. What was I going to do? I took a deep breath and tried to think things through.

First of all, he didn't know my name or anything about me. So...it would take time for him to find me, and I should be safe for now. There was also the fact that he was getting paid to kill Uncle Joey, so naturally he'd go after him first. I was just an afterthought, and he could deal with me later, right? And since Uncle Joey was bound to kill him before he got to me, I had nothing to worry about.

I let out a breath and relaxed my shoulders, but my stomach refused to cooperate and tightened into a queasy knot. I glanced around the precinct and took in the activities around me. It was business as usual. I was safe here. Now I just needed to figure out how to tell Blake that

I'd seen the assassin's face without letting on that I'd heard the dire consequences in his thoughts.

As soon as Dimples came out, I'd go back in there and ask him if he needed a description of the assassin. That should work. My stomach settled down, and I sighed with relief. My chair faced the right direction to watch the chief's office, so I kept my eye on the door.

"Hey Nichols," Bates said, coming up behind me.

I cringed at the sound of his voice, but managed to smooth the grimace off my face before I turned to look at him. "What?"

His brows drew together. He'd seen me cringe, and it bothered him. What was my problem? He was just trying to be friendly. For a woman with premonitions, I certainly didn't seem to have any. "I was just wondering if you brought that file on the other homicide at the underpass. I wanted to take a look at it."

"Oh, sure. It's here on the desk somewhere." I closed the files on Kramer and Haws and found Tom's underneath.

"What do you have these files out for?" Bates asked, motioning to the two I'd set aside.

"Um...we think they might have been involved in a burglary."

"I remember these two," he went on as if I hadn't said a word. "Never could get any charges to stick."

"Well...that certainly makes sense. Here..." I handed him Tom's file. "Take a look, and let me know if you see anything."

"It was like they had help from someone on the inside, you know?" He continued. "Someone pulling the strings and cutting them loose. Maybe it was Pete?"

"I couldn't find anything, but there are some pages missing. Who would do that?"

"Someone trying to cover their tracks," he said. "They should have copies of these files on the computer down in the archives. I'll bet we'll find all the pages there."

"Great. Why don't you go check it out? I'd come, but I'm waiting for Dim...uh...Harris. He's in the chief's office talking to someone."

Bates shook his head. "No he's not. He already left. I saw them leave right after you came out."

"Are you serious?" I hurried over to the office and knocked on the door. A second later, the chief pulled it open. I glanced inside, but Bates was right. They were gone.

"What's going on?" the chief asked.

"Where did they go?"

"You mean Beauchaine and Harris?" At my nod, he continued. "I don't know. Why?"

"There was just something I needed to tell Harris...but that's okay...I'll call his cell phone."

I hurried back to Dimples' desk and punched in his number, relief pouring over me to hear him answer. "Hey, it's Shelby. Where did you go so fast?"

"Oh...listen, we're going over to Blake's office with the thumb-drive. I'll call you back." He disconnected, leaving me with my mouth hanging open. What was going on? That wasn't like him to just leave me without an explanation.

Disgruntled, I glanced back to where I'd left Bates, but he was gone. I looked through the papers on Dimples' desk and found the files gone too. Bates must have taken them to the archives for the missing pages.

Drained by the whole thing, I decided I'd had enough of all this. Besides, it was time for my kids to get home, and I wanted to be there for a change. On the way to my car, I pushed the button on my cell for Uncle Joey. I should have forgotten about Blake and called Uncle Joey in the first place.

"Shelby? Did you forget something?"

"No, but I'm just leaving the police station...and I wanted you to know that I just met with Blake. He was here at the precinct as a special agent for the FBI. He's looking into a police detective's death, but his real investigation is with the attorney general's office."

Uncle Joey exhaled. "Now it makes sense."

"There's more." I opened my car door and sat down in the driver's seat. "I saw the assassin's face. Do you know what that means?"

"Uh...no."

"Blake doesn't know that I saw the assassin's face, but he was thinking that anyone who's seen his face is dead. That means the assassin is probably planning to kill me too."

"Ah...Shelby...that's too bad. I had no idea. But I'm glad we know. Listen...Ramos has a plan, and I wasn't going to ask you, but it might go better if you help. Will you come?"

I let out my breath. "Sure. Where?"

For the second time today, I pulled into the garage at Thrasher Development. This time Ramos was waiting for me, and the cold chill around my heart melted a little. I trusted Ramos. He'd saved me more times than I liked to remember, and if anyone could protect me, it was him.

Of course, now I had to participate in something dangerous and, from his thoughts, I could tell he wasn't real happy with me. "Did Uncle Joey tell you the assassin would be after me too?"

Ramos punched the elevator button and frowned. "Yes. But...this plan would have worked just fine without you."

"Well...if you're right, then I'll go home."

"No...you can't do that now." The elevator doors opened, and we stepped inside. "We left the bug on the flowers, so we should have him right where we want him. But something could always go wrong. That's where you'll come in. If he's there, you'll hear him, and you can tell me what he's planning."

"Okay. So where are we going?"

"We've talked about a scheduled meeting across town at The Depot this afternoon that Manetto can't miss. We've discussed our plan that we'll make it look like he's going, but he'll stay here in the apartment where it's safe, and I'll go in his place. Then we'll watch for the assassin to follow...and trap him."

"So what's the real plan?" I asked.

"The real plan is that he'll go to the meeting...and I'll stay here."

"What if the assassin doesn't take the bait?"

Ramos shrugged. "If I were him, I'd see this as an opportunity to get Manetto while he's only got one guard instead of five. It might be the best chance he'll get. But if he doesn't take it, we'll have to think of something else."

The elevator doors opened, and we stepped into the hallway. "Wait...so what am I doing?"

"Manetto wants you to go with him, in case the guy figures it out and goes to the meeting. You can warn Manetto, and the men I'm sending to protect him, if the assassin's there before anything happens."

That sounded kind of scary, and my stomach clenched. "Okay."

Ramos stopped and grabbed my upper arms, turning me to face him. "No...it's not okay...I don't like it, and you don't have to do it. Just tell Manetto you've changed your mind. He'll understand."

"Um...thanks Ramos, but let me think about it, okay?"

He took a deep breath, then dropped his hands. "Sure." He was thinking he could agree because he felt confident that the assassin would come here instead of following us.

That calmed my nerves a little bit, but I knew it was still a risk. "Does he know where the meeting is?" I asked.

"No...only that it's across town...we've been careful not to mention that."

"Where are the flowers?"

"On Jackie's desk. We haven't moved them, but we did find the bug," Ramos answered.

"Okay...I'll be careful what I say."

"No...you're not saying anything around those flowers. I don't want the assassin to know you're involved in any way."

I nodded and, after taking a deep breath, followed Ramos inside. I spotted the flowers right off the bat and turned down the hallway to Uncle Joey's office, trying to keep as quiet as possible. Ramos went the opposite direction to the surveillance room. At the front desk, the two goons from before nodded at me and kept their vigil.

As soon as the door to Uncle Joey's office closed behind me, I flopped onto the couch and exhaled.

"You okay?" Uncle Joey asked.

"Yeah...just resting for a minute," I lied, still unsure of what to do.

"Well, don't get too comfortable. We're leaving in a few minutes." He was thinking this plan had better work. Having an assassin after him was starting to get on his nerves. He'd sent Jackie to Seattle so she'd be under Kate's protection. He was grateful no one knew about Miguel, or he'd be worrying about him too. This needed to end. Today.

"I appreciate you coming, Shelby."

"Oh, sure," I said.

He smiled, hearing the hesitation in my voice, and pulled a sports coat over his bulky vest.

"Is that Kevlar?" I asked.

"Yes. Ramos insisted, although if this assassin is as good as we've heard, he'll go for the head shot, and it won't do me any good."

"Well...that's comforting."

He chuckled, relieving some of the tension in the room. "Don't worry...it's not going to happen."

"I certainly hope not," I said. A sudden desire to have one of those vests around my chest washed over me, but if Uncle Joey was right about the head shots, I probably didn't need it.

Just thinking about needing a bullet-proof vest made me realize how crazy my life was, especially that I was even thinking about doing something like this. What was wrong with me?

Ramos poked his head in. "It's time. You ready?" He was thinking all the men were in place and, with nothing out of the ordinary so far, everything was going according to plan.

Uncle Joey nodded, and I stood. The time to decide if I was going through with this quickly slipped through my fingers. If I didn't say anything now, it would be too late. Uncle Joey walked out the door, and the words got stuck in my throat. For some strange reason, I couldn't let him down. Straightening my spine, I followed him to Jackie's desk where he stopped to make his speech.

"I guess this is it," he drawled. "That white hair should convince him, but I'd keep my face down if I were you."

"Got it," Ramos said. "I'll call you with updates."

That was it. Ramos nodded at me and watched as we left the office and got on the elevator. Both bodyguards came with us, leaving Ramos on his own. My gaze caught his as the doors slid shut, and I heard his thoughts of 'be careful' which mirrored my own, and I smiled.

That's when I realized I hadn't called my kids to tell them I'd be late getting home. I checked the time. It was after three-thirty. They were already home by now. I explained to Uncle Joey that I needed to call them and pulled out my phone.

The elevator doors opened, and we walked the short distance to the waiting limo. The first bodyguard opened the door and I got in, hitting the button for home on my speed dial. After Uncle Joey took his spot beside me, the guard got in, with the other one sitting in front with the driver.

"Hi Josh," I said. "I'm going to be a little late, maybe another hour or so."

"Sure mom, see you soon." He disconnected before I could ask him if any of his friends were there, so I figured they were. What were they up to? I shook my head. I should be there too. With a sigh, I was about to put my phone away when I heard a string of swearing coming from the driver.

What was his problem? Then I caught him thinking that if I recognized him, it was all over.

Chapter 13

Fear slammed into my stomach, and my heart raced. With all the will power I possessed, I kept my gaze down instead of looking into the rear-view mirror like I wanted. The assassin pulled his cap down over his eyes and was thinking that this could still work. I hadn't spotted him yet. All he had to do was get us to the meeting. Once we were out of the car, he could still pop one into the back of Uncle Joey's head.

Killing me would be a bonus, but he didn't think he could get away with it before the bodyguards responded. Although he might be able to do it if he could get the shot off fast enough. It grated on him to leave me alive, so he figured it was worth a try.

My mouth went dry, and I swallowed, then pulled up my contact list on my cell phone and found Ramos' number. I pushed the message icon and wrote, *"The assassin is our driver,"* and sent it. I nudged Uncle Joey with my elbow and continued to write, detailing the assassin's plan to shoot Uncle Joey in the head once we got out of the car. I pushed send and tried to catch my breath.

Uncle Joey cursed in his mind and started thinking, *show the guard, show the guard.* I nodded to let him know I'd heard but, with the guard sitting across from us, I wasn't sure how to accomplish that. Thinking fast, I improvised, and poked Uncle Joey with my elbow and held up my phone. "Wow...look at this picture. Isn't that something? My son just sent it. Maybe I'd better skip this meeting and get home."

"Holy hell," he said, playing along.

"I know." I glanced at the bodyguard. "You should see this." I scooted close to Uncle Joey to make room for him, but he just shook his head, thinking there wasn't enough room. "Come on, there's plenty of room. Seriously, you've got to see this."

He glanced at Uncle Joey who sent him a stern nod. With a resigned huff, he moved his bulky frame to the space next to me. I held the phone so he could see the message clearly, but before he could read it, a message came through from Ramos, saying, *"I'm on my way. Show the guard."*

I tapped back to the first message so he could see them all and said. "There it is, see?"

As comprehension dawned on the guard he said, "Holy hell."

"Yeah...right," I agreed.

This caught the attention of the guard in the front seat. "What is it?" he asked.

The assassin stiffened, thinking that if I moved forward to show the guard, I might recognize him. He slipped his gun into his left hand under his jacket just in case he had to shoot me.

"Oh...I'll show you in a minute." I quickly typed another message. *"The assassin has a gun in his left hand."*

Uncle Joey read it and swore in his mind. Beside me, the guard's brows drew together, and he glanced at me like I had horns growing out of my head, wondering how in hell I knew that.

"Are we almost there?" I asked.

The driver ducked his head before he answered. "Yes, ma'am. Just a few more minutes."

"Good. I'm starving. I missed lunch. Did you say there'd be food at this meeting?"

"No," Uncle Joey said. "But if everything goes well, I'll take you to dinner afterward. How does that sound?"

"Great," I said. "I think I might have a granola bar in my purse. Is it okay if I eat it?"

Since the guard was basically sitting on my purse, he moved back to his seat and slowly removed his gun from the holster under his jacket. I breathed easier, knowing he was ready, then rummaged through my purse. I found my stun flashlight and put it in my lap. I wasn't sure how it was going to help me, but I felt better with it handy.

Uncle Joey smiled, thinking the flashlight was pretty useless as a weapon, but if it made me feel better then what the hell? Since he'd worn the bullet-proof vest, he hadn't brought his regular gun, but his compact pistol was strapped to his ankle. He'd just have to wait for the right moment to grab it.

Knowing they were both ready calmed my nerves, but it didn't stop my heart from racing as we got closer to our destination. I knew Uncle Joey wasn't planning on leaving the car, and I thought that made sense for me too.

I also remembered that Blake had asked that we take him alive, but I wasn't so sure that was going to happen. The guard was trying to decide if he should shoot the guy as soon as we stopped, or wait for him to get out of the car.

I was beginning to think he should shoot him once we stopped, and not wait around, even though that was pretty callous of me. Before I was quite ready, the limo pulled to a stop in front of a tall brick building on the west side of town.

He put the car in park and quickly jumped out, leaving his door open. The guard in the front seat did the same. With my heart about to burst, I watched as the assassin opened the back door for Uncle Joey to get out, holding the gun out of sight by his side, ready to shoot.

The guard took that opportunity to exit first, effectively blocking the assassin's view of Uncle Joey. In response, the assassin backed up a step into the street. At that same moment, a motorcycle barreled by. The bike clipped the assassin, sending him spinning to the ground. The gun flew out of his hand to rest under the car in front of us.

The assassin lurched to his feet and tried to make a run for it, but he didn't get far before the guard tackled him. Ramos jumped off his bike and, with the guard, brought the assassin's arms behind his back. Before I knew it, he was cuffed and lying on the ground.

It was over.

"I guess we can get out now," I said.

Uncle Joey smiled, then put his gun back in his ankle holster, a little disappointed that he didn't get to use it. He got out, and I quickly followed. Ramos hauled the assassin to his feet and roughly pushed him against the car.

"I'm a little disappointed you didn't kill him," Uncle Joey said to Ramos, still thinking it might be a good idea. He gave the assassin a hard frown but kept his distance. "I guess I'll give Blake a call so he can haul him off."

While Uncle Joey did that, I took his place. "Thanks Ramos...I was sure happy to see you drive by. I'm glad it all worked out."

"That's for sure," he agreed, thinking I'd saved the day.

That brought a smile to my face. I glanced at the assassin. With blood dripping from a cut on his brow, and a bruise forming on his cheek, he seemed more dangerous than ever. Then his gaze trapped mine, and he sneered.

Pure loathing and hatred, with a little crazy thrown in, washed over me. Even with the handcuffs and Ramos holding him, a chill traveled up my spine and sent goosebumps over my arms. I swallowed but held my ground.

"Um...how did you know Uncle Joey would be in the car?" I asked.

He frowned even more defiantly and pursed his lips tightly together, but I heard the answer in his thoughts.

"Holy hell." I'd been hearing that a lot today, so it came out of my mouth pretty easily. I glanced at Ramos. "He planted a bug in the elevator...and in the plants by the entrance to Thrasher. He heard everything you told me."

The assassin's eyes widened in shock, and it gave me quite the rush. I narrowed my eyes as evilly as I could to keep him off balance and continued my questioning. "What happened to the limo driver?"

The news wasn't good. "You killed him?" I shook my head and turned to Ramos. "He's in the trunk."

Seeing all the gory details in his mind was about as much as I could take, and I turned away in disgust. My legs shook a little from the ordeal, but I wasn't about to get back in the limo, knowing there was a dead body so close in the trunk.

Just then, a car pulled up beside us, and I let out a relieved sigh to see Blake and another agent. He jumped out and greeted Uncle Joey. Then he spoke to Ramos, who told him what happened and also mentioned the dead body in the trunk. Blake couldn't have been more satisfied with events.

A police car arrived and cordoned off the area under Blake's supervision. After several questions, Blake's partner pushed the assassin into the back of their car, and I breathed easier with him out of the way. While his partner opened the trunk of the limo, Blake made the rounds, asking the guards, then Uncle Joey and Ramos, several routine questions.

He finally came to me with the same questions but, at the end, surprised me with one I hadn't expected. "I'm curious. How did you know about the body in the trunk? I'm sure the assassin didn't tell you." He was thinking that even though Ramos had told him about it, he was pretty sure it was because of me that Ramos knew.

I shrugged, trying to make light of it. "My premonitions, I guess...or you could call it a hunch if you prefer."

"Anything else you'd care to add?" he asked.

"Uh...no...that's all I've got."

Blake was thinking it might be to his advantage to have me help with the assassin's interrogation. He was sure the guy wouldn't talk, but maybe I could pick up something that would make his talking unnecessary.

I tried to quell the instant panic that brought, and I sent him a tremulous smile. "That guy's one scary dude. I'm sure glad I don't have to talk to him again. Are we done here? I really need to get home."

Blake studied me with narrowed eyes. "Yes...for now. I got the thumb-drive from Harris. Maybe we can talk after I have a chance to look at it."

"Sure. I'd be happy to."

"Good. I'll be in touch."

I exhaled as he turned away from me and leaned back against the car, shoving my hair away from my face.

"Babe," Ramos said, coming to my side. "You did great. Did Blake say something to upset you?"

"Oh...a little, but I handled it." I smiled at him, not about to tell him about the interrogation part, or the fact that I was helping Blake with the investigation into the attorney general's office. Who knew what he might do?

His right brow arched. He thought I was hiding something but let it go. "I'm going back to the office for Manetto's car. Do you want to wait for me to get back, or would you like to go with me on the bike?"

My heart surged with happiness. "Holy hell, yes!"

Ramos chuckled. "Okay then. Let's go."

I'd probably overdone it with the holy hell part, but I was so relieved that it just slipped out. Maybe it was starting to become a habit? That wasn't good, but now that I knew, I could stop...only I kind of liked saying it. What was up with that?

I grabbed my purse from the limo, making sure my stun flashlight and phone were inside, and hurried to the bike, slinging my purse over my shoulder.

Ramos unclipped my helmet from the back of his bike and handed it to me. "I brought it just in case," he said with a wink.

My heart melted a little, and I put the helmet on to hide my blushing cheeks. He got on the bike and started her up, then I got on behind him. As I settled onto the seat and put my arms around Ramos, I figured that if being targeted by an assassin had a silver lining, this was it.

The ride back to Thrasher took a little longer than it should have, mostly because Ramos left the freeway behind and took the side streets instead. He did it for my benefit, and I appreciated the time to unwind and enjoy myself. Plus, it didn't hurt to have an excuse to put my arms around him.

By the time we pulled into the parking garage, I was back to my old self and feeling good. I dismounted and pulled the helmet off my head. "Thanks Ramos." I handed it to him. "That was awesome."

He took it from me with a smile, popping open the trunk to his car, and setting both helmets inside. "I guess I'd better get back, but I'll walk you to your car."

I nodded, and we walked slowly to my car. "I'm glad that went okay. You were right that something could go wrong. Who would have thought he'd plant all those bugs?"

"Yeah...it was a good thing you were there." We stopped at my car, and our gazes met. His desire to hold me in his arms washed over me. My knees went weak, and my breath caught, but he held back at the last minute. A slow smile spread across his lips. "I'll talk to you later."

I could only nod and watch him walk away. With a deep sigh, I turned around and got in my car. I didn't remember driving home so, when I pulled into my garage, I was grateful I hadn't run any red lights or caused an accident.

The kitchen surrounded me with warmth. Being home, safe and sound, filled me with gratitude. It was nice not to worry about an assassin coming after me. Even if I'd only known about him for a few hours, it still took a toll.

Laughter bubbled up from the basement, and I smiled. Josh and Savannah were actually having a good time together. Would wonders never cease? Then I realized how crazy that sounded and listened more closely. Nope...that wasn't Savannah down there.

"Hey!" I yelled. "I'm home!"

The laughter immediately stopped, and Josh called, "Oh...hey mom. Uh...Chloe's here. We're just watching some TV."

"Where's Savannah?" I asked.

"She's at Ashley's house."

I heard some whispering, but I knew it was Chloe telling Josh they ought to go upstairs and talk to me for a minute. I thought that was a good idea, so I took my jacket off and hung it in the closet while they headed up the stairs.

"Hey Chloe. How are you doing?" I asked. "Did you go back to school today?"

"Yeah...but just for half of the day. I found out how far behind I was, but Josh said he'd help me catch up." She glanced at him with a smile, and he turned a nice shade of red.

"That's nice," I said. "Well, at least it's Friday, so you have lots of time over the weekend."

"Yeah, really," she agreed. She bit her bottom lip, trying to decide if she should ask me something about the dead cop she didn't understand.

"Is there something you wanted to ask me?" I prompted.

She caught her breath and glanced up at me. "Yeah...actually there is. I was just wondering...did you ever find out how that cop knew I was staying at Aunt Holly's house?" She'd worried that the police had let it slip, and she felt betrayed. Worse, she'd spent a lot of time wondering what might have happened to her if she had opened the door. Would he have killed her?

"No. I can only guess that he overheard it. But I don't think he was going to kill you. I think he was trying to work things out, and probably wanted to take you someplace where you'd be safe until he found a way to deal with the threat."

She nodded, liking the sound of that scenario lots better than the one she'd thought of. "Really? That's good to know. Thanks for telling me."

"You bet," I said.

"We're going to work on our homework now," Josh broke in, thinking about studying in his room so he could show her his cool videogame posters.

"Okay," I said. "Why don't you go in on the dining room table? There's plenty of room there, and you can spread your work out."

"Sure," Chloe agreed. "My backpack's downstairs. I'll go get it."

"I'll come with you," Josh said, thinking he could still show her his posters. Then he thought about his unmade bed and all of his soccer equipment scattered on the floor and changed his mind. "I want a soda from the fridge. Do you want one?"

I smiled at his quick thinking and escaped to my room to take off my shoes. I was exhausted. My day had started at six-fifteen with Dimples' phone call about Pete's death, and so much had happened since then that it made my head spin. I wanted to lie down for a minute and regroup, but decided I'd better not with two hormonally-charged teenagers downstairs.

I came back to find them busy working at the table and breathed a sigh of relief. Watching them with their heads together was going to take some getting used to. Josh and a girl? At fourteen? I wasn't sure I was ready for that.

An hour later, Chloe's mom came to pick her up. While Chloe got her stuff together, I took the opportunity to ask Kira a few questions. "So how are you holding up after all this?"

"I'm so relieved it's over," she said. "It made me realize how awful our relationship was. I want to fix it, and that means giving her more time with her dad. But that's okay."

"Yeah...kids need both parents in their lives. Um...I was just wondering...did you tell anyone where Chloe was staying? It's just been bothering me that the cop found out."

Guilt washed over her, but she shook her head. "No, it wasn't me. Someone in the police department must have told him."

"Oh...yeah...of course. I'm sure that's what happened."

"Come on Chloe, let's go." Chloe came to her mother's side, worried about her mom's defensive tone of voice.

"Thanks for letting me come over," she said. "Bye Josh."

I closed the door behind them, and a huge weight hit me in the chest. She'd only told one person, and that was her lover, Matt Swenson. If he was the leak, what did he have to do with this? I tried to remember everything I'd heard about him, but the only thing I came up with was that he and Scott were friends. I'd have to call Scott and find out what he knew.

I could also check him out on the Internet, but Chris came home from work before I could, and I was grateful for the excuse to put it off.

After holding Chris in my arms a little longer than normal, he pulled away and glanced at me questioningly. "What's going on?"

"You won't believe the day I've had," I began, and I told him the whole story. I even told him the assassin part. I knew he wouldn't like it but, in this case, it wasn't right to keep it a secret, especially since everything turned out so well in the end. I couldn't always say that.

By the time I got done, he was sitting down at the table and shaking his head. "How do you do it?"

"Do what?" I asked.

"Get into so much trouble?"

"Hey...I saved the day, don't forget that part."

"I know...I know...it's just a lot to take in." He was wondering how this was all going to turn out.

"Yeah, me too," I agreed. "But I think with Blake on the case, he'll help out a lot. I just need to look into Matt Swenson and see if he's involved or if it was just a fluke."

"Uh...can you do it tomorrow?" he asked, checking his watch. It was almost seven-thirty. "I'm starving. What's for dinner?" He was thinking he'd had a pretty big day himself. One of their high-profile clients was getting sued, and he had to go into the office tomorrow.

"Hey...since you won't be here tomorrow, how about we all go out to dinner tonight." I hadn't cooked anything, since going out to dinner was my plan all along, and he'd just given me the perfect excuse. "Go change, and I'll get the kids."

Later that night, I snuggled beside Chris, but I couldn't fall asleep. Every time I closed my eyes, I saw Pete's bullet-riddled body in my mind, then it morphed into Tom's blood-soaked body and then back to Pete's. Had I missed something? The only thing I knew for sure...whoever had murdered them was a cold-blooded killer with plenty of secrets.

I hoped that talking to Matt Swenson would help me put the pieces together, but there was a possibility that he had nothing to do with it. I also worried about what Blake would find on the thumb-drive. Especially since I was pretty sure one of the companies I'd seen receiving a regular payout was PLM Investments. He'd asked Uncle Joey about that before he got the thumb-drive. So what did he know? And how was Uncle Joey involved?

With all that on my mind, it was no wonder I had nightmares.

After seeing Chris off to work Saturday morning, I got Savannah up, and we attended our Saturday-morning Aikido class. We had so much fun throwing each other around that we stayed for two and a half hours. I knew I'd be stiff the next day, but practicing my new moves seemed like a good idea.

Everyone at Aikido was happy to know Billie was going home from the hospital today. I picked up from one of them that it was too bad she couldn't have used her mad

Aikido skills against the intruders but, with a gun involved, a bullet was hard to fight. I didn't have the heart to tell them that it was her own gun she got shot with.

I spent the rest of the day doing laundry and all of the other housework I'd neglected during the week. The leaves were falling, and I enjoyed going outside in the crisp fall air and raking them up, especially once I got my kids to help.

Later, I called Scott about Matt Swenson and found out he owned a realty company, but he also did some consulting work for an investment firm.

"Oh, yeah? What's the name of his realty company?" I asked.

"It's called Countrywide Homes. You've probably seen their signs. They're all over the place."

My breath caught, and a chill went up my spine. That was the realty company on the billboard by the freeway where both Tom and Pete had been killed. It couldn't be a coincidence, could it?

"Uh...Shelby?" Scott asked. "You still there?"

"Yes, sorry. I got distracted. Thanks so much for the info, I'll chat with you later."

I disconnected and sat heavily on my couch. With this new information, Matt had just become my number-one suspect. But how was he tied to all this? I knew Billie was probably home from the hospital by now, so Dimples was with her and I hated to bother him, but this just couldn't wait. I pushed his number and waited for him to pick up.

"Hey Shelby," he answered. "What's up?"

"A lot," I said. "Do you remember Kira's boyfriend? Matt Swenson?"

"Yeah, sure. Why?"

"I think he's involved. He might even be Pete's partner...and probably Tom's killer too." I explained that Kira had told Matt where Chloe was staying. "He probably told Pete, and that's how he knew. And get this...he owns the realty company, Countrywide Homes."

There was silence on Dimple's end before he spoke. "Okay...the leak I get, but what does Countrywide Homes have to do with anything."

"Oh, that...well," I stammered. How could I be such an idiot? Of course he wouldn't get that part since I hadn't told him. "You might find this hard to believe, but I really do get premonitions once in a while...must have come with the knock on the head. Anyway, remember the billboard we were looking at under the freeway? It said Countrywide Homes on it...and I just had a feeling that the killer was tied to that sign. So...now that we know he's the owner of Countrywide Homes, it makes sense. At least to me."

"Hmm...yeah. Okay," he said.

"So what should we do?"

"Um...hang on." I heard some rustling noises in the background followed by voices, then he came back on the phone. "Sorry about that. We just brought Billie home, and I'm helping her get settled. She says 'hi' by the way."

"Oh...right. Tell her 'hi' back."

"I will. Okay...obviously you need to talk to Matt. You can ask him some leading questions and then you'll know exactly what he's..."

"Stop!" I shouted, cutting him off. "Is Billie listening? I don't want her to know my secret."

"Uh...right, sorry."

"Look. How about this? I'll call Matt's office first thing Monday morning and set up an appointment to chat. After I talk to him, I'll call you, and we can decide what to do from there."

"All right, but maybe I should come with you," he said.

"I'm not sure that's a good idea. Having a detective snooping around might tip him off. I think I'd better go by myself."

"But will you be safe? I mean if he's the killer..."

"Hey...I'm not going to go in there and accuse him of murder. I'll just ask a few questions. I'll be fine." I said that quite forcefully, so he'd know I wasn't an idiot.

"Uh...sure. Okay...good."

"If you think of anything before then, just let me know...and tell Billie I'm glad she's home. Oh...and that everyone at Aikido was asking about her, and they're glad she's all right."

Dimples said he would, and we disconnected. Guilt swamped me that I may have been a little hard on him, but he was an easy-going guy; he'd get over it.

I spent the rest of the weekend trying to figure out what to say to Matt without giving myself away. Chris helped calm me down, telling me I was good at getting people to talk, and not to worry so much. Then he reminded me that even if I found out Matt was the killer, we needed some kind of evidence or we were never going to prove it anyway.

"You're right," I agreed. "But maybe he'll think of something that will point to some hard evidence."

"Yeah...that could work," Chris said. His brows furrowed with worry, and he gathered me in his arms. "Just promise me that you won't say anything to provoke him or tip him off. Otherwise, I can't go along with this."

He was remembering how I sometimes said things without thinking, and he didn't want me in a bad situation. It killed him to think I'd be talking to a potential murderer anyway, but he also knew he couldn't ask me not to do it.

This was the part of my life that he both hated and admired. Hated because of all the close calls I'd had, and admired because I was helping people and solving cases that wouldn't be solved otherwise. It put him in a hard spot.

"Oh...Chris, I won't. I've learned a lot, and I'm not going to give myself away. You don't have to worry. Besides, Dimples will be in on everything. I won't make a move or say anything that will get me in trouble."

"I know you mean that, but Shelby..." His intense gaze caught mine, and his hands tightly clutched my upper arms. "I don't like how many times you cross over the line. I'm doing my best, and trying to be supportive, but it's hard. Just... please don't let this be the one time that ends up with you dead. Okay? Promise me?"

I swallowed, sorry that I worried him so much. "Of course I promise...with all my heart. Don't worry, Chris. It will turn out just fine. Besides, he might not even have anything to do with it."

He nodded, relieved by my assurances, but couldn't stop the small wisp of fear he tried to ignore in the back of his mind.

"You shouldn't worry so much," I said. "Now it's making me worried."

"Hmm...well if that's the case, I'll have to see what I can do about putting it out of your mind." His mischievous, but totally sexy grin spread across his face.

"Oh yeah?" I raised my brow in challenge. "How do you plan on doing that?"

He pulled me close and nibbled on my ear until my breath hitched, then deftly trailed kisses to that sensitive spot on my neck. Next, he rained kisses up to my chin, finally capturing my lips with soft, teasing caresses. My heart began to race, and my breath came in little moaning gasps.

"How's this working?" he asked, pulling away just enough to let me answer.

"Pretty good, but I think I need a little more passion to take my mind off it entirely."

He chuckled, but instead of kissing me like I wanted, he started tickling me like a madman. I yelped with laughter until I thought I would die. Then his lips found mine. This time all my worries went right out the window.

Chapter 14

Monday morning dawned with gray overcast skies and a chill in the air. With intermittent rain forecast, gusts of wind pulled more leaves off the trees, sending them rustling into bushes and fences. At eight a.m. sharp, I called the realtor's office to make an appointment with Matt Swenson, but the receptionist told me he wasn't in.

"Today he's at Plum Fidelity, the investment firm he consults with," she said.

"Can I reach him there?"

"Possibly...unless he's in a meeting, but you can talk to the executive assistant and work something out. Let me give you the number." I copied the number down and put the call through.

"Hello, I'm trying to reach Matt Swenson with an important matter," I began. "I know it's short notice, but is there any way I could talk to him today? I only need about five minutes, and I could come in to the office at any time."

"Um...well, let me look at his schedule," the assistant said. "It looks like he might have some free time after the meeting he's in right now, unless it goes over. Say about nine-thirty? Who is this?"

"Shelby Nichols." I was met by silence, so I hurried to explain. "I'm a consultant."

"I know who you are," she said. "This is Kira Peterson."

"Oh!" I said, surprised. "That's great. You can introduce us. I'll see you soon...oh...wait. What's the address again?"

After another moment of silence, she gave it to me, and we disconnected. Whoa. That was unexpected...although in hindsight, I shouldn't have been surprised since he was the 'someone in the office' with whom she was having an affair. I certainly understood her reluctance to have me pop up in the picture, and I hoped it wouldn't be too awkward.

Then it hit me that she might have told Matt all about me and how I'd helped Chloe. If she had, my cover story was blown. On the other hand, it might help me with my questions, since he'd be thinking about Chloe.

I wasn't sure what to do except go ahead with my plan, but it was a little nerve-wracking just the same. I chose my clothes carefully, deciding to dress up a little, and wore black slacks with a chiffon, smoky-green, flowered blouse accented by a black belt and my boots. I topped it off with a black drape-front cardigan and, with my smoky eye shadow, I looked pretty darn good.

After a fortifying swig of antacid, I left home and arrived promptly at nine-fifteen. I was early, but I didn't want to miss my window of opportunity.

As I hurried toward her desk, Kira caught sight of me and flinched a little. She was having second thoughts about introducing me to Matt, even hoping she could keep me away from him since she didn't want me talking about their affair, and I knew I had to do some damage control.

"I forgot that you worked with Matt when I called earlier," I said. "But I'm so glad you do. It's always easier when I talk to a new client when I have a former client vouch for me. You were satisfied with my investigation, right?" I wanted to add 'especially the non-paying part,' but thought I'd save that just in case she needed more persuading.

"What do you mean?" Her brows drew together. "What did he hire you for?"

"Oh...he hasn't hired me yet but, once I get a chance to talk to him, I'm hoping he will," I said, making this up as I went. From her confused expression, I could tell I was doing a terrible job. "Don't worry. This has nothing to do with you. In fact, I can pretend we don't know each other if that will help. You didn't tell him I was working on Chloe's case, did you?"

"No, I didn't, and I would appreciate it if you didn't mention that we know each other," she said, thinking that hiring me was something she didn't want Matt to know.

"I can do that." I smiled, hoping she'd relent.

She pursed her lips, but gave me an affirmative nod, thinking she didn't know why she was protecting Matt anyway. He'd basically told her they were done over the weekend, and her heart was bruised and raw. She'd hoped seeing him today would change things, but he'd completely ignored her. Being here with him was ripping her apart. She never realized how much she hated his condescending ways until they were directed towards her.

Maybe it was over, and she was just kidding herself to think he'd change his mind. In hindsight, she realized that things had gone downhill right after Chloe's disappearance. It all started when Matt found out she'd told the police about her affair with him. He'd been furious.

Her breath hitched, remembering his rage and how scary it was. She never realized he had such a bad temper. But the next day, he'd apologized, and even brought her flowers. He said he wanted to put this episode behind them, and he asked her to tell him everything that was happening with the investigation so he could support her through this hard time.

Of course she told him the little she knew, and they'd shared a wonderful night together. Then, on Friday, he had a complete change of heart. He said he couldn't get over her betrayal and, even though he'd tried, he couldn't trust her anymore. He couldn't worry about their affair coming out, so he had to end it. They were done.

She'd told him it wasn't even her fault. If Chloe hadn't gone with that stupid boy that day, everything would be fine. But he wouldn't listen. His mind was made up. Now, she was left with the unpleasant task of facing him, as if he hadn't stomped on her heart and left it in bloody little pieces.

Wow, she was pretty upset. I pulled away from her sad thoughts and shook my head, feeling sorry for her. Still, it confirmed my suspicions about Matt. Obviously, he'd gotten Kira to share Chloe's hiding place and sent Pete after her. That left me with only one conclusion. He had to be the killer.

The door to the conference room opened, and several men filed out, talking among themselves as they left. Kira jumped up to intercept them and stopped in front of a handsome, distinguished man in his late forties. He made her wait by holding up a finger until he was finished talking, then turned and raised an imperious brow.

"Yes?"

Kira lifted her chin, determined not to let him see the pain he'd caused her. "Excuse me Mr. Swenson, but there's someone here to see you." Kira gestured to me and continued. "She's right over there. Her name's Shelby Nichols." He frowned and took a breath to say he was too busy. Kira picked up on that and quickly added, "And she's a friend of mine."

That caught his attention, and I held my breath as he glanced my way and met my gaze. I smiled brightly and stepped forward to shake his hand. "Mr. Swenson it's an honor to meet you. Thanks so much for seeing me."

"Of course," he responded, giving me the once-over and thinking he liked what he saw. "What can I do for you?" He glanced at his watch, thinking that he didn't want to seem too eager to talk with me, even though he didn't have another appointment for an hour.

"I just have a quick question to ask you. Is there someplace we can talk in private?" I gave him a flirtatious smile and hoped it was enough to pique his interest.

"Yes, certainly," he agreed, taking the bait. "We can go back into the conference room for a minute or two."

"Perfect. Thanks so much."

I'd been thinking of some questions, but coming face to face with a killer was playing havoc with my nerves. I needed to ask him questions about Pete, or Tom, without making him suspicious of me, but how was I going to do that?

Then inspiration struck. As we sat down at the table, I put on my best smile and began. "I understand you're a member of the Fraternal Order of Eagles. Is that right?"

"Oh...yes," he agreed, surprised.

"How long have you been a member?"

"I think it's been about ten years now. My father sponsored me. It's kind of a family thing."

"That's really great. I hear they do wonderful work for all kinds of charities and good causes."

"Yes," he agreed, wondering what I was getting at.

"This may sound silly, but I think I found your tie clip. It's got the symbol of the eagle with the initials F.O.E. on it. Did you ever own something like that?"

"Um...yeah, I did," he said, puzzled. "In fact...my mother gave it to me, but I lost it some time ago. What makes you think the one you found belongs to me?" He thought his mother had something engraved on the back, but he couldn't remember what it was for sure.

My breath caught. It was his! Relief swept over me so powerfully, I could have cried. "Oh...that's easy," I began. "Because of the engraving on the back. It says, *Love Mom*, and the date is from about ten years ago. You probably think I'm crazy, but after I found it and saw what the order was all about, I really wanted to return it to the owner."

"Wow...that's impressive," he said, thinking that for something worth about forty bucks, I was going a little over-board.

"Well..." I rushed to explain. "With that inscription on the back, it seemed like it was a special keepsake. I've been searching for you for about a month now, and it took me some time to find the member of the club who had joined on that date ten years ago."

"Yes, I'm sure it did." He waited expectantly, unwilling to share more, and wondering why I hadn't shown it to him yet, especially if I was so eager to give it back.

I was trying to figure out if giving it back was the right thing. What if it was evidence? But it was too late for that now, and I hoped I hadn't just messed everything up.

"I've got it right here in my purse." Unzipping the inside pocket, I rummaged around until my fingers closed over it. Pulling it out, I smiled and held it up, then handed it to him. "Here you go."

He examined it closely, then turned it over to read the inscription.

"Is it yours?" I asked.

"Yes...this is mine. Thank you. Where did you find it anyway?"

I took a deep breath. This was it. "Under the freeway overpass, not far from the homeless shelter on the other side of town. Have you ever been in that spot before?"

His gaze caught mine with a penetrating glare which quickly vanished as his brows rose in denial. "Uh...no, I haven't. I can't remember where I lost it exactly." His thoughts contradicted his words, and I picked up his memory of struggling with someone in that very spot. It came as a revelation to him that Tom must have pulled the clip off after he'd shot him. He'd always wondered what had happened to it. Now I'd found it there.

His brows drew together in a fierce frown as he contemplated the implications. Did this have something to do with Pete? The fact that he'd killed him in the same spot heightened his sense of self-preservation. How had I figured it out? He'd been so careful. But I must know something, since mentioning that spot seemed a calculated risk to either blackmail him or get him to talk. Overcome with fierce determination, he didn't plan on doing either one.

"Thanks for returning it to me," he said. "I have to go, but would you consider letting me take you to lunch? It's the least I can do, and I'd love to chat some more." He needed to find out how much I knew, or if I was bluffing. He also wanted to know before I did something rash, so he'd have plenty of time to put a stop to it. "I'm free at noon today if that fits with your schedule."

"Um...sure why not? That's very generous of you."

"Great. How about that nice, Italian restaurant downtown, The Farfalle? You know it?"

"Yeah, sure. I'll meet you there," I agreed.

We both stood, and he reached out to shake my hand. "Thank you Shelby. What kind of work do you do again?"

It took a strength of will to place my hand in his, and I let go as fast as I could, forcing myself not to rub my palm against my pants. "I have my own consulting agency, but I'm like a private investigator as well, so I do all kinds of interesting work."

He smiled, but raised his brow. "Like finding lost items and returning them to their owners?"

"That's definitely part of it," I agreed. "There are also some things people don't want found, and I help with that too."

As his direct gaze caught mine, he was thinking, *and do you charge them an arm and a leg to keep their secrets? Is that your angle?* He opened the conference room door, then motioned to let me go out in front of him. As I passed him, I caught a blaze of anger toward me along with his sudden desire to plunge a knife through my neck.

My eyes widened, and the hairs on the back of my neck stood on end. As a chill swept down my spine, it took all my willpower to keep from hunching my shoulders.

"See you soon," he said.

I nodded and smiled, but couldn't manage to make my mouth work around the menace he sent my way. With his gaze drilling holes through my back, I tried not to run to the elevators or hyperventilate. My stomach churned, and my fingers shook as I pushed the call button, but I kept my back to him just the same.

Then I caught his thoughts that he needed to ask Kira how she knew me, and if I had been involved in Chloe's case. How else would I have known about him? She was the only link that tied him to Pete's death. Did Kira know more than he thought? Had she overheard a phone conversation or seen a text message? He'd been so careful, it was hard to believe he'd messed up. Too bad he'd broken things off with her, but he felt confident she would fall prey to his charms again. He just had to...

The elevator doors closed, and I lost his train of thought. With three other people in the elevator, I had to keep my cool and act normal, even though my heart raced. I felt a little guilty that I'd left Kira to fend for herself, but I had hope that she could hold her own.

Besides, what could he do to her in the short time before lunch? I didn't think he'd kill her. Plus, she didn't know anything, so it was a dead end anyway.

I got in my car and locked all the doors, then slowly exhaled and tried to think straight. I pulled out my phone to call Dimples, relieved more than I could say that he knew my secret and I could just be upfront about what I'd heard.

"I talked to Matt," I blurted, after Dimples answered. "It's definitely him. What should I do?"

"Wow! That's huge. Why don't you come down to the station, and we'll figure it out."

"Okay, I'm on my way."

Well...that was quick. I started up the car and began the short drive, arriving at the station a few minutes later. After slipping on my ID badge, I left my car and hurried inside, grateful to find Dimples waiting for me.

"Good job, Shelby," he said with a smile. "We're meeting in the chief's office." He ushered me down the hall, thinking this was the break we needed and he was so proud of me.

That lifted my spirits, and my lips turned up in a smile. It lasted until I stepped inside the office and found the chief, Bates, and Blake, all waiting with bated breath to hear my story. I had hoped to tell Dimples what I'd heard from Matt, but how was I supposed to do that with all of them here?

After greeting everyone, I sat down and tried to figure out where to start. "Okay...so, I believe Matt is our prime suspect. He's the only one who knew where Chloe was staying...because Kira told him...and he must have told Pete, and that's why he showed up at Holly's house."

They pretty much knew that part already, so what else did I have? I licked my lips and told them about the tie clip. "After he examined it, he said it was his, but I had to let him have it. I hope that's all right."

Blake was the only one who agreed with me, where the others were having heart attacks that I'd given it away. "What did he say to make you believe it was him?" Blake asked.

Now I had to come up with something quick. "He didn't really say anything, but I got lots of good premonitions about him. When I mentioned that I'd found the tie clip under the freeway, I got a flash of a dead body propped up against the pillar, just how we found Pete...and the same with that other guy, Tom. He said he lost the tie clip about a year ago...which is when Tom was murdered there. See? It's got to be him."

Blake raised a brow. "So that's it?" He was thinking that, without evidence, even if it looked like he was the killer, it still added up to absolutely nothing.

"No," I said. "From our conversation, I think he has an idea that I know something. He's probably assuming that I'm going to use it as leverage to get him to pay for my silence. He invited me to lunch, and I think he hopes to find out how much I know and what my terms are. So I'm meeting him at noon today."

I had decided to leave the realty company part out, but had totally forgotten about his consulting work. "I also found out that he's a consultant for an investment firm. Does that help?"

This time Blake's gaze sharpened, and excitement buzzed over him. He was thinking that could be the missing link. "What's the name of the firm?"

"Plum Fidelity. Ever heard of them?"

"No...but it sounds familiar. I'll have to check my notes and see." He glanced at me, then at the others in the room. "Since this is my investigation, I'll call the shots." The other men nodded their agreement, but I just shrugged. I mean, seriously, what did it matter?

"We don't have a lot of time to get things set up, so here's the plan. I have a bug Shelby can wear on her sweater. It looks like a pin, so he won't notice it." Blake turned his gaze to me. "You'll try and get him to talk about Pete. Maybe get him to say something incriminating. Say you have evidence even though you don't, or something like that. Do you think you can do that? I don't have a lot of time to train you, but I might be able to give you some pointers once things are ready to go."

I opened my mouth to agree, but Dimples broke in. "Sir, that won't be necessary. Shelby is a natural at getting people to talk. We've seen it a lot here, right chief? She's the best. You don't have to worry about training her. She'll know what to say."

Blake's brows lifted in surprise at the praise Dimples heaped on me, then he nodded and held back a smile, clearly understanding that Dimples had a lot of admiration for me...kind of like Manetto. I must have some real talent to impress both of them.

"Good," he agreed. "We'll have a surveillance van parked nearby, and we'll be listening to everything Shelby says. To be on the safe side, I'd also like to have one of you..." he nodded toward Dimples and Bates, "in the restaurant for back up."

"I'll do it," Bates said, standing and pulling his pants up around his waist. "I know that place. I can sit at the end of the bar and see everything from there."

My heart sank. Why did he have to volunteer? I'd much rather have Dimples inside.

"All right," Blake agreed. He glanced at me to see if I'd object, so I kept my mouth shut. "Let's get started."

We had a little over an hour to get the van ready, the bug on my sweater, and Bates inside the restaurant. Before they put the bug on me, I gave Chris a call to let him know what was going on. Happy that I wasn't going to be alone, he begged me to ask Blake if he could sit in the van and listen to the whole thing. Thankfully, Blake turned down that request pretty quick, and I was glad he did. I hoped that didn't make me a bad wife, but I was nervous enough as it was and didn't want to be distracted by my husband.

The time passed quickly and, since they had to leave early to get into place, I was left behind to twiddle my thumbs. I thought about using the restroom but nixed that idea. With the bug on my sweater, I knew they'd pick up every little sound. Just thinking about it tightened my stomach, and I tried to calm down before I made myself sick and had to use it for real.

I also couldn't hear anything from their end of things, so I felt like I was in the dark, but at least I had backup, and I took comfort in that.

I drove to the restaurant with my stomach a bundle of nerves. Even though I was grateful Dimples had such confidence in me, I wasn't so sure I could pull it off. I mean, talking to Matt earlier didn't seem nearly as scary as it did this time.

Now it was like both my job and my reputation were on the line, and the pressure was killing me. Turning on the radio and singing along usually worked to calm me down, but with this damn bug, I couldn't even do that.

Parking was limited on the street, so I pulled into the public parking plaza near the restaurant and parked on the upper level. Before opening the car door, I took a deep breath, then slowly let it out. Talking to Matt wasn't that big of a deal. I could do this. What was the worst that could happen anyway? At least I didn't have to worry about getting shot, or killed, right?

With renewed confidence, I hurried to the elevator and rode it to the street level. I pushed through the parking plaza doors onto the sidewalk and began my short trek to the restaurant. Without trying to be too obvious, I glanced up and down the street for signs of the van but couldn't see it anywhere. Before letting the flutter of panic take root, I reasoned that it was probably just around the corner out of sight, and tried to quit worrying.

I hesitated at the restaurant doors, then swallowed my fear and pulled the door open. I smiled at the hostess and told her I was meeting someone. She looked over me with interest. From Matt's description of me, she knew I was the one meeting him and wondered who I was, especially since he'd asked for the table in the back corner that was more private.

"Right this way," she said.

As I followed her through the restaurant, I glanced toward the bar near the back and found Bates sitting in the corner with a drink in his hand. He ignored me, but I knew from his thoughts that he'd seen me come in. I listened to his thoughts pretty hard, needing to know if he was ready to protect me with his life.

Since I knew how he felt about me most of the time, I figured he'd probably just as soon have me dead but, from what I could pick up, he seemed to take his role seriously.

That came as kind of a shock, but it also relieved some of my nervous tension.

I knew it the minute Matt caught sight of me. His thoughts hit me with enough animosity to send emotional daggers through my heart. He was pissed. I caught that he'd tried to get Kira to open up about me, but she had refused to talk to him. That brought a smile to my lips and, all at once, I wanted to nail this sucker flat.

Matt smiled back, thinking I looked too smug for my own good, and he couldn't wait to take me down a notch or two. He stood while I took my seat. "Thanks for joining me," he said, pouring on the charm. "I still can't get over it."

"What?" I asked.

"All the work you did to give me back that tie-clip."

"Oh...well, like I said, I'm pretty good at finding things. I sort of have a natural talent for it."

"I believe it," he agreed. He was thinking he needed to keep his cool, no matter what I said, and try and get under my skin so I'd tell him where all of this was coming from.

The waiter filled our glasses with water and asked for our drink order. After he left, I glanced through the menu, hardly seeing what was listed. I found my favorite, Chicken Marsala, and set the menu down. I'd order it but, with my stomach a bundle of nerves, I wasn't sure how much of it I could eat.

Matt set his menu down as well, thinking he'd order the lasagna, and turned his attention to me. "So tell me about yourself. You said you had your own consulting agency. What do you do?"

"Well...let's see. One of my first clients was a bank manager. The bank had been robbed, and he hired me to find the missing money. Even though the bank robber was captured, he wouldn't disclose where he'd hidden the money. Then he was killed during his trial, and the trail went cold."

"So...did you find it?"

"Yes I did," I said, proudly. "After that, I got a lot of cases, some big, some not so big. I've also helped the police as a consultant from time to time."

"Anything you're working on now?" he asked.

"Yes, but I don't think I'm allowed to talk about it. So...tell me about yourself."

The waiter came back to take our orders, then left with the menus, and Matt told me about his realty business and how he got started. By the time he'd finished, our food orders had arrived. I actually ate some of it, realizing that, as much as I didn't want to be with him, he'd managed to put me at ease. That ended once he came back to the reason he'd asked me there.

"So Shelby," he began. "Tell me...how did you find my tie clip? I'd like to hear that story."

"Sure." My stomach tensed, and I couldn't take another bite. I blotted my lips with my napkin and took a sip of water to calm my sudden bout of nerves. "I was actually there the other day. One of the detectives I've worked with was murdered there, and the chief called me in. After they took the body away, I was scouring the area for clues and found your clip in a crack in the concrete."

Matt's brows rose. "That's nuts. I wonder how it got there."

This was my chance, so I went for the jugular. "I think it was probably when you killed Tom Souvall there a year ago. He must have pulled the clip off of your tie in the struggle before you shot him."

Shock ran through his body, but he hid it well, then scrunched his brows together in confusion and managed to straighten in his chair like he was offended. "Wow. That's quite an accusation. You don't waste any time do you? But just so you know, I've never heard of anyone by that name."

"Oh, I think you have," I countered. "But what I don't get is why you killed Pete in the same place. Was it some kind of arrogance on your part? Or did it have something to do with the drugs."

This time Matt's eyes narrowed, and worry stopped his breath. How in the hell did I know that? "I don't know where you're getting your information Shelby, but you couldn't be more wrong."

"Hmm...I don't think so. What I think is that you and Pete had a nice drug ring going, but he got cold feet when you ordered him to kill Chloe. After that, you were afraid he'd turn on you, so you killed him. See? That wasn't so hard to figure out."

Matt tightened his lips into a thin line, thinking I could make all the accusations I wanted, but that didn't mean I had any proof. He was safe from me. Still, he couldn't figure out where my information had come from. Most of his crew had no idea he was the big boss. That left only one person. Anthony Kerby. Had he let something slip? Sometimes he was too cocky for his own good.

He caught my gaze and sneered. "You talk a lot," he said. "But talk is cheap. Where's your proof?"

I smiled and raised my brow. "Oh, I have proof. If you don't believe me, just call my bluff, and I'll take it straight to the police." He shook his head, thinking I was a piece of work, so I pushed him a little harder. "I know where the gun is."

"That's impossible," he gasped, but sweat popped out on his upper lip. He should have gotten rid of the damn thing instead of locking it up in his safe at work, but he never thought Pete's death would be traced back to him. Not in a million years.

"No it's not," I said, knowing I should probably relay that information to Blake as soon as possible so they could get it first. "It's in your safe at your realty office. Not too bright of you, but you had no idea I'd find out, did you?"

His mouth dropped open in shock. He'd never told a soul about that. Not one single person. "That's insane. You're...wait a minute. This is crazy. You don't know what you're talking about. You're just guessing...and you're wrong. I don't even own a gun."

He was scrambling now, so I decided to push a little more. "Your drug business has me puzzled though. What does Anthony Kerby have to do with it? How did he get involved? You made some kind of a deal with him, right?"

"Stop. Just stop." He didn't know how I did it, but every time I asked a question, it was like I plucked the answers right out of thin air. "No more questions. We're done here." He threw his napkin on the table, jumped up, and practically ran out of the restaurant.

I glanced at Bates, who nearly dropped his drink, and he hurried to grab some bills out of his wallet. He threw them on the bar before taking off after him.

"Um...in case you don't know," I said out loud. "Matt just ran off. I hope you got that stuff about the gun in his safe. You should probably send someone to his office to get it first, before he gets there. Oh...and I think he's carrying a gun on him somewhere, so you'd better warn Bates. He just took off after him. Uh...I guess I'll pay the bill and leave now. Then I'll head back to the precinct."

The waiter stopped with the bill, mid-stride, and wondered who I thought I was talking to. "Is everything all right?" he asked, handing me the check.

"Oh, sure. Thanks. My...uh...friend had an emergency." The waiter nodded and quickly left, thinking I was a little crazy and wondering if I'd forgotten my medication or something. I smiled and shook my head, then paid the bill with cash. I slipped the receipt into my purse and hoped that I'd get reimbursed. That was an expensive lunch, and it was the least the FBI could do, right?

I let out my breath and stood, ready to get out of there. Matt had surprised me with his abrupt departure, but he was spot on about how I was getting my information. Plus, I'd gotten what we needed to put him away, so I couldn't feel too bad. I just hoped it wasn't too good of a show, since I didn't want Blake to get any ideas.

My step was lighter on the way back to my car, and I could hardly believe it was over. I'd need to talk to Matt some more to get the whole story about the deal he made with Anthony Kerby but, once he was arrested, I was sure Dimples would let me do that.

I took the elevator to the top level of the parking garage, filled with relief and satisfaction that I'd done a good job. Even better, my life was never in danger. Chris would be so pleased that I'd kept my promise.

I stepped out of the elevator, and a rush of pure hatred filled my mind. Before I could take a breath, Matt grabbed my upper arms and shoved me up against the wall. He pulled out a gun and held it to my head while his eyes burned with anger. "How did you know?" he growled, his teeth clenching with rage. "Who told you?"

He pushed the gun so hard against my head that I thought my neck might break. "I'll tell you, I swear...just back off. I can't talk when you're hurting me." My eyes filled with tears of pain and fear.

Seeing this, Matt eased up with the gun. His breath whooshed in and out like he'd just run a marathon, but he managed to get enough control to speak. "I don't really care if it hurts, so start talking before I put a bullet through your head." He planned to do that anyway but was willing to wait until I told him everything.

If I was going to get out of this alive, I knew I needed to stall long enough for my backup to get there, and I prayed they were still listening. "Okay...I'll tell you everything. Just, please don't kill me, okay?"

"Sure," he agreed. My fear soothed him, putting him back in the driver's seat, and he lost that crazy gleam in his eyes. "All I need is a name...so start talking."

I swallowed and closed my eyes, knowing that as soon as I told him, he was going to shoot me. "Okay...but it's a little more complicated than that. You see...I found that tie clip, and then there was that billboard sign near the freeway. It was for Countrywide Homes. So that gave me a connection between you and the murder since the pin was yours and...you own the real estate company."

"What are you talking about? You think I'm an idiot or something?" He moved his free hand to grab me by the neck and started squeezing. I clawed at his fingers to pry them loose, but he held me too tight. Gasping for air, I let go and brought my hands up to poke him in the eyes.

He saw it coming and let go of my neck, moving his arm and body to trap me against the wall. As I wheezed air into my lungs, he watched with satisfaction that I was suffering.

"Okay," he sneered. "I'll give you one more chance. The name... now." He cocked the gun against my head, and I squeezed my eyes shut. He was going to kill me anyway, so I wasn't about to tell him anything. As tears coursed down my face, I sent a silent thought to Chris, telling him I was sorry for breaking my promise.

"Drop your weapon! Now!"

Matt tensed in surprise but yanked me around in front of him, using me as a shield. He held me in a choke hold with his elbow around my neck and kept the gun pointed at my head. "Get back!" he shouted. "I'll kill her, I swear it."

Blake, Dimples and Bates all had their guns pointed at us. From their thoughts, I knew each one of them wanted to take a head shot at Matt, but none of them trusted their accuracy enough to do it.

Blake was the first to raise his gun in surrender, and the others soon followed. "Let her go, Matt," Blake said. "It's over."

"No it's not," he hissed. "Put your guns down." He was thinking that if he could get me to my car, he might still be able to get away. Right now, there were only three of them, but he had to act quickly before any more cops showed up. He took a few steps in that direction, dragging me with him, but stopped to yell. "I said put your guns down! On the ground!"

Dimples and Bates did as he asked, but Blake hesitated. He knew if we got in a car I was dead, and he'd rather take his chances here and now. Matt recognized his hesitation and pulled the gun from my head to point it at Blake.

In that moment, I used every ounce of strength I could summon and, as swiftly as I could, pulled down on his elbow, took a quick step back, and grabbed his wrist, just like I'd learned at Aikido. I forcefully pushed outward with his elbow still bent, pushing down with all my might, to throw Matt forward to his knees.

The gun slipped from his hand before he could get a shot off, and I heard a satisfying pop as the bone in his arm broke. He screamed in pain, but I kept pushing him forward, forcing him to lay flat on the ground until his face was mashed against the asphalt. I held him there, even as he screamed, not about to back off until I knew he was completely subdued.

Dimples rushed to my side and grabbed Matt's arm. "I've got him Shelby, you can let go now."

It took a few seconds for Dimples' words to register. With a heavy breath, I relinquished my hold and stepped back. Dimples cuffed Matt's hands behind his back, happily ignoring his groans of pain, then stood and wrapped his arm around me while Bates took over.

My breath hitched, and I sagged against Dimples. Then my legs began to shake, and I was afraid I'd collapse, so I turned into his chest and wrapped both my arms around him, holding on for dear life. He held me close, patting me on the back and telling me over and over that I was safe now, and everything was all right.

A few minutes later, I felt strong enough to pull away and wipe the tears from my eyes. By then, a whole boatload of cops and FBI had arrived. As I tried to take it all in, the scene took on a surreal quality. I stayed close to Dimples, and mostly responded when someone talked to me but, for some reason, an odd detachment had come over me.

I hardly noticed when someone put a blanket around my shoulders and escorted me to a car where I could sit down. They even handed me a few tissues along with my purse, and I gratefully blew my nose and dabbed at my eyes. Several minutes later, Blake came to the car and crouched beside the open door.

"How are you doing?" he asked. His hazel eyes held a hint of worry, and he was thinking that I was in a state of shock. He hoped I snapped out of it soon because, if I didn't, he'd have to send me to the hospital, and he really wanted to talk to me while it was still fresh in my mind.

My eyes widened. I was in shock? No wonder I felt so strange. That realization cleared the cobwebs out of my head, and I sat up a little straighter. "I think I'm doing better. Lots better. In fact...I think I'm ready to finish this up and talk about it. Uh...get de-briefed or whatever it is you call it."

"Yeah?" he asked, his brows lifting. He thought that was a quick recovery, but he'd take it, even if it meant I might crash later. "That would be great if you could. I've already sent Matt to the precinct with Harris and Bates. I could drive you in your car if that's okay."

They were gone? How had I missed that? I glanced around. There were only two police cars left in the lot, and I was sitting in one of them. "What about his arm? Didn't I break it?

Blake smiled and shrugged. "His shoulder's dislocated, not broken. I thought we'd get someone to pop it back in once we were through questioning him."

"Oh." I nodded, then grinned back at him. "Sounds good to me."

"Let's go," Blake said, and he helped me stand. Since I wasn't cold anymore, I left the blanket on the seat and walked with Blake to my car.

"I could probably drive," I told him, getting the keys out of my purse.

Instead of answering, he just took them from my hand. With a polite smile that brooked no arguments, he opened the passenger-side door and waited for me to sit before shutting me in. Once he started driving, I was grateful for more time to recover before I had to negotiate through the busy traffic.

"Where did you learn how to throw a person like that?" Blake asked, thinking he'd never been so shocked. If anyone looked like a damsel in distress, it was me. But then I pull something off like that? It surprised him and, more important, completely caught Matt off guard.

"I take Aikido. I just started, but that's a move I've been working on."

"Nice," he said, thinking it probably saved my life.

"Yeah," I agreed. Coming so close to death washed over me with a vengeance, sending a river of dread over every inch of my body. I closed my eyes and concentrated on breathing evenly until it passed.

"Um...just so you know, your husband called," Blake said. "I told him the basics but smoothed over the part where Matt held a gun to your head. No use getting your husband all upset now that it's over. I told him you'd call him after we were done."

"Oh...good, thanks for telling me." I'd totally forgotten about calling Chris. Thank goodness Blake had talked to him, and I could fill him in later when I was more composed.

It wasn't long before Blake parked at the precinct and turned to face me. "Before we go in, I just have to say that I've never seen anything like what you did. Your technique was..." he hesitated. "A bit unconventional...and your questions...it was like you asked him something, and then told him the answer." He was thinking that it was the answers that broke Matt, probably because they were right. How had I done that? It couldn't have been a lucky guess. He never would have put those same things together like I had, and he was an expert.

"Thanks," I said. "I guess it's my psychic ability at work. Sometimes I get these images in my mind, so I just go with it." Not wanting to discuss it further, I opened the car door and got out, leaving Blake to follow behind.

Even though I wasn't anxious to face Matt again, I wanted to get this part over with so I could go home and take a bath. But I still had my work cut out for me, and worrying that Blake would figure things out wasn't helping.

We spotted Dimples near the chief's office. He smiled with relief to see me, and he held up a cell phone. "This is how he knew where you were parked. He got a text telling him. I guess he had someone watching you."

"Oh yeah? I wondered about that," I said, even though the thought hadn't even crossed my mind.

"He's this way," Dimples said.

Dimples led us to an interrogation room where we found Bates and the chief discussing the case. The chief smiled and told me I'd done a good job. I thanked him, then picked up that Bates wanted to tell me I'd done a good job too, but the words got stuck in his throat. He was feeling guilty that Matt had slipped through his fingers after he left the restaurant, and it was his fault Matt got to me.

Twisting his lips, he caught my gaze. "Hey...listen Shelby, I'm sorry I lost Matt. I should have done a better job."

Wow...that was a shock. I should probably enjoy it while it lasted. "Thanks Bates, I appreciate it. I think he took us all by surprise. I'm just glad it turned out okay."

"That's for sure," he agreed, mentally wiping his forehead that I'd taken it so well. "That guy's a piece of work, isn't he?"

We glanced through the mirror to find Matt sitting in a slouched position with his hands cuffed to the table in front of him. "The chief made us pop his arm back in the socket," he explained. "I didn't want to, but Matt was threatening a lawsuit, and the chief wanted to play it by the book."

"That's fine," Blake said, expecting no less. "I'm taking Shelby in with me to question him." He turned to me. "You ready?"

"Yes," I agreed, even though my legs shook a little. I followed Blake inside and sat across the table from Matt.

"I'm not saying a word until my lawyer gets here," Matt said, freezing me with cold fury. But then I picked up that the fury was a front for the fear that surged over him. He was afraid of me and thought I was some kind of a crazy lunatic. The things I did weren't natural.

That settled me down, and I smiled. "That's okay, Matt. I don't really need you to talk. I can read you pretty good. Right now you're showing anger but, behind it, you're really just scared." Wow...that was probably not the smartest thing for me to tell him, but it sure felt good.

"So how does Anthony Kerby play into all this? Pete was in on your drug ring, I know that much. His time as an undercover narcotics agent helped you find the dealers and set up shop. But Anthony made some kind of a deal with you. What's his job anyway?"

Matt shook his head and held his lips tightly together, but it didn't do him any good. "Oh my gosh!" I exclaimed, and I turned to Blake. "Anthony Kerby is the assistant state's attorney involved with the prosecution of drugs and narcotics. No wonder he's part of this."

I glanced back at Matt, whose face had paled to a pasty white. "He made a deal with you. Inside knowledge on pending cases and, with Pete's help, dropping charges against your people. Of course, he got a big cut of the profits, but it goes even deeper than that..."

Matt was a fountain of information but, with each revelation, he was starting to close down. He kept thinking that this couldn't be happening, and it was hard to get to the knowledge behind his panic. Then I found it.

"Grayson Sharp?" I blurted. "He's in on it too?"

"Stop!" he said. "What are you doing to me? You're violating my rights. Get her away from me."

Up until now, Blake had watched this exchange with quiet fascination, but Matt's reaction floored him. Matt obviously thought I was doing something to his mind to get the information. Blake glanced at me wondering if Matt was right. My premonitions were nothing like he'd thought.

Accurate and succinct. Not guesses at all. Somehow I knew, and it blew him away. How did I do it?

Damn it all! I was doing too good of a job, and now Blake wondered about me. This could go very wrong. I had to say something, so I chuckled and shook my head. "I'm not doing anything to you, Matt. It must be your guilty conscience. I guess killing two people will do that. I get why you killed Pete, but what about Tom? Why did you kill him?"

Matt shook his head, thinking he wasn't even going to think about it.

"He figured it out, didn't he?" I said, pushing him to remember. "He knew you from your charity work with the Fraternal Order of Eagles. He confronted you, so you killed him. You might as well tell us. The gun in your safe will confirm it's a match for the murder weapon, so it's not just me making this up."

"Shut the hell up," he said. "Where's my lawyer? I want my lawyer."

I wasn't sure I should keep up with my questions. I'd gotten the main points out of him, but if I pushed any harder, Blake was sure to figure out what I did. Maybe it was time to back off.

"Let's get back to Grayson Sharp," Blake asked, surprising me. "How does he fit in with all this?"

Of course, Matt didn't answer, but I heard it in his mind. Should I say something? Had I gone past the point of no return? Blake glanced at me and cocked his eyebrow, waiting for my response.

"I think the thumb-drive we gave you has something to do with it," I answered. "It's all tied up with Matt's realty business and his investment firm." I closed my eyes and concentrated on Matt's thoughts. "I think Grayson Sharp helped with the sale of the properties...or I should say the drug houses, through some deal he made. Matt bought them, then sold them to fake buyers under the umbrella of his investment firm...or something like that."

Matt's jaw dropped open, and he glanced at me with horror. This was unraveling so fast it made his head spin. He hadn't said a word, but I knew. How? Just a few hours ago, he had everything under control. Then I walked into his life, and it all fell apart. What the hell was going on? Who was I? What was I?

"Uh...I'm not feeling so well," I said. "Can I go now?" There was more that I'd picked up from Matt, and the implications hit me like a one-two punch to my stomach, sending a wave of queasiness over me.

"Of course," Blake answered, concerned. He quickly stood and walked me to the door, thinking I looked like I might throw up or pass out. Opening the door, he ushered me into the hall where Dimples stood waiting. "Make sure she gets home safely," Blake said, handing Dimples the keys to my car. He turned to me. "Thanks Shelby, we couldn't have done it without you. Get some rest. I'll talk to you later."

I nodded my head and gratefully took Dimples' arm. He walked me from the building, concerned that my sudden sickness had something to do with what I'd heard in Matt's mind. "Are you all right?" he asked.

"Yeah," I lied. "But all of this has suddenly caught up to me."

"I can see that," he agreed. "Did you hear something that upset you?"

"Well...a lot of it upset me, but I think it's the nearly-getting-killed-part that's hitting me so strong. I just need to go home and lie down." I hoped Dimples bought it, especially since it was partly true. "Do you think you can drive me home?"

"Sure," he said. "Give me a minute and I'll arrange for someone to follow us to your place."

It wasn't long before Dimples pulled my car into my garage. He even unlocked the garage door for me to go inside. He was bursting with questions, but wisely kept them to himself, although in reality I heard every one of them and chose not to answer.

He handed me the keys. "I didn't tell you this, but what you did today...it was simply amazing. I can't tell you how proud I am to know you." He smiled, but wasn't quite finished. "Look, I can tell something's bothering you, and I think I know what it is. You're worried that everyone will figure out that you're reading people's minds, but it's not going to happen. Unless you tell them, they won't believe it, I promise. Having premonitions is the perfect way to explain it, and I think they'll accept that and won't think it's anything else, so try not to worry. Okay? Everything will be fine."

"Wow...that was exactly what I was thinking. Are you sure you can't read minds?" I teased. This time his grin broadened, sending his dimples into swirling whirlwinds. "Thanks for driving me home...and coming to my rescue...and everything. I'm glad to have you on my side, and don't worry...I don't regret telling you my secret."

He chuckled, since that thought was rattling around in his mind. "Good. Get some rest."

I closed and locked the door, grateful to have the house to myself and time to gain some composure before I faced my family. I ran a bath and filled it with my soothing eucalyptus-scented bubble bath, hoping it would somehow calm me down.

It wasn't until I had soaked in the tub for a few minutes that the full weight of what I'd heard from Matt hit me, and I knew I had to face it. The awful truth that Uncle Joey was involved in the whole thing shouldn't come as such a big surprise, given that he was a mob-boss, but it certainly wasn't something I wanted to know.

I wasn't prepared to deal with it. But I also knew that if this came out, he was going to prison for a long time. That probably meant Ramos and most everyone else in his crew would end up there too. As a sinking feeling that I had just doomed them all flooded over me, tears started flowing down my cheeks. I didn't know what to do, or how to help, but I had to do something. Was it too late?

Matt had been thinking of the deal between Grayson Sharp and Uncle Joey where, in return for looking the other way on some of his business dealings, Uncle Joey had agreed to sell the drug houses to Matt and let him take over the business. But what made my stomach ache the most...I was pretty sure Uncle Joey was still taking a cut of the profits, and the proof was probably on that thumb-drive.

Before I changed my mind, I got out of the tub and called Uncle Joey.

"Shelby," he answered. "How are you doing?"

The sound of his voice hit me so strong that I burst into tears. "I'm so sorry, but I think I just messed up. Real bad. You'll probably want to kill me now."

"What's happened? Are you hurt?"

His voice held real concern, which made it even harder to explain through my tears, but I did my best, finally ending with telling him that Blake had the thumb-drive with proof of money transfers into his investment company. "I didn't tell them about Matt's thoughts about you, but I'm worried that Blake will figure it out from the information on the thumb-drive, or it might come out from Grayson Sharp himself, if he's ever charged with anything."

"I see," Uncle Joey said. He took a deep breath and let it out. "This is disturbing news Shelby but, whether you believe it or not, I'm innocent. I did give a large campaign donation to Grayson Sharp in the form of several properties, but I'm not in the drug business...anymore."

"Really?" I said, hopeful for the first time.

"Yes, but that doesn't mean they won't come after me. That company is not mine, so I think I may have been set up but, thanks to you, I can get my lawyers on it right away. Try not to worry too much, and if I need to, I can have a nice chat with Blake."

"Oh...okay," I said. What did that mean? Did he have something on Blake?

"In the meantime, please tell your husband everything. If we do end up in court, I'll want him to represent me. And you can help him. But I doubt it will get that far."

"Right...okay."

"Good. Get some rest, and I'll call you soon."

We disconnected, and I set the phone down, surprised that I felt a little better.

The kids came home, bringing some normalcy back into my life. I even got dinner made, and managed to act normal when Chris walked in the door. He was so proud of me and, with a brief explanation, told the kids that I'd solved the case. We even went out for ice cream to celebrate.

It wasn't until later that I broke down and told him the rest of the story. "I'm so grateful for my Aikido training."

Chris sat open-mouthed, so I quickly went on to explain my little chat with Uncle Joey as well. At the end, Chris let out a big sigh, and tightened his arms around me.

"Shelby," he said, shaking his head in exasperation. "What am I going to do with you?" I shrugged, not knowing what to say. "It's all right," he said, kissing the top of my head. "We'll figure it out. Try not to worry. I'm a great lawyer. We'll get through this."

As much as I appreciated how good of a lawyer he was, I still couldn't vanquish the worry that tightened my stomach and, until this was resolved, I knew it wasn't going anywhere.

Chapter 15

The next morning I got a call from Billie. "Shelby! I'm so glad you're all right. Drew told me what happened. I'm sorry I missed out on all the action, but he said you used an Aikido move to take him down! I'm so proud of you." I thanked her, and she continued. "Did you hear the news about Grayson Sharp?" she asked.

"What news?"

"He resigned this morning. Isn't that something? I think Drew said they were getting the evidence together to arrest him and his assistant attorney, Anthony Kerby. I guess it's all hitting the fan now. Since I have the inside scoop, I'm writing the first of several articles for the paper, isn't that great? But don't worry, I'm doing it from home."

"That's good," I said, grateful I still had her copy of the thumb-drive. There was no way I was going to give it to her now. Hopefully, she wouldn't ask for it. "So how are things going with you and Drew?"

She sighed. "Things couldn't be better. I really love him, you know? He's just the best man I know."

"He is," I agreed. "I'm so happy for you." We chatted a little longer before disconnecting, and I hoped with all my heart that things worked out between them.

Not an hour later, I got the call from Blake I'd been expecting, asking me to meet him at the precinct. Naturally, I agreed, but couldn't stop the trepidation that curdled my stomach.

Last night, Chris said he didn't want me talking to the police about the case since I'd basically incriminated myself by alerting Uncle Joey, making me an accessory to whatever he might be charged with...if he got charged...which was still up for debate. But I needed to find out what Blake knew and what he was going to do about the whole thing.

I arrived with time to spare and an enthusiastic hug from Dimples. It made me feel better until I wondered what he'd think of me if he knew I was working with Uncle Joey. I shoved that unhappy thought away and hurried into the chief's office where Blake awaited me.

"Thanks for coming," Blake said. He'd closed the blinds for privacy and was thinking how much I puzzled him. Whose side was I on? I'd definitely helped his investigation, but I'd also alerted Manetto. It put him in a tight spot, but he thought he had a solution. Although he had to admit it was a solution that completely rested on my shoulders. What would I do?

If I wasn't nervous before, I certainly was now.

"I just wanted to give you an update," he began, coming to sit beside me on the couch, wanting his close proximity to garner my trust. "Matt still hasn't said a word, but we found the gun in his safe like you said, and we're formally charging him with the murder of both Tom and Pete, along with kidnapping and attempted murder on your life."

"Okay," I said. "Did you find out any more about the whole drug thing?"

"Yes." He paused, glancing at his hands, knowing that I wouldn't like what he had to say. "It looks like Manetto was involved, but I think you already knew that, since you called to tell him."

I could deny it, but I didn't, locking my gaze with his instead.

Blake sighed, realizing that I wasn't going to make this easy. "Look, this is off the record, so I'm going to be straight with you. From everything I've found, I think Manetto was set up, but that doesn't mean some lunatic in the state's attorney's office won't file charges. Even if an indictment comes down against him, I don't think there's enough evidence for it to go to trial, but I don't know for sure."

He was thinking that if Manetto had sold PLM Investments like he'd said, then Matt had used the company name to launder his drug money and, at the same time, point the finger at Manetto as the real drug leader. It made Manetto look guilty as sin and left Matt in the clear. Blake worried that someone might see the connection before he could do something about it.

"That's nice to know, but how does this affect me?"

"I can use my influence to help. I'll make certain recommendations that nothing be filed against Manetto. If they are, I will use my considerable influence to have all charges dropped and the case dismissed."

"Sounds good," I said. "What's the catch?"

He smiled. "I could use someone like you in the field with me. To put it bluntly, you're the best interrogator I've ever seen. I know you have a life and a family, so it would mean only helping occasionally with some of the hardest cases that come along. If it makes a difference, you would also be helping your country."

"Um...I don't know." His offer overwhelmed me, and I wasn't sure it was a direction I wanted to go. Ever. Plus, now that I knew about the PLM Investments thing, I could tell Uncle Joey and Chris. "What if Uncle Joey isn't charged?"

"That could happen," he agreed. "And I understand your hesitation. Still...is that a chance you're willing to take?"

"Maybe it is," I said. "Especially if Uncle Joey was set up. If it's the truth, it shouldn't be too hard to prove."

Blake shook his head. "I wouldn't count on it. The state's attorneys have been trying to get Manetto for years, and they wouldn't hesitate to push it through whether it had merit or not. Think about it...even a jury wouldn't be sympathetic to a mob-boss." He let that soak in before continuing.

"So here's my deal. Agree to help me occasionally, and I'll make sure none of this can be traced to Manetto."

How could I refuse that? I certainly didn't want to go through a trial and worry about everyone, myself included, going to jail. Still, I didn't like the open-endedness of his deal with me. "How about this? For every time you help me...or Uncle Joey...that's one time I'll help you."

His brows rose in surprise. He hadn't expected that. "You drive a hard bargain." He didn't like it, but it was better than nothing. Of course, he could always help Manetto with other things in the future. That might work. "All right, I agree."

I took a deep breath, then let it out with a whoosh and threw caution to the wind. "Okay. It's a deal."

"Good." Blake nodded with relief. "I promise you won't regret it."

"I'd better not," I said.

"I'll be in touch."

I left the precinct, hoping I'd done the right thing. It seemed like the right thing at the moment, but what did I know? I probably should have talked it over with Chris, and maybe Uncle Joey, but it was too late now.

Besides, it wasn't something I needed to tell anyone yet. It didn't sound like Blake was going to need me any time soon, so maybe I could just wait until then. With that happy thought, I left for home, allowing myself to think about the one thing I'd caught from Blake that caused my heart to flutter with excitement. The mission he needed me for involved going to the one place I'd dreamed of visiting since I was in the third grade.

Paris.

A few days later, I stood beside the grave of my old high school flame. Although the sun was shining brightly, a slight breeze carried a promise of winter. Sorrow laced through my heart that Tom had met such a bitter end, but I tried to focus on the life he'd lived and the memories I held dear.

Before coming, I'd rummaged through an old box of high school memorabilia I'd kept, and I found the rose he'd given me on my seventeenth birthday. I'd kept it wrapped in a box all these years, so it was dried and perfectly preserved. Now I held it in my hand.

"Tom...you may be gone," I said. "But you'll never be forgotten." I gently placed the rose against the headstone. The breeze caught my hair, blowing it across my face. I raised my hand to push it back, but froze as the scent of Irish Spring and cut grass filled my senses. My hair playfully danced around my face and tickled my nose. My smile turned into a laugh of delight. Then it was gone, and my hair fell back into place. A sense of peace filled me, giving me the comfort I needed to move on.

I strolled back to my car at the top of the hill, then turned to look out at the city below. The view was amazing and, for now, I just wanted to sit back and enjoy it. Just then, my phone rang. I shook my head at the interruption but answered it anyway. "Hello?"

"Babe," Ramos said. My heart picked up speed like it had a mind of its own.

"Hi," I answered, a little breathless. "What's up?"

"The boss wants to see you. Do you think you could come in to the office?"

"Sure," I agreed. "In fact, I'm here at the cemetery, so I'm not too far away. I can be there in a few minutes. Will that work?"

"Hmm...how about this, why don't I come get you? I know it's a little chilly for the bike, but I could use an excuse to get out of the office. What do you think?"

"Really?" It was on the tip of my tongue to say "holy hell, yes," but I held it back, not wanting to scare him off. "That would be wonderful." I told him where I was, and we disconnected.

A few minutes later, I heard the roar of his motorcycle and watched as he pulled up beside me. He parked the bike and pulled off his helmet along with the backpack slung over his shoulders.

"I brought you something," he said, a playful glint in his eyes. Unzipping the backpack, he pulled out a neatly wrapped bundle, which he proceeded to unfold. My breath caught to find the most amazing black leather motorcycle jacket I'd ever seen in my life.

"Holy hell!" I squeaked. "Is that for me?"

He chuckled. "Put it on. If it fits, it's yours."

"Woo-hoo!" I shrugged out of my coat and slipped my arms through the luxurious leather, inhaling the musky scent and closing my eyes. The jacket fit perfectly, and I zipped it up with a huge smile. "What do you think? Does it fit?"

He nodded, thinking I looked great. "I guess you'll have to keep it now."

"Saweet!"

"Let's go."

I threw my coat and his backpack into the trunk of my car and locked it up, then grabbed the smaller helmet Ramos had clipped to the back of his motorcycle. After snapping it on, I threw my leg over the bike and we were off.

Before my hands had a chance to get cold we pulled into the parking garage of Thrasher Development. I was a little disappointed that the ride went by so quick, but I couldn't complain. Ramos was thinking that Uncle Joey was anxious to see me, or he wouldn't have hurried so much.

"We'll take the scenic route back," Ramos promised.

"Awesome!" I said. "This is the best. Really...thanks so much."

He smiled, but shook his head, thinking that seeing how much I enjoyed it was thanks enough.

We walked into Thrasher Development and trepidation filled me. I didn't think Uncle Joey would find out about the deal I'd made with Blake, but what if he had? He probably wouldn't like it. But...maybe this was something else entirely. A girl could always hope, right?

After a quick hello to Jackie, we headed straight to Uncle Joey's office. He stood with a smile. Then his brows rose to see us both in leather motorcycle jackets. He glanced at Ramos with a quirk on his lips, then nodded, thinking I deserved to be indulged once in a while, and turned his attention to me.

"Shelby. Thanks for coming. Sit down, we need to talk." After we sat, he continued. "It looks like my worries about your investigation with the police have disappeared."

"Really? That's good."

"Which brings me to my next question. What did you promise Blake in return for making this go away?"

"Um…" My mouth went dry. He didn't know. Uncle Joey's brows drew together, and his eyes narrowed. He was hoping I hadn't told Blake my secret, but if I had…

"No, I didn't tell him that! He just asked me if I'd help him on a case in the future. It seemed too good to pass up, so I agreed." I wanted to keep talking about how much I didn't want any of us to go to jail, but the thunderous look on Uncle Joey's face stopped me.

"Shelby," he said, shaking his head. "You didn't need to do that. I have enough on Blake that I could have taken care of it."

"Oh…I didn't know that. But…just so you know, I only have to help him one time. Well…it was more like for every time he helped you, then I'd help him. Like a trade-off?"

Uncle Joey cursed under his breath and his eyes widened. What the hell had I done? Then he took a deep breath and calmed down. I was out of my league dealing with Blake. He'd just have to make sure it never happened again.

"All right. We'll have to work with that. In the meantime, I want to know when he contacts you, and I want to be there to negotiate what you'll do for him. Is that understood?"

"Yes, of course."

Uncle Joey didn't trust Blake worth a damn and, alarming as that was, having Uncle Joey on my side both scared me and helped me feel protected. I probably shouldn't have agreed to help Blake, especially since Uncle Joey had such strong feelings about it.

"Good. Now that we have that out of the way, I'm going to need you for a meeting tomorrow. I'm on the board of directors for Plum Fidelity, and we're picking a new CEO." He smiled, knowing from my shocked expression that he'd surprised me.

"Okay," I agreed. "That should be interesting."

"Good." He gave me the details, and I realized Uncle Joey had more going on behind the scenes than I'd ever know. I also realized that I was nuts to underestimate him and his influence, and I regretted my decision to help Blake without talking to Uncle Joey first. What was I thinking?

I left his office in a daze, grateful I wasn't on Uncle Joey's bad side, especially since I'd agreed to help one of his enemies. Beside me, Ramos wasn't too happy with my decision either and worried that Blake could just whisk me off somewhere without a moment's notice.

"You think he'd really do that?" I asked.

"I don't know. If he's a spy, he could probably do just about anything he wanted."

I moaned. What had I gotten myself into now?

"Hey...don't worry about it too much. You've got Manetto to watch out for you. And don't forget, I'm part of the package, so you'll be fine. Okay?"

"Okay," I said, half-heartedly.

"Good. Hey, I heard that you took some guy down with your new Aikido skills. Is that right?"

"Yes. Hard to believe, huh?"

"No. I always knew you had it in you. You'll have to show me how you did it." He raised his brow in a challenge.

"Yeah...right," I said, with a laugh. "I learned my lesson the first time. So unless you actually try to kill me, I think I'll pass."

He chuckled, thinking he was sure glad I'd been able to get out of that mess. He hated knowing that I could have died...again. "So, how's the leather jacket working?" he asked, changing the subject and hoping to coax a smile out of me.

"It's great," I said, a small smile on my face.

"I don't think you've had enough time on the bike to know that for sure. How about we try it again?"

I nodded eagerly, and this time my smile was huge. We exited the elevator and, with a flutter of excitement, I took my seat behind Ramos on the bike. True to his word, we took the scenic route back. I knew it was probably the last ride I'd get before winter set in. But it didn't bother me too much, since I also knew there were plenty more to come.

What I didn't know was what I'd gotten myself into with Blake, and that worried me. But what could I do? Worrying about it wouldn't help and, like Ramos said, with him and Uncle Joey on my side, it couldn't be too bad. I decided that, until Blake contacted me, I was going to put him out of my mind. Life was too short to spend it worrying.

I tightened my hold around Ramos, feeling his solid warmth beneath my arms. The breeze rushed by, and leaves skittered along the street and fluttered over the sidewalks. It was a beautiful day, and here I was, riding on a hot motorcycle, behind an even hotter guy, and wearing my new leather jacket.

Right now, things were pretty great, and I was determined to hang on and enjoy the ride.

Thank you for reading **Crossing Danger: A Shelby Nichols Adventure**. Ready for the next book in the series? **Devious Minds: A Shelby Nichols Adventure** is now available in print, ebook and on audible. Get your copy today!

Want to know more about Ramos? **Devil in a Black Suit** A book about Ramos and his mysterious past from his point of view is available in paperback, ebook and Audible. It takes place between **Crossing Danger** and **Devious Minds**.

If you enjoyed this book, please consider leaving a review on Amazon. It's a great way to thank an author and keep her writing!

NEWSLETTER SIGNUP For news, updates, and special offers, please sign up for my newsletter on my website at www.colleenhelme.com. To thank you for subscribing you will receive a FREE ebook.

ABOUT THE AUTHOR

USA TODAY AND WALL STREET JOURNAL BESTSELLING AUTHOR

As the author of the Shelby Nichols Adventure Series, Colleen is often asked if Shelby Nichols is her alter-ego. "Definitely," she says. "Shelby is the epitome of everything I wish I dared to be." Known for her laugh since she was a kid, Colleen has always tried to find the humor in every situation and continues to enjoy writing about Shelby's adventures. "I love getting Shelby into trouble...I just don't always know how to get her out of it!" Besides writing, she loves a good book, biking, hiking, and playing board and card games with family and friends. She loves to connect with readers and admits that fans of the series keep her writing.

Connect with Colleen at www.colleenhelme.com

Made in the USA
San Bernardino, CA
13 May 2020